THE AWKWARD AGENDA

Beth Morton

www.BethMortonAuthor.com

Book Cover by Michael Ardan
Illustrations by Stacy Williams
First Edition: March 2026
ISBN: 979-8-9919365-5-2 (Paperback Edition - Grey Scale)

For My Mom,

I'd buy you ALL the Sinupret

TRIGGER WARNINGS

Mental health issues (anxiety, bipolar disorder)
Internalized ableism
Character suicide (referenced)
Parent death (referenced)

PROLOGUE

Hoyden: *(noun) a high-spirited girl*

CALIFORNIA BARTON had Luca Genna on the ropes. Fifteen rounds of words from the tricky *colonel* to the insultingly easy *laughter* had come down to the two of them. The word was *freight*.

"F-R-E-A..."

California's smile grew under her mop of messy blond hair, and she pushed the long strands behind her ears. That spelling bee trophy was as good as hers.

The unexpected arrival of Mr. Welch, the fourth-grade guidance counselor, interrupted Luca's turn. "Excuse me, Miss Barbato, could we see California Barton in the principal's office?"

"Ooooh...." The chorus of fourth-grade voices echoed around the room, and California felt all eyes rest on her in scandalized glee. Miss Barbato shushed them all, and California stood up and pleaded her case.

"Mr. Welch, can it wait a minute? I'm about to win the class spelling bee."

Luca gave a disbelieving scoff, and she looked back at him with a satisfied smile. Luca was her biggest bully, and there was no small amount of gloating in her tone.

"There's no A in *freight*."

Luca's face turned scarlet as he puffed up. "Well, maybe I was spelling freak, 'cause that's what you are, California–a freak!"

It was an old insult, and California had walked straight into it. That was Luca's favorite choice of abuse–old news. Typically, he chose to comment away from teachers' ears, but the loss of the spelling bee trophy had apparently goaded him to comment out in the open, and Miss Barbato looked mad enough to spit nails.

"Luca Genna, for that comment, you will be going to the principal's office, and I will be placing a call to your mother. California is correct about your spelling and will receive the spelling bee trophy when she returns from Principal Lang's office."

California gave Luca a surreptitious stink face to his obvious rage, then followed Mr. Welch out to the hall. She wasn't sure why she was being called to the principal's office. Last time, it was because her mom hadn't gotten California her flu shot yet. Her mom always forgot stuff like that when she was in one of her funks. Those days, California picked up the slack–making meals for the two of them, doing laundry, even making sure her mom got out of bed to shower and brush her teeth every other day. It was exhausting, but her mom would bounce back sooner or later, and then they'd go on an adventure together.

The funks were concerning, but the subsequent adventures made up for the exhaustion of caring for her mom. The plans were always spur-of-the-moment, like when they drove down to Disneyland from Sacramento at five p.m. on a Friday with nothing but the clothes on their backs. They spent three days living off of fast food and buying Disney T-shirts when the ones they wore got too dirty. It had been a gleeful, chaotic mess, an apt euphemism for life with her mom.

California didn't have friends. Scheduling playdates was too much work for her mom, and even if it hadn't been, California knew how kids like Luca and the rest of the class looked at her. She didn't know how to dress. Her hair was always messy–it knotted easily, and sometimes, her mom didn't have it in her to help her get ready in the morning. No, it was better this way. California and her mom were a team. Except for every other weekend, when her dad flew in from Arizona and they spent the weekend together.

When Mr. Welch led her into the principal's office, she was still thinking of her spelling bee trophy. Surely, it would help to cheer up her mom. She was surprised to see her dad sitting there with Principal Lang. Her dad had been in town the weekend prior, so she wasn't due to see him for two weeks. He had taken her to a science museum and to shop for clothes at Target. It had been a fun time—not the kind of fun she had on the adventures with her mom—but 'Dad fun' anyway. California was her mom's partner in crime. To her dad, she was a kid.

"Dad?" She gave him a quick hug. He was wearing a suit, and it made him look taller, more formal. She rarely saw him in work clothes. Had he flown in straight from work? Maybe he'd been traveling for business. "What's going on? Why are you here? I won the class spelling bee!" It was the first step in her grand plan to reach the Scripps National Spelling Bee. At nine-and-a-half years old, she was unlikely to go all the way this year, but she had five years to hone her game before she aged out of the competition.

"That's great, sweetie. I—I'm proud of you." His arms tangled loosely around her while he looked her up and down, almost as if concerned she was ill. "Principal Lang and I need to talk to you about something important."

"What is it? Where's Mom?" California looked around the room, half expecting her mom to pop out. Yes, she'd been in bed when California left for school that morning, but her mood could change quickly. It had happened before.

"Your mom is fine, Cali." Her dad and his wife, Grace, were the only ones to call her that. "But she needs to go away for a little while. She called me because she needs to see a special doctor and will probably stay there for a few months."

"A few months? What's wrong? Is she going to be okay?" California's eyes widened, and her stomach fell to her feet. "She can't go away—I need to help take care of her."

The men around the room shuffled uncomfortably as if California's admission made them feel...guilty?

Her dad's face contorted in something like grief. "That's not your job." His voice was harsh, as if he had a lump in his throat, but he took a breath and started over. "Cali, you're so good to your mom, but she needs medicine and doctors to help her get better. She called me because she knows I can take care of you. I'll take care of you so she can take care of herself."

"But...I can take care of myself. She needs me!" Panicked, California looked around the room at her dad, Mr. Welch, and Principal Lang, who regarded her with sympathetic expressions. Their eyes were kind but implacable.

"California," Mr. Welch knelt to look her in the eye. "Your mom told us what a great kid you are. She's so lucky to have you, but she wants you to have time to be a kid yourself. She wants you to have time to be with your friends and not to have to worry about her."

"The other kids are all mean jerks." California folded her arms and furrowed her brow in obstinacy.

"I'm sure that's not true. We can say goodbye to your classmates if you like. Perhaps you can get their email addresses so you can keep in touch?" California normally would've rolled her eyes in response to his good-natured nonsense, but saying goodbye to her daily tormentors and correcting Mr. Welch's assumptions were secondary to her fears about her mother's health.

She turned to her father. "Can I go with Mom? I promise I won't get in the way. I can help the doctor." She heard the pleading whine in her voice, a sure sign her request would go nowhere.

"No, baby, but we can call and visit her after she gets settled. I promise." He smiled at her. "Your mom packed up some of your clothes and your favorite stuffie, and I can get you anything you want at Target when we land...anything you want." Her dad ran a hand over her hair, trying to reassure her, placate her with the promise of a shopping trip—as if that could possibly matter. He was still talking, and she listened with only half an ear. "Grace and your younger brother, Michael, are so excited to get to know you better. Grace says you can renovate your new room however you want it."

"I don't want a new room!" California tore out of the principal's office, tears streaming down her face, and ran right into Luca Genna, who had been waiting for his turn with the principal.

"California, you freak, it's your fault I got sent to the principal. Here's your stupid trophy." He threw it to the ground, the cheap plastic breaking into multiple pieces. "God, you're just like your freak mom. My mom said we can't play with you because your mom is crazy. A pair of freaks. What kind of name is California, anyway?"

California looked at her beloved spelling bee trophy while Luca stomped its larger remnants into fragments with the heel of his Nikes. Her father caught up with her and rested a firm hand on her shoulder to prevent her from running off, but the fight propelling her to run had evaporated. Tears streamed down her face as she let her father hold her hand and take her out to the car. They would buy her new clothes, he said. Grace and Michael would be waiting for her when they arrived. It would be okay. She'd see. The words echoed in her ears without landing, and she only offered him mute nods when asked if she could hear what he was saying.

Something solidified in her stomach, a lead weight that grew from merely present to actively painful during the flight to Arizona. Her father and Grace tried to give her Pepto-Bismol, but California knew the truth of the matter. She was frightened. Frightened for her mom, whom she wasn't there to help. Frightened for herself and the unpredictability of the future. Frightened of being a freak by herself instead of part of the pair with her mom that she had come to rely on. With her mom gone, everything cruel anyone had ever said about her became true.

By day's end, California suspected the truth that would eventually come to pass. Her time living with her mother was over.

And she would never go by California again.

CHAPTER 1

Physiognomy: *(noun) the art of judging a person by their appearance.*

THE HOUSE CHARDONNAY was a mistake.

Cali should have known when the bartender, a twenty-something man in a Guns N' Roses T-shirt and man bun, smirked when she asked for it. Her coworkers had all ordered beer or quick cocktails–rum and Coke, Red Bull and vodka, and the like. They were all dressed in jeans and T-shirts, while she wore the black slacks, cream blouse, and Cole Haan pumps she'd worn during the day's training. She hadn't packed jeans. The outfits she packed were business-ready Theory or gym-ready Lululemon–ne'er the twain shall meet.

The drinks were plenty, and AC/DC played on the jukebox. Everyone was celebrating now that their three weeks of in-person training had ended. Tomorrow, they would all go home from the regional headquarters in Chicago and prepare for their regional rotations to start the following week. She and her coworkers were part of this year's management training program at Marcus & Meyers–a dozen recent MBA graduates gathered from around the country to learn the nuts and bolts of the country's largest pharmaceutical and medical device company. Over the next two years, they would work across the various areas to set them up for success and catapult them up the ranks. The average trainee became a manager by age thirty, with an executive role by age thirty-five.

Cali should have been feeling good. The leader of their cohort had named her as valedictorian of the class. It was as good a start as she'd hoped—but as she stared at her sad glass of wine, she was...lonely.

It could have been something to do with the rest of the trainees standing in groups of threes and fours around the various bar activities. The West Coast contingent played Skee-Ball, while the Midwest group enjoyed beer pong. She didn't see the other East Coast hires, so she lifted herself from the barstool, deciding to hunt them down.

The patio was open, celebrating the balmy weather of a late summer night, and the group was laughing around the cornhole game. Cali was walking to join them when she heard the raucous laughter and grating voice of Ryan Connolly, a Virginia native and her least favorite co-trainee. He always stared at her like a denied meal, which she supposed he had been. He'd made a sloppy pass at her on day four of training, which she had quickly—and politely—rejected. An unpleasant sensation climbed up her back, and she tamped it down with a frown. She ducked back, watching the group from behind a plant. When Ryan moved on—or more likely, passed out, based on how inebriated he currently appeared to be—she would join their conversation.

"Of course, she made valedictorian. She buried herself in her hotel room every night—she didn't come out with us even once," Buffalo-native Matt said as he aimed the beanbag at the other team's board. "If she made valedictorian, it's because she worked harder than the rest of us."

"Please...that girl never had to work hard," Ryan slurred with a wet-sounding burp. "No one that attractive has ever had to do more than bat her eyes to get her way." He paused, taking a long drink of his cocktail before collapsing with a thump in one of the outdoor patio chairs. "She's got that...what's it called...pretty woman syndrome."

Lauren from Westchester—her closest colleague geographically—let out a burst of loud, abrasive laughter, running a hand through her short, curly hair. "You mean hot girl syndrome, Ryan. Pretty woman syndrome is for girls who romanticize prostitution." Lauren looked up at Ryan, who appeared confused. "You know? Like the movie?"

Ryan stood there, looking as though he were trying to solve a math problem, and Lauren patted his shoulder with condescension.

"You'll understand when you're sober."

Ryan's eyes narrowed in response, and Lauren laughed good-naturedly, cutting the tension in half.

"What's hot girl syndrome?" Matt asked.

"Hot girl syndrome is when a woman has never been...unattractive. Think about it—when you were a kid, did you have an awkward phase?"

"Sure. I had bad acne and braces in high school," Matt admitted. "Oh, and I had my town's largest collection of locally recovered fossils."

"Mine was the largest collection of Archie comics." Lauren laughed. "Anyway, I'd bet good money Cali has always been as pretty as she is now. When you go through an awkward phase, you develop a personality. You can laugh at yourself. You try to be charming or funny because otherwise, no one pays attention to you." She threw the bean bag and whooped loudly when it went into the hole. "When I first met her three weeks ago, I thought I must have offended her or something because she was so...standoffish."

"I felt the same way," Matt admitted. "She seemed cold whenever I talked to her."

"When you grow up attractive, you don't have to *work* toward developing an engaging personality. People flock to you anyway."

"She's hot." Ryan agreed, his voice slurred.

"Pig." Lauren rolled her eyes and turned back to Matt. "Her being off-putting is going to hurt her chances at success."

"You think so?" Matt asked.

"Leadership is a social exercise. It doesn't mean you have to be likable, but you at least need to be able to relate to others and be..." Lauren paused, grasping for the right word. "Engaging. We're not managers yet. This job is all about networking and influencing stakeholders without authority. Little Miss Never-had-a-split-end doesn't know how to connect with people, and what's worse is that it doesn't look as though she's interested in doing so. It's why she's not here with us right now. It will be hard for her to influence customers and team members. Looks and intelligence only get you so far. Authenticity matters, connection matters."

"I guess it depends on how many of her customers are men," Ryan slurred. Looked like he had opted for hard liquor.

"That's enough for you, dude." Matt took the drink from Ryan's loose grip. "Here, have some water." Ryan stared at the clear plastic bottle as if confused by its presence in his hand.

"Thanks," Lauren said to Matt, sounding relieved. "Anyway, she's going to have to warm up a bit. To succeed in corporate life, you must have a cult of personality, at least to some extent. Look at Steve Jobs. Look at Sheryl Sandberg."

"That girl has *no* personality," Ryan grumbled as he considered the water bottle Matt had given him with eyes that were struggling to stay open.

Lauren looked at Matt and shook her head.

"She's a basic...basic bitch." Ryan's head lolled to the side, and his eyes slipped shut.

Cali watched as Lauren and Matt looked at him with something akin to disgust on their faces.

"He's a pig–but he's got a point." Lauren sighed, sipping her beer.

"That Cali is basic?"

"I don't think basic is the right word. Superficial, maybe–or snooty?" Lauren sighed. "She's not a bad person. I'd take her over the drooling dinosaur in the chair over there, but I don't see her getting other people to trust her. Competence, yes–that's why she's valedictorian, but inspiring confidence? Trust? Not so much."

Matt nodded at Lauren's point and the two went to collect the bean bags for their next match, leaving Ryan a drooling, snoring mess in a metal chair.

Cali leaned against the bar wall, wrapping her arm instinctively around her stomach, expecting the stomachache to come. Ryan's behavior, she could more easily write off as sour grapes. But hearing Lauren refer to her like that was an unexpected gut punch. Was this what her colleagues thought of her? Superficial? Standoffish? Lacking in all interpersonal skills?

They didn't know, of course. They didn't know what she had been through–what it had taken her to get here. Her adolescence hadn't been awkward, but what had preceded it was far worse. It led directly to her here and now, standing alone, sipping her boring glass of house Chardonnay.

Wondering if it was all for nothing.

THIS GIRL IN THE CROWN IS PRETTY. SHE WOULD BE A GOOD MATE FOR YOU - WHY DO YOU NOT ASK HER TO DANCE?
LIKE HELL IS CHLOE JURGENS GOING TO DANCE WITH ME, ZAP. SHE'S AAA STATUS. I'M A JUNK BOND.
RIDICULOUS. YOU ARE A SUPERHERO.
BUT NOT RIGHT NOW, I'M NOT!

ZAP!

BUMP

CAN I HELP YOU?
NOPE, NOPE, AN ACCIDENT. I'M SORRY.
ASK THE HUMAN GIRL TO DANCE.
I'M SO SORRY, CHLOE. CONGRATS ON PROM QUEEN!
PROM QUEEN

SUCH A FREAK, TWITCH...
PROM QUEEN

CHAPTER 2

Nodus: *(noun) a complicated problem*

FROM: George Melone
TO: Cali Barton
SUBJECT: Congratulations! Feedback from training.

Hi Cali,

I hope your travels back home were seamless. Reaching out because I received the report from your time at training. Congratulations on making valedictorian! I'm not in the least bit surprised at your success. I think there are some great things on the horizon for you at Marcus & Meyers.

Reviewing the feedback from your trainer, I think there is some room for improvement concerning team dynamics. Knowledge is essential, and you've got that in spades, but sales and management require a skill that inspires, influences, and encourages teamwork. One of the trainers mentioned that you struggled to connect with the other management trainees. These colleagues would be the people you lean on in the coming two years—your cohort, if you will. Let's connect on some tactics to help you engage and better connect when I return next week.

Can't wait to see what you're capable of! Have a great weekend!

George Melone
Senior Director - East Coast
Marcus & Meyers Medical Device Division

HUH. There it was.

And, like clockwork, it started. *That* feeling in the pit of her stomach, the stabbing pain she had named Phantom Tumor, the pain that roared inside her whenever something went awry. Oh look, bad news—Phantom Tumor strikes. Exercise typically supplanted the worst of the Tumor's effects, but when it was bad, like now, it overwhelmed her.

Where do you think you're going? it said. *You're not going to run me out of town on the treadmill now, Cali.*

Cali barely reached the bathroom before her gut painfully ejected her breakfast into the toilet, leaving a sour taste in her mouth. Leaning back, she drooped against the bathroom wall, resting her head on her bent knees, grateful she worked from home so that no one could see this glorious moment. The Tumor was temporarily appeased. Angry tears leaked from her eyes. Her face was on fire, and a fine sheen of sweat sent an uncomfortable chill up her back—as though the act of vomiting caused a fever rather than the other way around.

She wasn't sick. These incidents weren't common, but they were predictable enough for her to know there was no actual tumor in her stomach. Her body responded to extreme anxiety with gut pain.

Struggled to connect...

No personality...

Those were two references to her inability to engage with others in as many days. An aberration? No—both statements had the uncomfortable ring of truth to them. She felt utterly unglued to campus life in college until the sorority recruited her. In middle and high school, cheerleading filled the same role. Both of those opportunities had come to her.

Hot girl syndrome.

Had that been why she had fit in? Because of her appearance?

At her college sorority, Kappa Kappa Gamma, they called her Committee Queen. Be it for formals, fundraising, or recruitment, Cali was the one to call when you needed a...workhorse. She never chaired the various groups, but she picked up the slack of her sisters when they had a final to study for, a breakup to mourn, or a hangover to recover from. She was the ultimate henchman...peon...minion.

And it hadn't bothered her until that disastrous night in the fall of her senior year when they gave her a Minions T-shirt during a roast event hosted by the newest pledge class. Everyone laughed, and she half-heartedly chuckled along as she processed how close to home the gift had hit. The girl who had wanted nothing more than to fit in had become a background character in her own life.

Grad school hadn't been much different. Oh, she wasn't a minion anymore. Now she was a Girl Friday–responsible for conducting research and assembling the PowerPoint decks for group projects. And her partners always listed her name last in those group presentations. Why did she let others lead the way while she carried out orders? Why hadn't she ever led the charge?

Jealousy ate at her each time a lead teammate won accolades, and she smiled tensely. She wanted to lead. She wanted to be the person who waved a metaphorical banner high, saying, "I did this! Me!" and not just a supporting player.

When Marcus & Meyers came to campus at Northwestern to recruit for their management training program, she applied, knowing the role would help accomplish two of her lifelong goals–one, to help shape research in women's and mental healthcare, and two, to prove to herself she could be more than a space filler.

She swore things would be different. She would learn to use her voice. She wouldn't hide behind a facade any longer.

It had never occurred to her that after so many years of quieting her voice, she had effectively gone mute in the process.

She stood and washed her hands. Before she could assess the damage to her appearance from the crying and vomiting, her doorbell rang.

"Great timing," she muttered before lifting herself off the floor. She crossed her fingers that it was a delivery so she could get on with her plans to shower off the icky duo of being sick and feeling like a failure. She looked through the peephole and spied her upstairs neighbor carrying a large arrangement of daisies and roses...her favorites.

Just as quickly as the image appeared in her peephole, there was a large crash of glass breaking, and the flowers scattered on the floor, followed by a muttered "Damn it!"

Simon smacked his tongue against the roof of his mouth. The side effects of Haldol were numerous, but the ones affecting him the most were insomnia and dry mouth. The insomnia sometimes fed creative binges like the one he experienced last night, but the dry mouth—ugh. The most unpleasant way to wake up was assuredly with a furry-coated feeling on his tongue.

The primary benefit of quitting his nine-to-five job was that Simon no longer needed to set an alarm clock. Waking up before 9 a.m. was abhorrent to him.

Stretching, he took stock of what woke him up and belatedly realized someone was ringing his doorbell.

"Go away!" he tried to shout, but it came out as a hoarse croak. He grabbed the water bottle on his nightstand and took a long drink, intending to repeat the direction, but the ringing had stopped. Unfortunately, the damage was done. He was officially awake.

Grumbling, he left his bedroom, shaking out the pins and needles in his legs. Simon had lived in his one-bedroom townhouse apartment for the better part of three years. Now that he had quit his day job, he was home a lot more and was considering upgrading to a space with a yard. He could investigate it when his lease expired in six months.

Whoever had been knocking had left by the time he opened the door, but a floral arrangement sat on his "Knock Thunderously" Thor doormat. Well, he couldn't fault the delivery man for his efforts, could he? Curiously, he lifted the hefty vase of yellow roses and daisies and carried them inside, where he fished out the card.

Cali–congrats on making valedictorian! We are so proud of you! –Grace and Dad

Oh, it was for his neighbor.

Well, fuck.

Not that he disliked his neighbor. It was just–she wasn't *his* kind of people. She'd moved into the townhouse unit downstairs around six weeks prior. He'd been there the day the moving truck had arrived, carrying her furniture and other possessions, and he had thought perhaps she was the most beautiful woman he'd ever seen. Blond and petite with wide green eyes, she looked like something out of a Disney movie. She had smiled when she saw him standing on his balcony porch and gave a little wave, and he'd immediately and involuntarily grimaced, which embarrassed him enough to make him retreat into his apartment.

Two weeks later, she knocked on his door in the late morning. She had pulled her hair back in a ponytail, and she wore black yoga pants and a light pink hoodie as she stood outside his door, holding a plate. She looked at his mailbox, likely to ascertain his name. He opened the door, flinching at the sunlight, and she practically pounced when he appeared.

"Hi! Simon Goldberg, right? We haven't had a chance to meet yet. I'm your new neighbor, Cali Barton. I don't know if you like cinnamon rolls, but the recipe made way more than I could possibly eat, so I thought you might like some." She spouted the introduction and offer in such quick tempo that, in retrospect, he realized it indicated she was nervous to approach him. She held the plate toward his face, and the soft fragrance wafted into his nose. Given his tendency to eat whatever was quickest or prepackaged, the smell of fresh-baked goods caused his mouth to water, but for some reason, the smell of cinnamon always caused his body to react erratically.

And, before he could say thank you, his eyes rolled, and his lip curled up in a sneer that flickered on and off as Cali stood there looking at him. He saw the emotions flicker across her face—confusion, hurt, and finally, anger.

"Well, I'll leave these here," she said tartly while Simon tried to get the tics under control. She thrust the plate at him and stomped off, her shapely form storming down the stairs back to her unit.

Simon groaned at the memory of how hurt she'd appeared. He wanted to explain, but what was the point? In the weeks since, she'd determinedly ignored his presence, her nose firmly in the air whenever they crossed paths. He didn't blame her—she must have thought him a complete asshole. Watching her perfectly coiffed and dressed like something from an episode of *Gossip Girl*, he realized how little it mattered. She was Lois Lane to his Ant-Man—characters from different universes that weren't meant to interact.

Well, the least he could do was to bring her the arrangement. He brushed his teeth to eliminate the dry mouth and put on something slightly cleaner. He hoped she wasn't home so he could leave it on her doorstep.

The large arrangement took both hands to deliver, and he struggled to ring the doorbell while keeping his arms wrapped around the glass vase. As he managed to press the bell with his pinky, the vase slipped in his grasp, and before he could regain his grip, it had careened down to the porch pavement at his feet.

"Damn it!" he muttered. Bending down, he carefully gathered up the flowers, hoping to salvage the floral part of the arrangement at least, when a piece of unseen glass gave him a minor gash across his palm. "Ouch!" He sucked in a breath, watching the thin line of blood blooming across his skin.

Cali opened her door. "Simon?"

He looked up briefly. He was not the only one having a bad moment, if her dried tears and red eyes were any indication.

"I'm sorry. The delivery man brought your flowers to me by mistake, and I was bringing them to you..."

Her eyes flickered down to his palm.

"Come in, let me get you a towel."

He stepped over the mess on her doormat, and she indicated he should sit on the cream couch with sage throw pillows in her living room. He held his hand up, wary of staining the fabric. She reappeared a moment later with a towel, a glass of water, and a first aid kit. Dipping the towel in the water, she pressed it against his cut while he took a steady breath in through his nose. The urge to tic began to build up, and after a moment, he shrugged involuntarily and cleared his throat. As she worked to disinfect the cut and apply a bandage, he looked around the room.

The interior layout of her unit was a carbon copy of his, but where his home featured artwork and a bookshelf of board games from the classics, such as Monopoly and Connect Four, to the relatively newer–Ticket to Ride and Settlers of Catan–to the bizarre like Exploding Kittens, her home looked like something out of a Pottery Barn catalog. Around the room were a handful of acrylic picture frames with staged photos of Cali, an older couple he assumed were her parents, and a younger brother. He turned around, looking for something noteworthy that would give him a glimpse of her personality. A piece of art...a souvenir shot glass from vacation...a refrigerator magnet? The space was exquisitely staged and exquisitely boring. It was like walking into a marketing professional's wet dream of the stereotypical twenty-something's home. Where was his neighbor in this room?

"You should be good to go," she said after affixing gauze and a bandage to his palm.

Simon flexed his hand, relieved it was his non-dominant one, so his artwork wouldn't have to take a backseat for a few days. He hoped the pain from the cut didn't exacerbate his tics, but the sting was currently minimal. "I'm sorry about your flowers. Let me help rescue some of them."

"Thanks." She sighed, shaking her head as if the circumstances couldn't be helped. He recalled that he'd walked in on something that had upset her deeply, apart from the broken vase. Her tears did something primal to him. Maybe it was the years he'd spent in the world of comics and heroes, but the thought of a *damsel in distress* came unbidden to his mind.

She attempted a smile, but it had the feeling of brittle twigs to it. Even with her proverbial mask in place, she glowed, the green of her eyes brightened by her misery. It practically hurt to look at her; she was so pretty. The two of them worked to clean up the broken glass and recovered a handful of roses and daisies, which Cali placed in a glass pitcher. He admired their work critically. Maybe it was a guy thing to think, but it didn't look half bad. He chanced a surreptitious look at her to ascertain if she agreed, but she wore a dull look of misery, as if the flowers reminded her of something she'd rather not think about.

Simon considered how to proceed before breaking the tension. "A broken vase and a need for first aid is not the thank you I should be giving you for the cinnamon rolls you made." He paused and considered whether to make his escape before deciding to be a gentleman. "Do you want to talk about what's bothering you?"

"Bothering me? Why would you say that?"

"I'm sorry. It just, it looks like you've been crying."

"Oh, yeah. That." Cali ducked her head and gave it a shake but continued staring at the arrangement. "Nothing worth discussing." She was trying to reassume a more contained mien–the kind she adopted after he had offended her the day they'd first met. He'd seen it happen before when other people witnessed his tics and then took on a practiced neutral expression, but whatever had caused her to don this protective layer had nothing to do with him.

"I feel like I owe you an ear at least for the baked goods and the broken vase."

She shifted her eyes from the flowers to him. "It's stupid and not something I'd usually share with someone I barely know." She waved a listless hand in front of her face before looking away.

Simon made one more try. "Maybe sharing it with someone you barely know will help give you an unbiased perspective. I'll even promise to tell you if I think it's stupid."

Cali looked him head-on, her lips pressed together, a seeming war waging behind her eyes before she let out an aggrieved sigh. "You know what? Fine." She fell back on the couch with a muffled thump, and Simon joined her, sitting on the chaise outcrop kitty-corner to her, their knees inches from one another.

"Do you know the company Marcus & Meyers? I'm part of their management training program. I got back from three weeks of training a couple of days ago."

"Yeah—congrats on being valedictorian."

Cali's eyes narrowed, trying to make out how he could possibly know.

Simon explained, "Your dad and Grace wrote about it on the card in the flowers. I looked to see who they were for."

Cali nodded, pressing her lips together.

"Yeah, they like to celebrate my wins. Anyway, the training went fine—at least, I thought it had. On the last night, there was a party, and I overheard some of my coworkers talking about me behind my back."

"What did they say?"

Cali's eyebrows lifted as she looked up at the ceiling. "What did they say? That I'm snotty and standoffish, and I have no personality, so I'll likely fail at this job because I won't be able to connect with my customers and colleagues. If I can't do that, I won't be able to effect change and I won't get promoted and—"

"Was this after you got valedictorian?" he interrupted, considering her situation as she nodded. "It sounds like resentment to me. They're probably jealous of you."

"Yeah—I might have been able to convince myself of that as well, but I got an email from my manager. He was pleased with my grades, but the head of the program there noticed I didn't connect with the others. My boss says I need to work on being a team player." She looked at Simon. "That probably sounds silly, but I took this job as a way to break out of some of the patterns I keep falling into with others, and—" She bit her lip and huffed. "My colleagues said something else I can't get out of my head."

Simon waited while she seemingly debated whether to share this detail. "Go on," he prompted.

"They said I had hot girl syndrome." She spat out the words quickly, as if this were the ultimate humiliation. "They said I never developed a personality because I never went through an awkward stage." She looked at him. "Is that necessary to form a personality? To relate to others?"

When his tics began in elementary school, Simon remembered how he would have given anything to be invisible instead of constantly drawing attention to himself. Cali embodied the epitome of what would have been his fantasy back then—being unscathed during adolescence—sitting here crying because of the barest taste of the torture he and so many others experienced in their childhoods.

But he thought of the first time he had been able to fight back against the bullying with a clever quip.

"Twitch, you freak, what's with those ugly faces you make?"

"Higgins, I work hard to make these ugly faces—we can't all be naturally hideous like you."

It hadn't been the most brilliant move—Higgins had nearly beaten him up. Still, he'd survived, and his skin had gotten infinitesimally thicker with each new verbal assault and carefully crafted comeback. That he had developed a group of friends meant his armor grew broader and the attacks against him much less potent. He looked at Cali, thinking about what it would be like never to have built up that skin and never to have sharpened your tongue in retribution for defense against an insult. Never to have to spar with an opponent set on cutting you down.

"I think..." He sighed, trying to pick his words properly. "I think that when challenged in our youth, it gives us a higher degree of empathy and kindness. Also, it helps us to laugh at ourselves. If we can laugh at ourselves, we develop a sense of humor. When we are challenged, we better understand our capabilities."

"I...I didn't have an awkward stage...not in that way anyway."

"You never had pimples?"

"No."

"An embarrassing outfit?"

"Grace would never let me out of the house poorly dressed." She looked comically appalled. Her hand lifted to rest on her sternum as if clutching metaphorical pearls. This time, Simon pushed down the urge to roll his eyes, an instinct that had nothing to do with his tics. Was this girl for real?

"Did you ever fart or burp in public? Get toilet paper stuck to your pants or shoes? Trip in front of a crush? Draw a blank during a big presentation? Get caught picking your nose? Braces?"

"I didn't have those experiences. I saw other kids have them, but it didn't happen to me. Was that what your childhood was like?"

"Mine was a hell of a lot worse than that." He ran a hand through his flop of dark brown hair. Feeling on display with her wide green eyes watching him, he shrugged his shoulders methodically and tapped his thigh. "I mean–you can see why, right?"

She shook her head. "What do you mean?"

"Cali, I have Tourette syndrome." And as if on cue, his eyes rolled repeatedly to match the shrugs. His tics had been quieter thanks to his new work situation and the Haldol, but even quiet days meant at least several tics per hour, and nothing set them off more than a conversation about his situation.

"Is that why you rolled your eyes at me? When I introduced myself?"

"Uh, yeah."

"Oh." She sat up. "Oh! I thought you were just a jerk." She laughed. "Or like too cool for pastries."

"The pastries were delicious, and I've never been cool for a single day of my life, believe me." He smiled at her. "I was diagnosed with Tourette's in fourth grade. While you were riding the wave of perfection"—her face went dark—"I was uncontrollably blinking, shrugging, eye-rolling, smacking my thigh or tapping my foot..."

"Did you yell out obscenities?"

"No, that's relatively uncommon. Coprolalia—that's what it's called—only occurs in about ten to fifteen percent of people with Tourette's. It's the most common in the media because it's played for laughs."

Cali processed his words. He saw her mouth the word *coprolalia* as if memorizing it. "Thank you for telling me. I'm glad you're not a jerk."

Simon didn't hide his smile, though he ducked his head, trying to conceal the blush that rose unbidden on his face. "Yeah, so while you were busy flying under the radar, I was the star of the radar. My teachers thought I was doing it on purpose, and even after I was diagnosed, I was bullied mercilessly until I got to high school."

"What changed for you in high school?" She sat back now, one leg bent toward her thigh, holding her shin while she listened. As he talked to her, his body calmed, the overwhelming urges muting in the face of her gentle curiosity.

"I stopped trying to be something I'm not. I'm not normal. I'll never be 'normal.' It's freeing when you realize you can't fit in because it means you can stop trying to do so. It means doing what makes you happy rather than what makes you acceptable to everyone else. So, instead of sports, I took art classes. Instead of keeping my head down to try and make myself invisible, I made friends like me, unusual in their way. They're still my best friends to this day."

"That's great you have them," she said quietly, thoughtfully. "I've lost touch with most of my high school friends. Hearing you say it, there wasn't enough to keep us together, apart from the proximity of being in the same school." Her eyes looked down as she contemplated her reality. "It sounds like my coworkers have a point about me. I guess I'll have to figure out how to better connect with others," she mused. "I guess it's too late for me to have my awkward phase. It would be funny, but not exactly professional, if my pants split open during a customer meeting."

"I mean—that's only one example. We could recreate a few awkward experiences—if you wanted to."

Simon clenched one fist tightly, his fingernails pressing into the skin of his palm. What was he thinking? Why did he have any desire to spend time with this woman?

Such a freak, Twitch...

The look on her face as she considered his offer appeared as both gratitude and confusion. "You'd do that for me?"

She wanted in? Simon had to bite his tongue while he considered how to respond. "I mean—I'd do it for me. This would exorcise some of my demons from middle school—you know, torture the pretty girl..." Simon swallowed his self-consciousness and wagged his eyebrows in gleeful, wicked intent.

A humored, wry smile broke through the brittle one from earlier. "I'm not getting braces." She paused, then added, "And I'm not farting in public."

Simon tented his fingers on both hands together with mock villainous intent. "Oh—you'll probably wish for those by the time we're done."

CHAPTER 3

MomI'mBoardGameClub CHAT GROUP

TheMagnificentZap (Simon)
You guys remember the neighbor I told you about?

MuppetMaster99 (Anton)
The one with the yappy dog that won't shut up?

TheMagnificentZap (Simon)
No - she moved out. This is my new neighbor.

CruellaTheHero (Kat)
The snotty hottie?

HammerDontHurtEm (Ben)
Why am I always the last to hear about the hottie?

CruellaTheHero (Kat)
Cause you're creepy, Ben. You gotta stop staring. 👀

HammerDontHurtEm (Ben)
I'm not creepy!

TheMagnificentZap (Simon)
Not since you got a gf anyway. We really should give Sheila a medal. But yeah - that one - her name is Cali

MuppetMaster99 (Anton)
Do you mean Callie?

TheMagnificentZap (Simon)
No, it's Cali. She texted me her contact info - it's definitely Cali. Anyway, I'm helping her out with something, and I thought you all might have some good ideas.

CruellaTheHero (Kat)
Do tell!

TheMagnificentZap (Simon)
It's kind of hard to explain, but basically, she wants to have the middle school treatment - she wants to experience some of the stuff we all did in our youth because she's having a hard time relating to her coworkers.

CruellaTheHero (Kat)
She...what?

TheMagnificentZap (Simon)
I swear it makes sense - sort of. You had to be there.

CruellaTheHero (Kat)
You want us to torture your snotty, hot neighbor so she'll know how to relate to her coworkers?

TheMagnificentZap (Simon)
In a nutshell.

CruellaTheHero (Kat)
And she agreed to this?

TheMagnificentZap (Simon)
Surprisingly, yes.

CruellaTheHero (Kat)
<<evil laugh>> 😈

TheMagnificentZap (Simon)
Back down, demon.

HammerDontHurtEm (Ben)
And you need our help for?

TheMagnificentZap (Simon)
Ideas. I can't exactly turn back the clock, but what would be the adult equivalent of a middle school awkward phase?

HammerDontHurtEm (Ben)
Wardrobe malfunction!

CruellaTheHero (Kat)
Ben, this better not be for her to have a Janet Jackson Super Bowl moment.

HammerDontHurtEm (Ben)
No! But maybe she puts on two different shoes, or she could have underwear or socks stuck to her from static cling or something.

TheMagnificentZap (Simon)
Not bad AND not pervy. Two thumbs up! 👍 👍

CruellaTheHero (Kat)
Ooh! She could get bangs!!! Or a perm!!!

TheMagnificentZap (Simon)
Are bangs or a perm embarrassing?

CruellaTheHero (Kat)
Hell, yeah, they are.

TheMagnificentZap (Simon)
Ok, keep 'em coming.

MuppetMaster99 (Anton)
Do you think she'd be willing to dress up like a pirate?

TheMagnificentZap (Simon)
If you weren't gay, I'd be assuming this was a very specific kink you're trying to get in on.

MuppetMaster99 (Anton)
I'm performing at the New York Renaissance Faire with my puppets next weekend. It's a pirate-themed show, and I could use a couple of volunteers to get attendees in to see the show and help boost my tips.

HammerDontHurtEm (Ben)
Ding ding ding! Winner winner chicken dinner.

CruellaTheHero (Kat)
That could be embarrassing if it's not your thing.

TheMagnificentZap (Simon)
Technically, the goal is to help her to laugh at herself.

CruellaTheHero (Kat)
If you can't laugh at yourself while talking like a pirate, what's the point of being alive?

MuppetMaster99 (Anton)
Argh, me matey!

CHAPTER 4

Cisvestism: *(noun) wearing strange clothes*

Simon (Upstairs Neighbor)
Hey Cali, I got our first mission lined up. You okay if I pick you up at 9 on Saturday?

Cali Barton
Sure! Should I be wearing anything in particular?

Simon (Upstairs Neighbor)
Nope. See you on Saturday!

"WHAT ARE YOU DOING up so early?" Cali breathlessly answered the phone as she ran on her treadmill. She was surprised to receive a phone call from her stepmother at 8:30 a.m. in New Jersey—or 5:30 a.m. in Arizona, where Dad and Grace lived.

"Your dad and I are off to a sunrise hike on Camelback Mountain. We wanted to check in. Are the flowers still alive?"

"Yes, thank you. The daisies and yellow roses are pretty. Right now, they're brightening up my kitchen."

"Your dad and I are so proud of you for having such success at training. Your boss must be proud of you too."

"They aren't like parents, Grace. They want us to do well, but I don't think they get proud. That's for you and Dad."

"Well, we are proud of you! You work so hard–you're the Little Engine!" Grace often complimented Cali's indefatigable work ethic. Cali was the Little Engine–I-think-I-canning-it through high school, college, grad school, and now her first grown-up job.

"Thanks, Grace. That means a lot." Cali turned off the treadmill. "All right, let me get going. My neighbor is taking me out."

"On a date?" Her stepmother wanted her to find romance more than anyone she had ever met. In the background, she heard her dad tell Grace to mind her own business. "Stop it, Mitch. I can ask her if she's going on a date. What's his name?"

"Simon, but it's not a date. He's..." She considered saying he was just a friend, but she wasn't sure they were that either. "He's doing me a favor."

"Well, have fun. I'll call you tomorrow."

Simon hadn't told her where they were going, but had said not to stress about what to wear. Did that mean she was going to get dirty? She threw on some gym clothes and was putting the finishing touches on her makeup when she heard Simon at the door.

"Morning!" Simon entered, carrying an outfit on a hanger. *What in the world was he wearing?*

"Are you dressed as a...pirate?"

"Aye! And soon you will be too, ya landlubber!" He bent his arm at a jaunty angle and swished it back and forth several times in succession. She sensed the first swish was purposeful, but the rest were involuntary. She'd looked it up the night before, and everything she read said she should ignore his tics unless they were harmful to him.

"Why am I dressing as a pirate exactly?"

"You're joining me on an adventure to the Tuxedo Park Renaissance Faire, where we'll advertise my friend Anton's pirate puppet show."

"Oh God." Cali put a hand to her head. What had she gotten herself into? "Is it too late to get braces?"

"Come on, Cali, live a little. This is gonna be fun... Well, for me anyway."

'Live a little' brought up images of vacationing in an exotic locale or purchasing an out-of-budget pair of shoes, not dressing up like the entertainment at a five-year-old's birthday party. Still, Simon patiently waited for her to make her move, and if he was willing to make a spectacle of himself, then what was her excuse? She grabbed the costume and changed.

She considered asking–okay, begging, *imploring*–Simon to pull his car around so that she wouldn't risk exposing her current attire to the view of her neighbors. Instead, she pulled the lapels of the pirate coat closed and speed-walked to the parking lot at the rear of their building.

It appeared Simon had gone authentic with the pirate costume he bought her, though she wished he had foregone the boned corset until they got to the faire. It dug uncomfortably into her chest. She wore a white blouse underneath, and the combination transformed her lack of bountiful cleavage into something slightly more impressive. She had been given a blue waistcoat and a matching tricorn hat. Underneath, she wore a blond-colored skirt and matching breeches. He'd given her some mock half-boots that slid over her sneakers for footwear.

She picked at the corset again to keep it from digging into the skin beneath her chest.

"You okay?" Simon asked.

"Yeah–the corset is a little snug."

"We can fix that when we get to the faire. It's only about a half hour from here."

"I can already smell the countryside." Cali looked out the window of Simon's dark blue SUV. In almost no time, they had transitioned from suburban tracts to apple orchards and horse farms. She enjoyed the abundant greens and subtly shifting golds of the northeast, so different from the reds and browns of the arid desert where she'd spent so much of her youth. So different and yet beautiful in their ways. If it weren't for the boning of her costume digging into her ribs, she'd probably be cheered by the outing.

"You don't seem uncomfortable in your pirate getup. Aren't you worried people are gonna stare at you?"

"You clearly don't know anyone with Tourette's, or you wouldn't be asking. People always stare at me. As for the pirate costume, you do get that a lot of people are going to be in costume, right? It's not like we're wearing this out to the River Palm Terrace. Although..." He gave her a wicked smile.

"They'd probably make a new sign for the door–no sandals, no shorts, no swords."

"A pirate sword is called a cutlass."

"Yeah, but that's not alliterative." She paused. She already knew that fact but didn't want to sound like a know-it-all. "No cutlass, no cutoffs, no..."

"Caps?" he suggested.

"Not bad. I feel like we can do better."

"Clogs...coveralls...crop tops..."

"You're good at this." She hemmed. "Cargo pants! They're universally unflattering, and no one should wear them to a fancy restaurant."

"Nicely done." She saw him smile out of the corner of her eye. "No cutlass, no cutoffs, no cargo pants. I like it. I think we can make a thing of it."

She turned toward him. When focused on the road, his tics lessened. She wanted to ask why but didn't want to make him self-conscious. She had to admit, pirate outfit notwithstanding, he was handsome–and frankly, the pirate look was off-kilter sexy. He had dark brown hair, a broad smile, and dark brown eyes. His hands sported visible calluses, and she felt an unexpected urge to feel their texture–beyond wrapping his injured hand. He looked about 6', taller if she counted the tricorn hat he wore for the occasion. She sniffed a laugh and looked out her window.

"So, who is this friend of yours? The one with the puppet show?"

"Anton? Oh, we met in high school. He still lives locally in Wayne." Wayne was a few towns away from their two-story townhouse in Ridgewood.

"That's nice that you've been friends for so long. Does he do puppet shows for a living?"

"Ha—he'd like to. No, Anton works in marketing. This is his passion project."

Puppets...huh? Cali remembered watching *Sesame Street* with her mom, who took it upon herself to create their own puppets from some old socks and a few years' worth of extra buttons collected from clothing purchases. She smiled to herself, remembering that, and immediately sobered, as she did anytime a memory of her mom surfaced. *Grown men don't play with puppets,* the Tumor relished reminding her. She sat up straight and wrapped her arms around herself. The whole point of this exercise was to get out of her comfort zone. Simon grunted repeatedly, snapping her out of her reverie.

"So—we should give you a pirate name," he said when his tics calmed.

"I can't be Cali the pirate?" She tilted her head toward him.

"No, Cali isn't a pirate name." He looked over at her. "I'm not sure what kind of name Cali is. I'm assuming it's short for something. Caroline? Callysta? Caliente?"

Cali inwardly grimaced. The name California in his possession scared her. The last time she'd told anyone her birth name was when she had to have her first name changed on her passport.

"It's been a long time since I've been anything but Cali. What's your pirate name?"

He looked over at her with an assessing glance in reaction to her unwillingness to share. He shrugged, letting her off the hook. "I'm Cap'n Rusty Rattlebones!"

"See, alliteration always makes it better." She nodded in appreciation.

"Okay, go on Google and look up 'pirate name generator.'"

Cali took out her phone and did as he asked. The first one that popped up—and there were like twenty of them—asked for the first initial of her name and birth month and provided her with a pirate moniker.

"Mad McSwiggans."

"And it's even alliterative! It's destiny!"

"It's not destiny, it's demented, but... I put myself in the hands of the master so..." She indicated with a flick of her hand that they should continue, not that they had ever stopped.

"Where did you grow up, Cali?"

"I lived in Sacramento till I was nine, then I moved to Arizona. I went to ASU for undergrad and Northwestern for grad school."

"That's the job interview explanation, huh?"

"What?" She gave him a quizzical glance. What had she said wrong?

"Nothing. So Arizona. Did you live near Tucson?"

"No—I lived in Scottsdale, a suburb of Phoenix."

"Oh yeah, I've been there for work. Fun town."

"What do you do for work?" She realized she knew little about him except that he liked her baking and had Tourette syndrome. He had mentioned doing something with the arts.

"I was a graphic designer until recently, but I quit a couple of months ago. I write a webcomic, and it's about to be published in book form."

"I didn't know you could make a living doing that." Cali smacked her face. "Oh, my goodness, that was so rude of me. I apologize."

Simon laughed at the blunt statement. "Don't beat yourself up, my dad said the same thing. To answer your, uh, question, it's not easy. I've been working double duty on the comic since college. It took a while to build a following, but it started pulling in some decent revenue about six months ago. I got a publishing deal for the print rights—it'll be in bookstores by the summer."

"That's incredibly impressive. What's your comic about?"

"It's a superhero comic. You probably wouldn't be interested."

"Comics aren't my go-to reading material," she admitted. "But I'd like to read it. What's it called?"

"*The Magnificent Zap*. It's about a man in his twenties with superpowers."

"What kind of superpowers? Flight? Strength?"

"The power of electricity. He can hijack electric currents to stop bad guys."

"What's his origin story? How did he get his powers?"

"He has a sort of alien parasite that amplifies the natural electrical impulses in his brain. They work together to save people."

"But aren't parasites bad?"

"Maybe it would be more correct to say it's a mutualistic relationship."

"So, it's good for him?"

"Sometimes. Sometimes it's a pain in his ass. The parasite, Twitch, wants to hijack him all the time, but our hero, Daniel, keeps him in check. As a result, Daniel tics a lot."

"Your superhero has Tourette syndrome," she said softly, considering what he told her. "Why did you decide to do that?"

"I don't hear that question often." He looked at her with surprise.

"No?"

"They all assume I did so because I have Tourette's and want to create someone other kids with Tourette's can look up to." Simon motioned his head back and forth on his neck. "Or they assume I want to be inclusive 'cause there aren't many people in media with Tourette's that aren't, ya know, swearing or using racial slurs. They all make my intentions much loftier and altruistic."

"But they're wrong." It was a statement. Cali sat patiently. She liked it when Simon smiled at her, as if he were seeing her for the first time. "So, what's the reason, Cap'n Rusty?"

"I guess I wanted to feel powerful instead of victimized. I was bullied a lot–I mean *a lot*–as a kid, and sometimes, I imagined being able to fight back against my bullies. I had dark, vengeful daydreams. But when I found my tribe, I realized I wanted to be a hero—not a villain."

"So, there's a parallel universe where the Magnificent Zap is a supervillain?"

Simon chuckled in response and nodded. "That's a good idea. I should write that down."

Simon helped Cali loosen the corset in the parking lot before they made their way into the Renaissance faire while he tried to ignore the sight of her cleavage. After she claimed improvement, they walked toward the entrance. He usually made his way up here at least once a season—sometimes to see Anton in action and often to enjoy a lovely day with a flagon of mead and a turkey leg. This was the first time he would be part of the entertainment, but he was game to give it a try. These were his people. The people who thought it fun to dress up as a jester, prince, or knight on a 75-degree Saturday in September. The people who wouldn't look twice if he did something unusual.

Cali looked tense. She also looked adorable—and honestly, sexy as heck in her costume—but she walked around like a newborn deer, still getting the hang of her legs. A crowd cheered at a nearby stall, and she nearly fell on her face. As they walked through the fairgrounds, people stared at her, and a few even smiled and proffered compliments on the quality of her costume. That said, the stiff look on her face showed she endured rather than enjoyed the day's endeavor. As a result, she came off as standoffish and a little rude.

"Hey, are you okay?" He stood in front of her, blocking her path.

Cali's eyes wandered about without settling on anyone, unsure where to make eye contact, as if anticipating a sniper attack but not knowing where the sniper lay in wait. "I don't enjoy it when people look at me like this," she admitted in a halting voice.

"And yet, working for Marcus & Meyers, won't you have to speak in front of crowds occasionally?"

She considered his question. Her shoulders rose, and she looked around at the crowd mingling around them. "Perhaps I should say, I don't like being stared at when I'm not in my normal attire."

"Hey, I get that. We all have our versions of armor." When she didn't settle, he decided to soften his approach. "Cali, look at me," Simon commanded gently. He gripped her shoulders. Her eyes met his, and he nodded encouragingly. "Take a deep breath." He watched her do so and let out a breath of his own. "Good. Now, our deal aside, you don't have to do this today. I can leave you at the food stalls and get you later. I promised my friend Anton that I'd help him, but if this is too much for you, please let me know. You won't lose any points in my book."

"Thank you," she said almost silently, mouthing the words more than speaking them. She raised one of her hands to touch one of his as it rested on her shoulder, and his reaction to her touch surprised him. He fought the urge to take her hand in his. "I want to try. I think...I *need* to try." Cali closed her eyes and took another deep breath. "Okay...Okay, I'm ready."

Simon appreciated that she was taking a big step and shifted into coach mode. "Then let's get started. Here's the thing, Cali. When you wear a costume like this to the faire, people expect you to get in on the fun. You're so nervous you're giving off a 'don't fuck with me' vibe."

"That's bad?"

"I mean, anything goes here at Ren faire. You could wear a scowl, and people would think you're playing a vicious character, but that's not what's happening here. You look unhappy."

"Are you about to tell me to smile more?" She gave him a look that would make most men's testicles shrivel into raisins.

"I wouldn't dream of it. I'm not here to tell you to be a Barbie doll, but you said you want to be approachable. If you're nervous at work, and your go-to is resting bitch face, it's not going to help you make friends with your customers and colleagues."

Cali nodded, listening with a furrowed brow. "Resting bitch face. I had no idea I was projecting that. What do you recommend?"

"Consider what you're putting out there. Most people are a little bit apprehensive when they meet someone new. If you're putting out annoyance or misery, they'll assume you're either miserable or thinking badly of them."

"So, how do I counteract that?"

"We're going to start with a little improv. Today, you're not Cali Barton. You're Mad McSwiggans, a fearsome pirate. You're a badass lass who slaughters British sailors and steals gold doubloons. You say 'argh' and 'matey' and 'walk the plank!'"

She swallowed a gulp. "Argh!" But she still sounded unsure.

"Louder." He gripped her shoulders, ignoring the jolt of awareness he got from touching her.

"Argh!" Her voice rose, but her eyes locked on Simon.

"Better—now give it to me from the gut."

"*Argh!*" she said, loud enough that the crowd around them turned to look. Simon took her hand, raised it above their heads, and took advantage of the attention.

"That's right, I'm Cap'n Rusty Rattlebones, and this is Mad McSwiggans, and we're here to invite ye all to the best pirate puppet show ye'll ever see at the Fortune Stage over yonder! Come see Amazing Anton's Pirate Revenge at eleven a.m., one p.m., and three p.m. today!" Simon looked over at Cali, who was fighting a smile.

"*Argh!*" Cali echoed triumphantly, and the crowd around them chuckled in amusement.

Walking over to the theater, Simon coached Cali through additional improv techniques, pirate terminology, and even some ideas for back-and-forth exchanges. That first shout unleashed a well of creativity within her, and unexpectedly, Cali had an odd internal database of pirate terminology, leading Simon to wonder about her hidden depths.

"Dance the hempen jig?" He looked over at her when she used the phrase.

"Being hanged," she explained, and Simon nodded, impressed.

"Are those my pirate advertisers?" A new voice joined their conversation as Anton joined them in his pirate get-up of green and gold. He had covered his short, curly blond hair with a long black wig pulled back into a ponytail. His significantly more ornate costume had likely been purchased from one of the faire vendors as opposed to a Spirit Halloween location.

"Aye, matey!" Cali responded more enthusiastically.

"Cali, er, Mad, this is my good friend Anton Adler. He's the one we're helping today."

"Thank you so much for the help. Of course, my show runs at the same time as Incredible Ivan the contortionist—he always draws so many people in because his advertisers walk around on stilts."

"Putting me on stilts would be a mistake." Simon gave his friend a comical look. "There is such a thing as bad publicity, and my landing on faire attendees is not the word of mouth you're looking for."

Cali gave a breathless laugh at his joke.

"Spoilsport," Anton responded, but he smiled. "Okay, if you could, please try to hawk the show. The first performance starts in about forty-five minutes, and remember—it's the *best* show here—no matter what the Incredible Ivan has to say." Anton led them to the theater entrance and left them to begin gathering the crowd, and Cali gave Simon a look as if to say, *Well, what now?*

"Ladies and gentlemen," Simon raised his voice above the murmured din of the crowd. "I'm Cap'n Rusty Rattlebones, and this here is the fearsome Mad McSwiggans, and we're here to invite ye to the best show at this here faire! Amazing Anton will show you pirate stories that will terrify your mother and put hair on your chest! Ain't that right, Mad?" Simon looked at Cali. She gave him a blank look. Her jaw dropped, and he gave her a gentle nod. "Ain't that right, Mad?"

"That's—tha's right, Cap'n Rusty! Amazing Anton likes to tell stories of pirates on the open sea, fighting sea monsters and British trading ships!" She paused, bringing a single finger to her chin. She was getting into this. "Why, I remember..." She stopped and looked at Simon, terror on her face warring with apparent exhilaration.

"What da ya remember, Mad?"

"I remember the story of the gigantic whale who directed Anton to the King of Spain's sunken treasure." At the word gigantic, she brought her hands back to mimic the great creature's size.

"The one who swallowed the treasure and spit it out through its blowhole?"

"Aye, the very one! It rained gold doubloons and rubies and diamonds."

"Tha's how young Billie lost one o' his eyes, ain't it, Mad?"

"Indeed."

And as if on cue, both looked at each other with identical sad faces and said, "Poor Billie."

The crowd laughed, and as the time grew close to the first of Anton's three shows, they trickled into the theater. Cali and Simon—or rather, Mad and Rusty—kept up the banter for the one o'clock show when Simon heard a voice in the crowd.

"Cali Barton? Is that you?" Cali stiffened at the voice and turned around. Cali's jaw dropped to somewhere around her collar as she tried to respond to the brunette with short curly hair watching her with wide, disbelieving eyes.

Simon put an arm around Cali in a gesture of solidarity. "Cali? Ain't no Cali here—this here is the feared pirate Mad McSwiggans. She's ruthless! She made the governor of Barbados dance the hempen jig!" Simon made eye contact with Cali, who looked to be on the verge of either laughter or a nervous breakdown. He raised his eyebrows playfully at her, and a smile fought through her tense expression. "Tell 'em about it, Mad!" he prompted.

Cali stood up a little straighter and responded to the woman who held the hand of a little girl in a Princess Anna costume. "That's right, I'm Mad McSwiggans. I give no quarter to my enemies, especially those that scuttlebutt about each other around a game of...cornhole." Cali looked straight into the woman's eyes as she dropped that word.

"Cornhole?" the woman questioned, and her eyes went wide, her jaw dropping in realization. There was a silent conversation happening between the women that Simon could only glean.

"Are you really a pirate?" The little girl holding the woman's hand tugged on Cali's coat, and she got down on one knee to talk to her.

"Aye, I is a pirate, and who might you be?"

"This is my niece." The woman indicated the young girl. "I take her to Ren faire every fall," the woman eagerly explained, but Cali ignored her.

"I'm Princess Anna. Are you a bad pirate like Captain Hook?"

"I's the worst pirate, Cap'n Hook afraid of me, ain't he, Cap'n Rusty?" She turned to Simon, who smiled from ear to ear.

"That's right. Cap'n Hook ran off to Never Never Land to escape Mad here."

"But you, princess, ain't got noffing to worry about. I grant you safe passage to the pirate puppet show put on by the Amazing Anton and his band of pirate puppets."

"You promise?" the little girl asked, her face serious.

"A pirate who breaks her oath will swim with the fishies in Davey Jones's Locker." And Cali offered her pinky to the little girl for a pinky swear. After a moment, the little girl joined her pinky with Cali's and offered a gap-toothed grin of glee.

Cali stood and nodded at the woman, who looked discomfited, her open mouth indicating she was at a loss for words. Turning around, Cali bantered with Simon, effectively shutting the other woman out.

Simon was prouder than he could say.

After the final show, Simon snuck away with Cali. Together, they raided some of the more popular food booths that had quieted down toward the end of the day. Armed with two flagons of mead, turkey legs, and funnel cake, they sat in an empty theater and enjoyed the twilight settling around them.

"So, who was that woman?"

"Who?"

"Come on, her face went white when you mentioned cornhole. That was some high-level shade you were throwing."

Cali waved a hand airily in response. "Oh, that. Yeah, her name is Lauren Polski. We work together. She was the one who said I had 'hot girl syndrome.' She didn't know I heard her talking about it around the cornhole game. I was letting her know I overheard what she had to say."

"Props to her for what sounds like a mean advertising slogan for what she sees as your flaws. In ninth grade, this asshole, Adam Higgins, got all the popular kids to chant 'Twitch' every time they saw me walking down the hall, the street, whatever. It got so bad that a couple of the teachers accidentally called me Twitch in class." He shook his head in disgust. "But it's how I got the name for the Magnificent Zap's parasite."

"Making lemonade?"

"Exactly!"

"Cheers to that." Cali raised her cup, and he responded in kind. In the distance, the crowd roared at one of the shows. The darkening sky was illuminated by the on-and-off glow of fireflies setting up camp for the night. "Sounds like quite a party over there."

"That'll be the joust. It closes out the faire every day."

"Do you typically go watch it?" Content in the quiet of the area, Cali had no intention of moving.

"Nah, I'm not a huge fan of being in packed crowds like that. You know the kind where you can't make an easy escape?"

"Me neither. Why don't you like them?"

"Ah, guess I don't like being stuck in a throng if I get a tic attack, which, of course, makes it more likely my symptoms will go crazy. What about you?"

Cali made a mental note to google 'tic attack' when she got home. "You'll laugh."

"Maybe. Is that so bad?"

Cali considered him with a critical eye. What had he said about being able to laugh at yourself? Cali had toddled, crawled, and baby-stepped her way into opening herself up to her neighbor. Taking the job at Marcus & Meyers had been done in an attempt to break patterns, but here in her pirate gear, with a mug of mead, she realized how little those efforts had accomplished. Simon forced her from her comfort zone, and she let him. Why, when she hid so much of herself away, was *he* the person she felt comfortable confiding in?

"Fine." She sighed. "At seven years old, my mom took me to Disneyland. We were exploring the park, and I had to go to the bathroom, but we got stuck on one of the parade routes. At most, we had to wait, like, twenty minutes to get out of the crowd, but that twenty minutes felt like forever, and ever since, I've hated being stuck in a group of people."

"Well?" He motioned with his hand for her to continue.

"Yes?"

"Did you make it to the bathroom in time?"

"That's what you took from this story?" She shook her head and gave him an incredulous smile, tamping down the urge to smack him on the shoulder, which she had never done to anyone.

"You're not answering. I might have to rescind my offer for the Cali Barton Embarrassing Experiences Tour if you don't tell me whether you wet yourself at Disneyland or not."

She laughed and put him out of his misery. "I made it—but it was a near thing." She took a bite of turkey leg and let out a small moan of enjoyment. "This is so good. Maybe I should tell Grace to make the whole turkey for Christmas this year instead of only the turkey breast." She continued around a mouthful of crispy turkey skin, "This is delicious."

"It wouldn't taste the same—there's something about the visceral feeling of the bone in your hands while sitting at the faire."

"I'll take your word for it." She swallowed the mead, which tasted like a sweeter version of beer.

"So, are you a Ren faire convert?"

Cali considered the day. "No to dressing up as a pirate again, but you can count me in for turkey legs, mead, and pirate puppet shows any day of the week." She swallowed a bite of turkey. "By the way, I know Anton took some photos–can you make sure he doesn't tag me on social media?"

She looked over at Simon and noticed his easy manner had fallen. He looked down at the food with his lips pressed into a thin line.

"You looked like you were having a fun time. What does it matter if you get tagged in a few photos?" he said quietly.

"I did have fun, but it's not something I want to share with the world."

"Too weird for you?"

"No, not at all." She looked at him. "If I want to keep something I've done quiet, does that equate to being too weird? I'm saying this helped me get out of my comfort zone, but I like my comfort zone. It's comfortable for a reason." When Simon sat, unmoved by her explanation, she dug in deeper. "My colleagues follow me on social media, and they already don't like me. It's bad enough Lauren saw me like that today, I don't need to be known as Mad McSwiggans at work," she offered, exasperation bleeding into her tone.

The camaraderie of the earlier conversation evaporated in an instant. "So, what was this then? Normal person on safari?"

"Why are you so offended?" She looked at him, perplexed by his shift in demeanor. "I didn't say I didn't have fun. I had a great time, and it was a fun way of seeing what I'm capable of and what I'm putting out there to others–but I'm not an entertainer and I don't aspire to be one."

"Wasn't the point of this exercise to break some of their impressions of you?"

"Yes, but I want them to think I'm authentic, not..."

"Not what, Cali?" Simon looked at her, his head softly shaking from side to side in apparent disappointment.

Her stomach churned when Cali recognized that she didn't know how to answer his simple question. Her mouth hung open in mute realization. *Not what?*

Not a freak.

"California, you freak..." Luca Genna's strident voice rang loud and clear in her mind all these years later. Maybe she *was* saying this was too weird for her.

"I think you had fun and don't want to admit to yourself that you might be something more than..." His voice dropped off, and Cali found herself getting angry.

"More than what?" She took her turn to challenge him.

He turned away, gathering their food trays.

"More than what, Simon? More than superficial? Shallow? If I'm shallow, does that mean I'm not interesting enough to be your friend? You must be *this* interesting to be worthy of Simon's friendship?" She held her hand above her head as if mimicking the height measurement tool on an amusement park ride.

Freak, shallow...were these her only options?

Simon looked at her, his nostrils flaring. She noticed him hitting his thigh with his hand in repetitive, jerky motions that had been largely absent throughout the afternoon. "Come on, we should get going to beat the faire traffic." And he stalked off while she raced to follow.

MANHATTAN APARTMENT

!

I'M SO SORRY, DAMN BOX WAS BLOCKING...

IT'S FINE... CAN I HELP YOU?
THIS WOMAN IS ATTRACTIVE BUT UNPLEASANT.

NO, I'M SORRY...

CHAPTER 5

Carriwitchet: *(noun) a puzzling question*

"WHAT ARE YOU thinking for game night food?" Anton asked as he put the bag he brought into Simon's fridge.

"There's a new Thai place in town. I want to give it a try."

"Ben gets ridiculously bad gas when he has Thai food."

"That's Sheila's problem. I'm in the mood for red curry."

"Your mood is more pissy than usual. What's going on with you?" Anton looked over at him from the open fridge, then turned back to take in the sorry state of expired products and soggy vegetables inside. Sometimes, Simon failed at adulting, much to his friend's chagrin.

"There's a fresh bag of chips in the pantry if you're hungry," Simon muttered before flicking on the Roku to find something to watch before the rest of the crew arrived. "And what do you mean, I'm pissy?"

"I dunno–it's a vibe I'm getting. You were so happy last week at the faire. What's changed?"

"Nothing. I don't know what you're talking about." But it had the taste of a lie. He had been off since that day, and he knew it had everything to do with his downstairs neighbor. He couldn't decide why Cali's attitude toward their day together annoyed him. She hadn't insulted him or Anton. She'd been a good sport. In those hours out in the sun with the hordes of attendees, she dropped her guard a little bit. He'd liked her in the pirate getup, charming and balls-out doing her best at being a hawker and pirate princess. When she said it wasn't her thing, he couldn't tell if she lied to herself or if she was as boring as she feared herself to be. He couldn't tell which possibility upset him more—that she didn't see her potential, or that she was happy being...less.

They had barely talked on the car ride back. When she got out of the car, she tried to say thank you, but he waved her off with a claim of exhaustion. They hadn't spoken since.

"If you say so." Anton returned with the bag of sour cream and onion chips. "By the way, I need to stop by Cali's apartment. I brought a gift to thank her for her help at the faire."

Simon stiffened. Of course, Anton brought a gift. It was his 'love language,' as he often said. "You didn't need to do that."

"Yeah, yeah, you always say that. But thanks to the two of you, I out-earned Incredible Ivan in tips for the first time."

"So, where's my thank-you gift?"

"It's sitting in your fridge. I picked up cupcakes from Magnolia in the city. Your favorite, right?" Anton shook his head. "Pissy, like I said."

"Thank you. That's nice of you." Anton wasn't just generous—he was thoughtful.

"I'm going to bring it to her now—you want to join me?"

He didn't want to join. He wanted to forget Cali Barton, with all her petty problems, even existed, but he also needed to have something resembling a decent relationship with his neighbor, and it would look weird if he didn't at least accompany Anton to drop off his thank-you gift.

"Yeah—fine. I'll join."

Laundry on a Saturday night might have been a letdown for some women. Cali had her share of nights out in college and grad school—where she was dragged places by boyfriends and sorority sisters alike. She smiled through nights at the clubs, baseball games, and spring break trips to Miami, but really, it exhausted her. Living on her own, a night doing laundry oddly recharged her, with nothing to look forward to but a Pilates class the next morning.

So when the doorbell unexpectedly rang, she wanted to ignore it. Then she realized whoever had rung the bell had certainly seen her living room light on from the door.

She looked through the peephole to see Anton and Simon standing outside, the former holding a shopping bag and the latter wearing a grimace.

During the drive home from the faire, Cali had begun to reconsider her opinion of her neighbor. Simon *was* a jerk. She felt the veil he drew between them when he thought she wasn't cool because she wasn't into dressing up as a pirate as a regular thing. Some people wanted to be entertainers, but she wasn't one of them, which was okay. She resented the heck out of the fact that Simon put her on the defensive about her personality.

But Anton had been nothing but nice, so she pulled on a sweatshirt and opened the door.

"Anton, it's so nice to see you." She gave him a warm smile and a hug. "Hi, Simon," she said politely.

"Cali." Simon nodded.

"I have a gift for you. Can we come in?" Anton held up a reusable grocery store bag.

"Uh–sure. The place is a bit of a mess though. You caught me folding laundry."

Simon snorted, but Cali forced herself not to acknowledge it. Perhaps it was a tic, though she was almost positive it wasn't.

"I'm sure it's fine. I had to throw away two packages of furry bread upstairs at Simon's place."

Cali laughed. Anton charmed her, and she'd have to be made of stone to refuse a gift. She waved them in and invited them to sit.

"Can I get either of you a drink?"

"No–we won't be here long." Simon stood against the wall by her door, his arms crossed.

Anton gave Simon an aggrieved look. "He means we have to be upstairs for game night in a bit, but I wanted to thank you for your help last week." Anton stuck his hand in the black Stop & Shop bag he had brought and came up with his hand inside a puppet. "I'd like to introduce you to your puppet doppelganger, Mad McSwiggans, the pirate princess."

Cali let out a bark of laughter at the puppet, meeting her eye to eye on Anton's arm. It wore a facsimile of her Renaissance faire outfit, complete with a corset and blue waistcoat. Even the tricorn hat matched.

"Anton, she's amazing! This must have taken you so much work." She moved closer and tentatively took the puppet's felt hand. "You did this all in a week? I'm so impressed."

"I cheated a little. I had already created the body and head for another puppet I had in the works. I only needed to customize the features–your hair, eyes, and clothing. Do you like her?"

Cali had never owned anything like it, and she had never done anything like her pirate act last week. She blinked away unexpected moisture in her eyes as she considered the puppet. "I love her so much. But how can I possibly accept such a generous gift?"

"Consider it appropriate repayment. Last weekend was one of my best at the faire, something you and Simon helped make happen."

"Did Simon get a puppet too?" Her eyes flitted to him, leaning with uncharacteristic quiet against the wall by her door as if waiting for the sign he could flee her presence.

"Nah, but I brought him his favorite cupcakes for game night." Anton looked at her laundry. "These are your plans for Saturday, I take it?"

"Yeah, I know. Boring, but I'm new in town."

"Come to game night! The whole crew will be there. Simon has told them all about you!"

"He has?" She turned to Simon. "You have?"

"Yeah, well..." Simon's face reddened. "I needed ideas for the project."

"You should definitely come. Do you like board games?"

"Yeah, they're all right." She nodded. Of course, it depended on the game, but she loved games with her Dad, Grace, and Michael.

"Anton, don't bug her. She clearly doesn't want to come."

"I didn't say that." Her eyebrows furrowed. What was Simon's problem? Why was he so determined to be unpleasant? Anton had issued a genuine, kind invite, and she had told herself she would put herself out there more. "I'd love to join. Can I bring anything? I just made cookies...or would you prefer alcohol?"

"We accept booze, food, and even traveler's checks. See you in about an hour? Bring your game face, McSwiggans!"

She doubted either man noticed, but inside, her gaze became steely-eyed and vicious. She hoped they played word games. She destroyed her family in word games. It would be interesting to see how she did against others.

"See you in an hour."

"Kat says she's bringing her mom's original copy of Balderdash from the 1980s. She's hoping we can give it a try," Anton said through a mouthful of chips.

Simon shrugged, still annoyed over Cali's upcoming attendance at game night. "How retro..." He unpacked the recently arrived Thai food and smacked a container of peanut sauce off the counter with a wave of his hand. "Shit."

"Okay, what's bugging you now?" Anton asked as he handed Simon a roll of paper towels.

"Nothing." He bent down, cleaning up the mess.

"Does nothing have blond hair and green eyes?" Anton gave him a knowing look. "You were a little rude to her."

"I wasn't rude. I don't want to give her a false expectation of friendship."

"Uh-huh—if you say so."

Simon looked up at him from where he knelt on the kitchen floor. "What does that mean?"

"It means the last time I saw you act so surly around a girl, it was Mena Jackson in high school, and you ended up losing your virginity to her after junior prom."

"First, I wasn't surly with Mena–I played it cool. I liked Mena the minute she showed up to junior year wearing goth makeup and black hair dye. Second, Cali is the opposite of my type."

"What type is that? Pretty? Smart? Makes a good pirate?"

"Girls like Cali end up married to stockbrokers or lawyers named Kyle who cheat on them with their country club friends. She has a future of being disappointed in life but well-dressed in matching sweater sets and pearls."

"That's a vivid fantasy for someone you claim to have no interest in."

"She's. Not. My. Type." Simon stood and leveled a murderous look at Anton, who wagged his eyebrows in gleeful mocking, clearly enjoying giving Simon the third degree.

"Who's not your type?" a female voice came from the open doorway. Kat walked in, along with Ben and Sheila. Ben, Kat, Anton, and Simon made up one of the tables in their high school cafeteria, set aside for the less cool contingent of students. None of them had minded–they had all been glad to find a group of friends. For Simon, it had built an invisible force field separating him from the jeers of others because he was no longer alone.

"His downstairs neighbor."

"The 'snotty hottie'?" Ben asked, using finger quotes. He looked over at his girlfriend, Sheila. "She's the one I told you about who's asking Simon to torture her."

"I hope you don't have anything too mean planned, Simon," Sheila offered with a disapproving frown. "Even if she is as snotty as you seem to think."

"She's not snotty at all. I met her last weekend. She's coming to game night," Anton said, offering the bowl of chips to the new arrivals.

"Yay! Now we'll have enough people for even game teams." Sheila clapped. As the group's newest member, she made an effort to fit in whenever possible.

"As long as we play Balderdash first. I don't think my mom even played this one time. I want to see what an '80s board game was like. This game is forty years old!"

"Probably lots of references to communism," Ben offered as a knock interrupted their conversation. Five heads turned toward Cali, standing in the open door, holding a platter of cookies and a bottle of red wine.

"I hope I'm on time?" She gave a tentative smile. As the host, Simon should've been the one to greet her and thank her for the food and wine, but Anton beat him to the punch. Simon snorted inwardly. If Anton weren't gay, Simon would have sworn he had a crush.

"Right on time!" Anton greeted her with a friendly kiss on the cheek. "Are these the cookies you made?"

"Yes, snickerdoodles. Nut-free, in case anyone has an allergy."

"Dibs!" Kat called, and she headed to take the platter. "Hi, I'm Kat. Snickerdoodles are my favorite." She immediately snagged a cookie from beneath the aluminum foil and took a bite while moaning in enjoyment. "Feese are gud," she said through a cookie-filled mouth.

"They're my favorite too! I'm relieved to have somewhere to bring them, or I would've eaten all of them myself." Cali smiled, and it was warmer than Simon had remembered. She seemed...relieved? Simon watched her quietly as he pulled out plates and utensils for the Thai takeout.

"I hope you'll take Thai food in trade," Anton said. "Let me introduce you to everyone. We're all survivors of Wayne Valley High School—except Sheila, Ben's girlfriend. She grew up in Ridgewood."

"Maybe you can give me some good recommendations. I'm new to town." Cali looked at Sheila, who smiled, pleased.

"Do we want to eat first or go right to games?" Simon asked.

"Eat," three voices immediately voted while Cali and Sheila remained silent. The two women's eyes met with shy smiles—two outsiders having an unspoken conversation. Were Simon and his friends being judged? He felt an itch climb up his neck, an irritation he couldn't quash. He grimaced involuntarily and shook his head as if to clear it.

"Okay, eating first it is." He forced a smile and offered up a buffet of different options. Everyone helped themselves heartily to their choices, except for the red curry with beef, which only he and Cali shared, to his surprise.

"Okay, Balderdash–the OG version." Kat held up the box. "I stole it from my mom, and it's my turn to make the first pick."

Simon shrugged. After their first sessions were a free-for-all on game choice–leading to lengthy debates and little gameplay–they decided to take turns with who got to pick. Kat tended toward word games like Scrabble and Scattegories, so Balderdash was right up her alley.

"Okay, you guys know the rules. Unusual words–make up a definition. Or, if by some bizarre coincidence, you know the definition, write it down. Correct definitions earn points. Votes for your incorrect definition earn points. Are we clear?" She held the deck of cards containing the odd words and their definitions close to her person, as if suspicious that the rest of them were a group of cheats.

"Rules are super important to Kat. The Scrabble word battle of 2020 is still discussed in hushed tones," Ben whispered to Cali. Everyone was friendly to her, and Simon knew Cali was making an effort as well. She was taking their first 'lesson' from the faire the previous weekend to heart.

"Okay, are we ready to go?" Kat asked, spearing Ben with a supercilious glare.

"Aye, aye, captain." Ben saluted.

"Okay, the first word is *amphigory*," Kat announced.

"Amphi-what?" Anton asked.

"Amphigory." Kat wouldn't be distracted. "You have ninety seconds to write your answer."

They quickly jotted down their answers on pieces of scrap paper, handing them to Kat with solemn expressions. The group was still sober, so their answers all had a ring of realism to them. Later in the night, when the group had imbibed more alcohol, they would undoubtedly be more humorous.

"All right, for amphigory, we have: an amphibian in a state of mutation between tadpole and adulthood, an ambiguous ending to a horror movie, a children's nursery rhyme, an allegory with mythological undertones, and finally, writing that appears profound but is nonsense."

"I like the mythological one," Anton said.

"So vote for it. No secret lobbying for your answer, Anton," Kat ordered.

"I didn't write it!" Anton protested.

"Whatever." Kat ignored his complaint and awaited their votes.

When the votes came in, all but one had voted for the mythological one. One came in for the nonsense answer.

"And the actual definition is 'a piece of writing that appears to have meaning but is foolish nonsense.'" Kat turned to the group. "And Cali got the correct definition. She gets 5 points–three points for the correct definition and two points for voting for it."

"That's an amazing guess!" Anton looked at Cali.

"It wasn't a guess. I've heard the word before," Cali admitted shyly, sinking into the couch.

"Where?" Simon gave her a look, and their eyes met, her surprise evident at his direct address.

"I like old and odd words. It's a hobby." Cali blushed, and she grabbed her glass of red wine and swallowed a large gulp.

"So are you gonna know all of these words?" Kat asked, looking both impressed and annoyed.

"Maybe? I haven't played Balderdash in a while, but I used to flip through the cards as a kid."

"Wait–I wanna see how many she knows!" Ben looked at Kat with a pleading look. "Please, game master supreme?"

Kat looked torn.

"What if we also let you pick the game for our next session?" Ben suggested.

"Hey, it was my turn next time," Simon protested, receiving glares from his friends. "Fine, " he muttered sullenly.

"Okay." Kat nodded, placated by the offer. "Let's see what the new kid knows."

Cali had never told anyone about her love of words—not since her fourth-grade spelling bee. But the fantasy of winning the Scripps National Spelling Bee had never died, and every night, it had become her hobby to memorize stranger and longer words. Her Oxford English Dictionary had more tabs than a 1980s mini-mart. She never used the words in conversation, writing, or otherwise, but sometimes, when she was anxious, she'd distract herself by coming up with as many odd words as possible.

As she reviewed how Simon's friends considered their discovery of her secret passion, she was embarrassed, self-conscious, discomfited, flustered, and discombobulated.

So why confide her secret passion now? For one thing, Simon's friends seemed like the kind of people who wouldn't make fun of her for it. They would see her fascination as something cool, and she *needed* them to like her. Recent events had shown that her struggles to fit in were related to her inability to connect with others. This outing tested that skill set. A step here, a pivot there, as she worked to be someone with whom others could relate, and maybe, letting them get to know her was the first step.

And then there was Simon, staring at her with thinly veiled derision while everyone else was so pleasant. He still judged her and found her lacking anything interesting. Well, she'd show him. She wasn't so plain and typical as all that. She had layers—or a pluripotent personality.

Splitting the remaining Balderdash cards among the group, they took turns finding out how far her knowledge went. Anton started them off. "Your first word is callipygian." Kat played the Jeopardy theme song on her iPhone.

Two notes in, Cali inelegantly snorted over her wine glass. "Callipygian–having a nice ass."

"Correct!" Anton called out, impressed and pleased.

"I like that word!" Ben laughed and looked at his girlfriend. "Sheila, your buttocks are truly callipygian."

Kat made a show of pretending to vomit. "Sheila–your boyfriend is as pervy as he was in high school."

"But he's so grateful for the affection." Sheila patted Ben on the shoulder and kissed him on the cheek.

Kat shook her head and rolled her eyes, but her wide grin indicated she'd gotten over her game night choice being hijacked. "Okay, my turn. Dewdropper."

"An unemployed young adult who sleeps through the day." Cali looked over and pointed at Simon. "Like him!"

Kat pronounced her correct, and a series of groans and laughs echoed around her. Even Simon shrugged in amusement.

"Hey–graphic novelist is a perfectly reasonable profession. But yeah...to the sleeping part anyway." He smiled a little when Cali's eyes caught his own. She tamped down her answering grin into a polite smile, but inside, a warmth bloomed at his regard. Part of her had agreed to attend game night as a petty response to Simon's earlier derision. She hadn't expected to enjoy herself, but here she was, having fun and vindicating her personality at the same time.

"Okay, I got one–fogo," Sheila called out, more participatory than she had been earlier in the evening. Cali liked Sheila, who seemed friendly and down-to-earth. Sheila shared her boyfriend's petite stature, and they were endearing together. Casual affections and teasing gave Cali a pang of longing. They were so comfortable with one another.

"Um–an overpowering and unpleasant stench," Cali offered, and the rest of the room laughed uproariously.

"Yes, and after the Thai food, Ben is sleeping on the couch, so I don't smell the fogo from his callipygian ass." Sheila waved a hand in front of her nose as if smelling something gross.

"All I heard is my girlfriend say I have a shapely ass," Ben said, unbothered at the references to his farting.

Sheila high-fived Cali, and Cali made a mental note to find her on social media. Perhaps they might end up as friends? Simon's friends were lovely, but they were his. Like her, Cali could tell Sheila stood on the fringes of the group.

"Okay, my turn," Simon interjected. "Accismus."

"A fake refusal of something you really want," Cali answered promptly. These were too easy.

The words came fast and furious, both bizarre and funny—ataraxia (a feeling of bliss), blatteroon (a person who boasts constantly), bumfodder (toilet paper or a useless document), fopdoodle (a buffoon), and sting-bum (a stingy, mean person).

"I'm so impressed," Anton said at last. "You haven't missed one. Why did you start memorizing words?"

They were all staring at her, and scrutiny brought an uneasy roiling to her stomach, her imaginary Tumor gleeful at her self-consciousness. "Well..." Cali took a deep breath. "As a kid, I wanted to win the Scripps National Spelling Bee—and they always asked such unusual words, so I started memorizing them. After a while, it became something I did—to see how many I could memorize."

"Did you ever compete in a spelling bee?" Simon asked.

"Once, but after I moved in with my dad, I lost interest."

"Then why did you keep learning new words?" Simon asked, his head tilted as he watched her.

"Well—I guess I like doing it." But she sounded unconvincing even to her own ears.

"Should we do a spelling bee next?" Anton asked.

"That's not necessary. I outgrew my desire for spelling bees a long time ago." She stood suddenly. "Is there any more red curry? I'm still a little hungry."

"Sounds like accismus to me." Cali heard Ben mutter under his breath, and Sheila elbowed him in the stomach.

Cali made her way over to the kitchen, where she perused the remainder of the Thai food. Her face was warm, and she pressed the back of her hand against her cheek and took a deep breath. Something was tight around her chest, a vaguely unpleasant sensation that shortened her breath. Uneasy. She felt uneasy, and she couldn't pinpoint why. She shoved down the sensation with a mental promise to examine it later, a promise she had no intention of keeping.

"You okay?" She turned, startled to see Simon standing close to her, his dark brown eyes focused in concern. His low voice and large frame made the conversation feel private. "You're a bit flushed."

Every instinct, every learned behavior, wanted her to smile banally and write off her behavior as too much wine. But...she knew Simon wouldn't buy it, and after their visit to the Renaissance faire, she felt barbed in his presence.

"I've never shared my word collection with anyone." Her mouth turned downward as her eyes shifted toward his friends. "It makes me nervous to share that part of myself."

"Didn't think you'd be a secret geek." He leaned his back against the counter, his arms folded in front of him. His eyes met hers, and he smiled with frank appreciation.

If her face hadn't already been red, it would've flamed brightly at that moment, but he spoke gently, and it helped to settle her nerves. "I prefer word nerd, thank you very much."

Simon snuffed out a laugh. "It looks good on you."

"Does this compensate for my lack of passion for all things Renaissance faire? Am I now worthy of your friendship?"

"Please don't say it like that. You make me sound like a jerk."

"If the shoe fits..."

"Okay, okay, you're right. I apologize for my judgmental behavior last week. I was out of line. How can I make it up to you, Mad?"

Cali considered him critically. She could tell him it was no big deal, and they would return to their pleasantly distant acquaintanceship. They wouldn't be enemies, but they wouldn't be friends either. There were already so many people in her life who fit that description. If nothing else, Simon wanted to get to know the real her, and it prodded her to take the olive branch he offered.

"Cali?" Simon asked, shaking her from her reverie.

"Okay–you can make it up to me. Next Saturday morning, you're going hiking with me."

"Hiking...in the morning." Simon pulled a face. "That sounds..."

"Fun to me. I love hiking. Fresh air. Exertion. Beautiful views."

"I was going to say horrible." He looked at her with exasperation. "Is this revenge for the pirate costume?"

"No, just a pleasant side benefit...but now that you mention it, maybe I should have you hike in a boned corset."

Simon laughed quickly and covered it up with a cough. "Come back when you're ready; we're playing Pictionary next. They're all excited to have even numbers for teams."

CHAPTER 6

***Telic:** (adjective) tending toward a goal*

ONLY THREE PEOPLE called Simon regularly. The first and second were his mom and dad, who were blessed with a ringtone based on "Sweet Caroline" by Neil Diamond, a reflection of their boomer tendencies to insist on hearing his voice every three days. The third was his agent, Joanne Kelly, who had been given a ringtone based on "The Imperial March" from *Star Wars* because, like Darth Vader, crowds parted when she walked into a room. Though relatively petite, her personality made up for her lack of physical stature, and she relished her ability to scare the crap out of editors, authors, and publicists alike.

In short, she was the kind of person you wanted on your side.

Simon liked her immensely. He smiled as he picked up the phone.

"I shouldn't have to wait three rings for you to pick up your phone, Simon."

"Would you have preferred I do so while peeing? I can bring the phone in with me next time."

"Don't be crude, or I won't tell you the good, the bad, and the ugly."

"I'm deeply sorry, Joanne. If you were here, I would prostrate myself before you. Now, please, what's up?"

Joanne made a contented sound at the prostrate comment. "Just got off the phone with Carson Mathers." They were Simon's publishing house. "One of their February releases was one-star bombed on Goodreads when the author said some offensive things on BookTok. They need to fill the slot, and they're so pleased with your latest pages that they want to push the print date up from May to February."

"February? That's less than five months away."

"Is that a problem?"

"Not necessarily—it's gonna be a bit more of a squeeze to complete the formatting." He ran a hand through his hair and sat at his drafting table. "Was that the good, the bad, or the ugly?"

"That was the good. February is a great month for releases."

"I was hoping to release it in the summer—closer to Comic-Con."

"Comic-Con hasn't been for comics in years. No, this is great because they're not treating you like a graphic novelist—they're treating you like a mainstream release. This means they're considering putting their marketing dollars behind you!"

"Don't they pay to market every book they publish?"

"Oh no, no, no—they only choose about five or six books a quarter to truly market, out of well over a hundred. So I need you to do me a favor."

"I'm sensing the ugly is about to start..."

"None of this is a done deal. If we want to keep their attention, your work needs to be on time, and you need to ramp up your subscription base on Webcomicz."

"I'm in the off-season right now. I was taking a break while working on the book's formatting."

"Well, you're now off the bench on both. We need to consider upping the ante on the web comic—adding some spice or something to broaden your audience and help escalate your profitability in line with their Emily Henrys and Joe Hills."

"Spice? Joanne, you've never offered editorial input before."

"Before, you were niche, and you had a strong following. However, you'll now potentially be exposed to a much wider audience. Have you thought of giving Zap a romantic partner?"

"There are females in the comic, other heroes, friends..."

"Yes, but your female readership might grow if the Magnificent Zap got a little action."

"Action..." Simon considered her words. Was his character's game about to be better than his own?

"Think about it. I'm sending over the updated timeline and contract. They're increasing your advance in exchange for the extra work they put on you–you're welcome."

Simon grimaced. "I'd rather have the extra five months than the increase...but thank you, Joanne."

"I'll remind you of this when you see the email I'm sending you."

"Then we should hang up now." He clicked over to his computer and saw the email pop up. He distantly heard Joanne end the conversation as he realized he would be working ten-hour days, six days a week, to get this done in time and push up the next season of his comic. Perhaps he could do a limited storyline–a half-season to help build interest?

Either way, these would be a trying few months physically. Any increased stress or physical discomfort wreaked havoc on his gestures and grimaces, which only exacerbated the underlying problem. He needed to chat with the crew about this. What would Cali say when he told her?

Simon stood up short. *When he told her*–when had that become a consideration? They were meeting tomorrow for hiking–that was it. She had only been at top of his mind.

Not remotely noteworthy whatsoever.

But later that evening, when he pulled out a piece of paper to begin drafting the Magnificent Zap's new partner/girlfriend, he gave her long blond hair, bright green eyes, and a pirate hat.

CHAPTER 7

Oppugn: *(verb) to call into question*

"COFFEE OR TEA?" Cali looked at Simon from the driver's seat of her Honda Accord. She looked way too perky for the ungodly hour of 8 a.m. on a Saturday. Simon got in on the passenger's side while she indicated two tumblers. "The tea is decaf. I wasn't sure if you're able to drink caffeine. Google wasn't clear on it."

"I can have caffeine. I take it you've already had some." He picked up the coffee and took a deep swig—it had been heavily doctored with milk and sugar.

"Just some apple slices and peanut butter. There's more in the bag if you're hungry." She picked up the tea and took a long sip, then glanced down at his feet. "I'm glad I picked an easier hike—those sneakers won't hold up to anything more strenuous."

"You take your hiking seriously."

"Don't want you to get hurt. Hiking with the wrong shoes can be dangerous."

"Where are we going?"

"The Kaaterskill Rail Trail—about an hour from here. The path will take us to Kaaterskill Falls."

"Sounds like you know more about the surrounding area than I do, and I grew up right near here." It amused him how he had traveled the national parks with his parents and sister as a teen but had never explored the area around his home. "How did you get into hiking?"

"My stepmom used to take me on her walks when I was younger. The physical effort got me out of my head, and there's something fulfilling about using my body to go places most people won't make the effort to see in person." She looked over at him. "Do you like to exercise?"

Simon nodded. "It depends on the exercise. I enjoy activities that help create muscle memory. Recently, my sister got me into barre."

Cali looked at him in surprise. "I love barre classes. I don't see too many men who enjoy it."

"I think there's a stigma because it's affiliated with ballet and is less about..."

"Building big muscles?" she suggested.

"Exactly. I like it because repetitive movements feel...meditative. They establish patterns for my body to follow. Also, I can do it in my apartment. For me, strenuous exercise can be trickier because physical discomfort can worsen my tics. But an easy hike should be fine." He took a sip of coffee. "This is good–what is it?"

Cali gave him a sly grin. "Starbucks Pumpkin Spice."

A smile came unbidden to Simon's lips. "Of course, it is."

"It's the fall, and it's what we shallow women crave."

"I can see why–it's good." He took a long sip, enjoying the taste more than he cared to admit. Cali seemed game to drive in silence, but Simon fidgeted restlessly. "So, how's the new job going? You throw any more shade to the catty bitch?"

"No, Lauren has been surprisingly pleasant lately. She even texted me a photo of me in costume with her niece, along with a nice note. I think running into each other at the faire is forcing her to reevaluate what she thought of me...or maybe she feels guilty that she was caught being such a jerk." Cali sighed wearily. "But I did get some news this week that's on my mind."

"Lay it on me, Mad."

Cali's nose crinkled impishly at the nickname. "The goal of the program is to prep me for a management role, but usually, that's a ways out. I'm supposed to spend the next year learning the ropes of the different divisions. It turns out the manager of the New Jersey region is pregnant and has been on bed rest for the last four months of her pregnancy, so they gave me the interim role. I'll be managing her team until she's back from maternity leave. It's an eight-month assignment."

"You're getting a head start on the management job. That's a good thing, isn't it?"

"I mean, yes, the other trainees would be champing at the bit for an opportunity like this, but given my recent...struggles...I'm not sure I'm ready for it. I'm worried I'll screw it up."

Simon considered her from the passenger seat. "You worry a lot for someone without a wrinkle line in sight."

"I have a fantastic skincare regimen." She pointed to her forehead. "The pricey stuff–from Sephora."

Simon laughed. Cali's sense of humor surprised him. Why did he feel like no one else knew that about her? Her quips gave him a small thrill, like he had been responsible for finding gold in a barren mountaintop or a rare number one issue of *Superman* at a garage sale.

"Tell me what you're nervous about–what's the worst-case scenario?"

"Worst-case scenario, I take over the team for eight months; they all hate me. They give a negative review to the leadership team, and I'm kicked out of the training program."

"Okay, now the best-case scenario."

"I do a good job, I connect with my colleagues, and I get promoted to the product development team in record time."

"And that's what you want to do? Product development?"

"I want a say in which therapies the company decides to pursue–like which diseases they want to develop treatments for."

"So why not go into research?"

"I thought about that. I even took a few pre-med classes in college, but, frankly, my grades in biology and chemistry were lackluster at best. There's no way I was getting into medical school. Math and business have always been in my wheelhouse. But there's so much unexplored in the women's and mental health marketplaces. I want to be part of moving that forward."

"Why the women's and mental health marketplaces?"

Cali's voice changed as she spoke, becoming decisive, passionate. "Did you know the FDA didn't start requiring the use of women in clinical trials until 1993? We haven't thoroughly studied or analyzed how medicine differs for women compared to men. There's even something to be said for current drugs whose patents have expired that haven't been explored in different women-centric disease states like PCOS, endometriosis, and menstrual pain."

"And mental health?"

Cali's lips tightened. "It's an important space."

Her clamming up was a clear sign she didn't trust him yet, and after the Renaissance faire, he couldn't blame her for that in the slightest. He decided to move forward.

"And this is the best way to do that?"

"It's the most predictable path, but it means slugging it out in the trenches. It's admirable—they want their leadership team to have worn all the different hats with the company. Makes us better-rounded."

"I think your solution is right there. Your company is sending you out to learn things, so focus on asking questions. People love to talk about themselves."

"I don't like to talk about myself."

"You do it with me."

"Huh." She considered his statement with a brow bent inward. "You're right."

"Most people like to talk about themselves, so ask questions. Come up with a list of questions for your team members. Ask about their lives. Ask about their goals. Ask what they like about the job."

"Your advice is so common sense, it makes me feel like Lauren had the right of it when she said I had 'hot girl syndrome.' Once I got to middle school, the 'cool' kids approached me to join their clique, and I accepted the offer. If I hadn't, I would have been the target of their bullying. They didn't care about being my friend—the only reason they approached me was because I fit the image of what they wanted to be."

"Were you always...so pretty?" Simon couldn't think of another way to ask the question and cringed when he realized how it sounded.

Cali's eyes widened at the question, but she laughed. "How am I supposed to answer that?"

She looked over at Simon from the steering wheel. He gave her an expectant look in response.

"Okay, I get it. I know I'm attractive, and you're right. I didn't have an ugly duckling phase, but I didn't always have it easy. My mom had a free-range approach to parenting, making me an odd duck in elementary school. None of the parents wanted to set up playdates with my mom, so it was kind of just the two of us. When I went to live with my dad, my stepmom, Grace, homeschooled me for a few months, and part of that schooling was social. She taught me how to dress, do my hair, what to say and not say—basically how to fit in."

Simon sat, eyes wide, silently appalled at her description. Cali didn't seem to notice. She continued to prattle about the half-year equivalent of finishing school her stepmother had put her through. He took a long drink from his latte, trying to tamp down his urge to call bullshit on Cali's upbringing. It sounded like she went from being herself to being a perfect little Stepford child. Surely, he was missing a piece of the puzzle, something she hadn't shared—or that he hadn't looked for because her facade had fooled him. He felt an uncomfortable sensation in his gut, akin to guilt.

"Anyway, by the time I started fifth grade, a new student in a new district, I had a strategic approach to fitting in. The being attractive...well... it helped." She looked troubled and sheepish at the same time.

"Was popularity everything you wanted it to be?" He tried to ask the question without a tinge of judgment creeping into his voice, but his tone was clipped, belying the bitterness he felt.

Her smile turned sad as she parked the car in a spot along a row of SUVs and bikes belonging to other hikers who had already set off on the trail. "I never said I wanted to be popular."

CHAPTER 8

Melee: *(noun) a confused fight or skirmish*

"I DIDN'T KNOW that hiking was so popular in this area." Simon perused the collection of SUVs lining the parking lot at the trailhead.

"Early October is one of the peak foliage times for the Catskills, so it's not terribly surprising. It could be worse; the chill is keeping the worst of the crowds at bay." Cali gave Simon's attire–a pair of cargo shorts and a T-shirt–a once-over and tossed him a sweatshirt.

"Take this–it's always better to start with layers."

Simon looked down at the light blue hoodie she had thrown him. "And this would be?"

"My sorority sweatshirt. Kappa Kappa Gamma sisters always come prepared. I use it for layering, so it's an extra-large–shouldn't be too tight."

Simon groaned, chagrined. "You could have warned me. I do own a few sweatshirts."

"You needed me to warn you to bring a sweatshirt to an early morning mountain hike? Besides, I think you'd look rather fetching in baby blue."

He pulled it over the black T-shirt printed with anime characters.

"What show is that?" she motioned to his shirt.

"*Howl's Moving Castle.* It's a movie by Hayao Miyazaki." The sweatshirt fell a bit short on his torso, but it sufficed.

"I've never seen it. What's it about?" she asked as they walked to the trail.

"A young woman has a curse put on her to appear like an old woman and journeys to save herself. In the process, she meets and falls in love with this mysterious wizard named Howl, who has some issues of his own—namely, he's merged with a demon."

"Kind of like your superhero."

Simon considered the comparison. "Huh—yeah, a little bit."

"I started reading some of your earliest comics last week. The ones on your old website."

"The website ones? Man, those are so old. It gets much better if you fast-forward to about three years ago when I put them on Webcomicz."

"No, I'm enjoying it. I don't usually read comics, but I admire Zap. I see you in him. Makes me feel like I know *your* secret identity."

"That's how I felt when I saw you whooping everyone's butt at Balderdash." He bumped her shoulder with his own and grinned. "Word nerd."

"That was fun," she admitted. "I don't get many opportunities to play."

"Here's my question: why not seek out those opportunities? Join a board game group or something."

"Oh." She seemed a little breathless at the idea. "I tried suggesting it to my high school and college friends, and the one time I managed to get a couple of people interested, it ended up turning into a beer pong tournament. After that, I stopped trying to make game nights happen."

Simon didn't say anything, but he felt the same distance he had at the faire—the sense that either she didn't know herself or actively suppressed everything unique about her to fit in. His gaze must have made her uncomfortable, for she cleared her throat audibly, then watched as Simon repeated the sound several times in quick succession.

"Is it like yawning?" she asked after he had stopped. "The tics, I mean?"

"Yes, I'm surprised you noticed. Tourette's is not contagious, but certain gestures can set me off—can become my new tics. Just like yawning. It's called echopraxia." He watched her mouth the word and connected the gesture to her collection of vocabulary words.

"What do the tics feel like?"

"Kind of like a pressure behind my eyes—like taking a sneeze, cough, yawn, any involuntary gesture and amping it up on steroids."

"Are you able to control it at all?"

Out of anyone else's mouth, Simon might have found the question insulting, but Cali's consistently gentle approach put him at ease—she asked questions easily, those green eyes absorbing without judgment.

"Think of it this way. Have you ever had bronchitis?"

"Yes, in high school."

"So you know how you might be able to suppress your cough for a minute or two, but eventually it's going to come out? Ticcing is like that. I can control it or suppress it briefly, but eventually it comes out, and when it happens, it doesn't matter where I am or who I'm with."

Cali's eyes widened at Simon's implication. "I imagine that could get you in trouble."

"Oh—you have NO idea."

"I'm sensing a story..."

"A good one. You'll feel bad for me and laugh at me at the same time."

They were well on their hike when they encountered a large fallen tree blocking the path. Simon paused and offered Cali his hand while she traversed it. Her fingers were soft—maybe the same cream from the pricey skin regimen? He wanted to take the time to feel that silky surface, to study it like a sculptor searching for veins in a block of marble. He ignored the creeping blush climbing up his neck. "Junior year of high school, I'd taken Mena Jackson, my crush, to prom."

"Describe this Miss Jackson. What kind of girl did you go for in high school?"

"She was a goth goddess—black hair, purple eye shadow, nose ring. She used to draw these tattoos around her upper arm with a ballpoint pen." Simon looked at the trees, remembering how she'd been the star of more than one high school wet dream. "We went to prom together, and she deflowered me in the back of my dad's SUV afterward."

"Sounds like something out of a teen movie."

"Yeah, well... The sex part was good—fantastic even. I mean, I'm sure I was garbage at it... At seventeen, I, um, lacked experience."

Cali sniggered under her breath.

"Anyway, I—uh—finished before she did, but I'm a gentleman, and um, I took care of her afterward—only she made this face when she..." His hand twisted rhythmically in embarrassment as he tried to finish the sentence.

"Came?"

"Yes—and afterward, I could *not stop* making the face."

"Oh no." Cali gasped, her hand clapped over her mouth while she tried and failed to keep from laughing. She was already beautiful, but when she laughed like that, unguarded, she glowed. "I'm so sorry, I shouldn't laugh."

"No, it's okay. I gave you permission. I can laugh at it now as well." He shook his head. "Anyway, it wasn't only that night. I made the face intermittently for the next two months, and it got worse around Mena." Simon ran his hand down his face, mortified by the memory. "I mean, it's not like Mena didn't know I had Tourette's, and she laughed about it as much as anyone. She was against everything traditionally cool; I think she loved dating a freak."

Cali's laughter abruptly stopped, and she turned to him, her face stony from where she stood a few steps up the trail. "You're not a freak."

"I'm just joking—I know I'm not a freak." He paused and tilted his head as he looked at her. "Are you okay?"

"I don't like that word," Cali muttered. They reached a steep part of the trail, and Cali summoned a reservoir of strength as she practically jogged up the trail with Simon following behind her. Her speed indicated how often she partook in this activity, and Simon was breathless, attempting to keep up with her.

"We're about halfway to the falls," she said after he caught up with her. "After that, the walk should be mostly downhill."

"It's been a while since I've had exercise like this," he admitted ruefully. "I'm guessing Mario Kart doesn't count as cardio."

"Did you play any sports as a kid?"

"Little league, flag football, you know the drill–but I stopped when I became symptomatic."

"What happened?"

"Coach decided I was distracting the team. It's not like I was a brilliant player they were missing out on, a star receiver or pitcher, or whatever. I tried taekwondo for a bit, which worked with my need to focus. My parents got me involved with some sports groups for kids with similar issues, but by then, I'd mostly lost interest."

"Sounds like your parents tried to keep you involved."

"Yeah, and my dad and I still travel together to see the Yankees play an away game every spring."

"Are you close with your family?"

Simon nodded. "I got lucky. They're good parents. And my older sister Rebecca is much less annoying as an adult than she was as a teenager. She lives in Texas. My parents go to Florida during the fall and winter, but they're back here in the spring, and their house has a pool, so I end up hitting it up most weekends. Anton, Ben, and Kat tag along."

"I'm jealous. Grace, my dad, and Michael–he's my younger brother–still live in Scottsdale. I'll go see them at Christmas."

"Cali...I want to apologize for bothering you with the word 'freak'."

Cali looked over at him as if surprised he would bring it up.

"No, it's not your fault. I overreacted, jogging off like that. It reminded me of something that happened back when I lived with my mom."

"Where does your mom live?"

"Lived. She died about ten years ago. She lived in Northern California."

"Cali from California," Simon paused. *California–no way, it couldn't be.* He shook his head. He could ask another time. "What happened to her? Your mom, I mean."

"She killed herself."

"Fuck, I'm sorry." Simon stopped, his eyes widening as he looked at her, another piece of the Cali puzzle falling into place.

Cali shrugged. "It happened a long time ago. I hadn't seen her in nearly five years when she died."

"But you grew up with her, you said once, until you were nine?"

Cali nodded but hastened her steps, putting distance between them. "The view of the falls should be right up here." They were momentarily interrupted by the logistics of walking on the viewing platform. The sun sent gentle rays through the canopy of red, yellow, and orange trees. The falls cascaded over two levels, surrounded by dark red rock with purple undertones. The area was filled with the oddly sweet scent of decaying leaves on the forest floor below. A pair of hawks circled in the sky above them, searching for an unlucky rabbit to hop into view. "I'm glad we missed the early rush. It's more peaceful to get the platform to ourselves."

Winded from the walk, Simon paused on the platform as the sight of the falls and foliage stunned him into silence. His artwork focused on the fantastic and supernatural, and he sometimes forgot how visually striking a natural vista could be. He understood Cali's affection for hiking. The betrayal of his body often angered him, but looking out at the hillside, he felt gratitude for his legs bringing him here and for Cali for dragging him along.

"So." She looked back at him, and her face lit up in a broad and unaffected smile–a further slipping of her carefully constructed mask. "What do you think?"

"Thank you for bringing me with you. This is something else." He walked up to the edge of the platform. Leaning on the railing, he closed his eyes, feeling the soft breeze on the sweat of his forehead. The wood creaked as Cali walked beside him to take in the view. He opened his eyes to see her leaning down on the railing, resting her face on her folded arms.

"Cali, why did you stop living with your mom?"

"She was sick. She had bipolar disorder, and she couldn't take care of me anymore."

"Jeez–that must have been a terrifying experience at 9 years old."

Cali looked at him, surprise plain on her face. "It was the best thing that could have happened to me–Grace and my dad saved me."

Cali had a tendency to say things that confused him, but when he had previously jumped to conclusions about her, he realized his preconceived perceptions were consistently wrong.

"When I first came to them, I was a mess. Think about how much parents do for their kids–not just making lunch and helping with homework. Really think about how parents turn us into functional people. What would your life look like if your parents didn't teach you to eat healthily or brush your teeth? Imagine life with no rules, where you made every decision for yourself at seven, eight, nine years old."

Simon's memories from ages seven and eight were fuzzy, but he remembered resisting his parents' directions whenever possible–because that's what you did as a kid. You tried to get away with a late bedtime, you tried to skip dinner and eat dessert. Kids were lousy self-managers.

Cali continued. "Imagine not having anyone to give you that lesson or a parent who is unable to care for you or themselves because they're either so manic everything feels like a party or so depressed they can't get out of bed."

"You think I didn't see how you looked at me when I said Grace taught me how to dress and fit in? I grew up with a fun mom, and then just as quickly, bedridden for a week or more. I had to parent myself. I had to parent *her*! No one told me to do my homework, so sometimes I didn't. That was another reason Grace had to homeschool me until fifth grade—so I could catch up on everything. She had to make sure I knew about hygiene. I used to walk to school with my hair like a rat's nest. If it weren't for Grace..." Cali turned around and leaned her back against the railing, and she looked up at Simon. Anyone else would have been crying, but Cali appeared stoic until Simon realized she practically quivered with anger.

"Are you angry with me?"

"I'm angry at myself because I know how you see me."

"How do I see you?"

"You think I'm a side character with nothing to contribute unless I do something you perceive as interesting." She looked at her feet, kicking the tips of her hiking boots at the grooves between the platform's planks.

"Cali, you are *not* a side character. You have more main character energy than anyone I've ever met. What infuriates me is how much you seem determined to bury that part of yourself. When Grace gave you rules for fitting in, did she remove your personality in the process?"

Cali's eyes widened at his question, and Simon shocked himself with the cruelty of his question. He was an outsider, first by circumstance and now by choice, but he'd never been unkind. What he said—well, Cali should slap him for it. He wanted her to slap him for it.

"Grace gave me boundaries and guardrails to help make my life a little easier. Think about it—if there had been a way to cure your Tourette's when you were first diagnosed, wouldn't you have leaped at the opportunity? I think you're annoyed because I found a way to fit in."

The blood drained from Simon's face. His head buzzed at her correct assessment. If someone had offered nine-year-old Simon a pill to cure his tics, he would've taken it in a heartbeat. He would've given anything to be more normal back then. How could he judge Cali for taking a lifeline to fit in?

The ugly duckling becomes a swan, and the guy with glasses gets contacts. How many stupid teen movies had he watched where the outsider gets a makeover as a hall pass to popularity, only to realize it's no better?

I never said I wanted to be popular.

Neither had spoken in a minute, and the clean autumn air felt bruised. Simon turned from her and looked at the multicolored canopy of trees around them.

"I used to have dreams where the doctor would call my parents up to tell them there was a new pill for Tourette's that would take away my tics. I woke up crying because I wanted the dreams to be true."

"Do you still have those dreams?" she whispered behind him.

"No, not in years. At some point, I accepted my reality. Then I embraced it because if I didn't have this life, I wouldn't have the amazing things that have come with it. Anton, Kat, and Ben, but also my artwork. What made me weird as a kid is helping me be more remarkable now, and I guess what frustrates me is that you've taken the easy way out. It's much easier to hide who you are than live authentically."

"Authentically, huh." Cali considered his words. "When I was younger, my mom was the 'fun' mom. The kind who made every day exciting by putting her own spin on it, and I loved her for it. We were partners in crime. She didn't get bad until second grade. I didn't understand why she couldn't get out of bed for days, but I loved her enough to try to fill in the gaps. I took care of her. When my mom gave me up to get help, I was convinced I was the only one who knew what she needed. I researched. Thought maybe she'd take me back if I knew enough about what she needed."

"But she never took you back," Simon whispered.

"You say I took the easy way out–maybe you're right. But I didn't know any better, and now I'm trying to rectify that. I thought we were becoming friends, but I see now that you'll always judge me for how I chose to survive."

Simon wasn't sure how it happened. Maybe the watery hiccup accompanying her confession instigated it, but he wrapped his arms around Cali, pulling her close.

"Christ, Mad, you know how to make a man feel like garbage, don't you?" He spoke into her blond hair. She pressed her forehead against his chest, wrapped her arms around him. He held her shoulders to his chest, wondering if she was crying or taking comfort in his embrace. "I'm so sorry. I'm a shit friend. I hope you can forgive my stupid assumptions." The smell of her sweat and whatever shampoo she used filled his nose, but the scent didn't overwhelm him. Instead, he held her tighter, her embrace washing over him and wiping away the sensations prickling inside him like a thousand reflexes shouting for his attention daily. With her in his arms, he was calm.

She nodded into his chest, and at length, she looked up at him, his arms slung low around her shoulders. She stood close enough that he could see the unshed tears gathered on her eyelashes, and they made her green eyes even brighter, if possible. His breath caught in his chest as he thought about what it might be like to kiss her, to brush his lips against hers. They would be soft, and his thumbs would seek the smooth texture of her cheeks before he deepened the kiss. His eyes flickered to her mouth, and he forced himself to look away.

Cali gave a shaky sigh and stepped back, oblivious to his train of thought. "I don't think you're a bad friend. I mean, you're the first person in a long time who's bothered to dig deeper than what I put out there." But her eyebrows furrowed. "And I appreciate that more than you know."

He nodded, both reassured and perplexed by his reaction to her. "You okay?"

"Drained." She gave him a wan smile. "You ready to head back?"

"Yeah, I think I did well for my first hike." Simon watched her as they began the return path to her car. He tried to figure out if she was okay or masking her emotions again. He stared at her so closely that he didn't see the knotted tree root across the dirt path until his foot made contact, and he went down with a thud.

CHAPTER 9

Gestic: *(adjective) bodily movement*

GETTING DOWN THE HILL had been a trial, though they muddled through with Simon's arm around Cali's shoulder as he limped down the gentle slope. Once they were back at the car, she shoved him in the back seat so he could elevate his foot while she found the nearest urgent care with Saturday hours.

"I take back everything nice I said about hiking," Simon grumbled from the backseat. Cali decided against teasing him when she could see his tics asserting themselves as if his body were angry at Simon for the pain he had subjected it to.

"What's going on back there?" she asked, spying on the jerky movements in the rearview mirror.

"My body doesn't do well with discomfort–makes the tics worse, which then makes the pain worse. Argh!" At that moment, his injured leg jerked. Simon squeezed his eyes closed in frustration.

Cali floored it back to Ridgewood. She clenched her jaw as Simon groaned every time his body moved against his will. She thought back to her mother, Winifred, and how her mind betrayed her to the point of alienating her daughter. In the early days of living with her dad, Cali had been sympathetic to her mother as she made her way through cycles of treatment. Like clockwork, she would call her mother and visit whenever possible. But at some point along the way, her mother gave up. Perhaps seeing her daughter do well with her father and stepmother helped Winifred feel absolved from continuing her treatment because no one depended on her. To Cali, it felt like a rejection. Her mother would rather have her highs and lows than her daughter.

There was no comparison between Simon and Winifred. Simon didn't want to be in pain. It renewed her resentment at her mother, who might have had peace from the disease that took her will to live. Why should her mother get to opt out of life when people like Simon worked their hardest to live, to make something out of what they were given?

And as quickly as the feelings of anger surfaced, so did the feeling of guilt. What kind of daughter harbored anger toward her mentally ill mother, toward her *late* mentally ill mother? This elevated her resentment of having to brush away her anger until the Phantom Tumor churned in glee at her unexpressed frustrations.

Pulling into the urgent care parking lot was an unexpected relief, if only because it gave her something to do instead of something to feel.

While the physician's assistant on call gave Simon the side-eye at his gestures, he ascertained that while Simon's ankle was most definitely injured, thankfully, it was only a moderate sprain and not a break. He directed Simon to follow the RICE protocol of rest, ice, compression, and elevation for no less than two weeks and to see a podiatrist or orthopedist if the pain continued after that time. Getting Simon back in her car, Cali breathed a sigh of relief that the damage was not more significant, though it was clear Simon was in pain.

Once they arrived at the shared townhouse, she let Simon lean on her shoulder again as she got him upstairs to his apartment. Dropping him gently onto his couch, she looked around the apartment and set to work, getting him a glass of water and some recently expired Motrin from his medicine cabinet.

"Making yourself right at home, huh?" Simon grumbled, his body tense as if awaiting the next wave of pain.

"I'll take that to mean you have a head injury because that is not a nice way of saying 'thank you.'" She gave him the glass and got him a pillow to put under his injured ankle. "What would you like to eat? I'll order us some takeout."

"I'm not hungry."

"Not even for some red curry?" She took humor in the thinly pressed line his lips formed before he nodded. She noticed how they'd both favored the dish at game night. She placed the order on DoorDash. Unfortunately, Simon's tics worsened as time passed, indicating his high degree of discomfort.

"Seriously, Simon, you're in a lot of pain. What can I do?" She took one of his hands in both hers and watched as an almost wistful expression crossed his features. His body stilled momentarily, and he gripped her hands. She'd noticed the texture of his fingers when he'd helped her over the fallen tree earlier in the day—calluses that had built up, she supposed, from hours spent drawing.

"Can you go to my bedside stand? There's a pack of cannabis gummies there—they should help."

Cali nodded, though it took Simon a moment to let her hands go. In short order, she had the package he'd asked for and opened it for him.

"My doctor prescribed these for me whenever I have a tic attack."

"You mentioned that at the Renaissance faire, but I didn't get a chance to look it up. What is a tic attack?"

"It's a severe episode of ticcing that involves my whole body. It can last from minutes to hours. I haven't had one in a while, thanks to the Haldol I take, but injuries can make everything worse...so..." He popped the gummy in his mouth. He chewed it quickly, his body still jerking around, exacerbated by the pain in his ankle. "It takes a while to start working."

"I'm here, what can I do?"

A series of emotions crossed his face, and Cali tried to make sense of the fleeting expressions. His face settled into something that could've been need or yearning.

"Can I hold your hand?" he asked through clenched teeth.

Cali tilted her head in confusion. She wanted to ask why, but at that moment, Simon grimaced, and she grabbed his hand in helplessness. She didn't understand why it would help, but he knew his body and needed her help.

Simon disentangled her fingers from his and slowly turned her hand. She watched, mesmerized, as he played with her fingers like an odd fidget spinner. The sensation was pleasant–not quite ticklish, but warm and friendly–and she found she didn't mind his tender ministrations. His expression morphed into something sweet, almost boyish. Watching silently, his body calmed in minute degrees until he breathed deeply, relaxing into the couch cushions.

"Thank you," he whispered many minutes later, his eyes hooded in relief. "It helps to have something to keep my hands busy. Silly Putty helps, but for some reason, human contact is the most effective."

"I should no doubt make some joke about being glad I could lend you a hand." She looked down at him. The combination of human contact, exhaustion, and possibly the gummy was doing its job. Their food would be arriving soon as well.

"Why don't you put on a movie?" he mumbled. "Since I plan on keeping your hand hostage for the foreseeable future."

"Could we watch the movie you mentioned earlier? *Howl's Castle*?" She'd liked the brief outline of the story he'd provided.

"*Howl's Moving Castle*? Sure." He directed her to the cable remotes–an interesting endeavor since he was unwilling to let go of his plaything for even a moment. When the movie began, he continued his soft caresses while Cali smiled down at him, pausing only when the deliveryman arrived with their food.

The movie was charming. Cali smiled at Sophie's efforts to change her life and come to care for Howl. She understood the heroine, who had spent much of her life making herself small and unremarkable before finding a well of bravery within. Perhaps she, too, could uncover the bravery to be more. She turned to Simon to say something to that effect, but his eyes were closed, his head on her shoulder, his breathing deep. He still held her hand in his own. She could disentangle herself now, but the movie had forty minutes to go, so she let him sleep with her hand in his while she watched to see if Howl and Sophie found their happily ever after.

CHAPTER 10

Compeer: *(noun) a person of equal rank, status, or ability*

OH, IT WAS AWKWARD. Even she could tell it was awkward.

As interim manager of the New Jersey team, Cali decided to spend a day with each of the seven reps reporting to her. Today, she was traveling with Jesse Andrews, a forty-two-year-old rep who had been with Marcus & Meyers for over a decade. The attractive middle-aged woman either had good genes or a fantastic deal on Botox and chestnut hair dye because she appeared about ten years younger. The car seats in the second row of Jesse's navy-blue SUV indicated she had two young children. Calm and collected, Jesse did not appear disposed toward being friendly.

Cali brought a cappuccino and a pastry to make friends. Jesse politely thanked her, but both items remained untouched while she sipped from her Stanley.

"Not a coffee fan?" Cali asked.

"No, never cared for the taste. Always liked the smell—but the taste is too bitter."

"Have you tried it with different flavored syrups? I'm a big fan of caramel macchiatos."

"Caramel sounds good, but it would still taste like coffee. I prefer English breakfast tea."

Trying again, Cali removed her notepad from her bag. "I'm looking forward to working with you today," Cali offered as Jesse nodded coolly at her. "I hope I can help you over the next few months until your manager returns."

"Thanks, that's nice of you." Jesse entered an address into the GPS, all business. "I have appointments today with two of my largest customers–Dr. Sandman and the Shermans."

Cali nodded. "Can you tell me about them?"

"Sandman is open with how he feels, good and bad, but he's loyal to our company. Some of his ideas on how we can improve are on point. He's a good bellwether for customer sentiment."

"And the Shermans?"

"The Shermans like to think they're the biggest game in town, but their volume has dropped for two straight years. Their marketplace is changing, but they don't want to admit it. It makes for some fun conversations."

"Maybe some of our new tools could help. I got a sneak peek behind the scenes for what's coming at the kick-off meeting in January," she blabbered nervously, which she did next to never. "The new marketing materials can help offices with their social media strategy. And our new programs aimed at helping offices grow worked quite well with the pilot offices in Italy."

"Italy–huh–the New Jersey of Europe." Jesse seemed unconvinced and cynical, and she looked at Cali as if to say *who the hell are you kidding?*

This was not going well. The Tumor gleefully churned, as if to remind her of the consequences of failure. A lump rose in her throat, and she tamped it down with a determined sigh.

They rode silently for several minutes while Cali rethought her game plan. Growing up, she had never had to ingratiate herself with others–they all went out of their way to connect with her. But high school, college, and even graduate school, to some extent, had been popularity contests. Grace had given her rules for fitting in geared toward going along with the crowd. But that's not what leaders did. Leaders inspired. Their ability to make things happen grew as an extension of the respect they commanded.

What did Lauren say about influencing without authority? Cali was only an *acting* manager. Jesse had no obligations to take Cali's suggestions seriously, knowing her regular boss would be back soon. Temporary, inexperienced, and about fifteen years younger than her companion, Cali needed a new approach. After all, a six-month interim assignment meant little to a rep who could measure their time with the company in multiple years. Cali tried to see herself through Jesse's eyes. What could Cali possibly have to offer a rep of her tenure?

And then she remembered the text Simon had sent her the previous evening after she'd checked in to see if he felt better. She'd confided in him about her nervousness surrounding today's work.

"Mad, if all else fails, ask questions."

How could she forget? How arrogant to assume she could teach anything to a rep who'd been on the job for ten years. Cali needed to flip her approach.

"You're right, of course. Italy is nothing like the US market." Cali paused. "I feel like we got started off on the wrong foot. I'm brand new and want to help, but I don't know anything about what you're seeing in your day-to-day. I'd like to hear what you think. Perhaps we could stop for lunch somewhere after the appointments. Where do you think we're missing the mark with these customers?"

Jesse gave her a side-eyed look and tilted her head. Her lips pressed together in something resembling a good-natured smirk.

"As long as we're back by 4 p.m. My youngest has a doctor's appointment." She gave Cali a guilty expression as though this were a failure of her dedication to the company. "I couldn't reschedule."

Something thudded in Cali's heart as her colleague talked about being there for her child. "I'm glad you didn't. This is a job—your family comes first." And Cali meant it. Maybe younger managers would look askance at an employee putting family before work, but Cali found it impressive. After slipping through the cracks in her early childhood, Cali found Jesse's dedication to her children reassuring. She belatedly hoped that Jesse didn't think she was being condescending, but the statement appeared to have landed well.

Jesse gave her a satisfied nod and warmed considerably. "You ever had soup dumplings? There's a great place in Fort Lee when we finish our second meeting."

"Never had them, but I'll try any food once." Cali released her breath and got to work.

During the appointments, Cali listened to customers discuss their concerns about the industry and the company, taking notes and realizing with dismay that training had not adequately prepared her for some of the objections the reps received. Jesse had a deft approach with her customers, acknowledging their concerns and asking questions to further investigate the matters they raised. They trusted her guidance, and Cali realized how much she could learn from her colleague.

And that included from a culinary perspective! It turned out soup dumplings, or Xiao long bao, as Cali learned they were formally called, were little pockets of delicious pork and broth wrapped in dumpling dough. The potent flavor soothed, the fat and salt warming her from within. She wondered if Simon would like them if she got some to go. She hadn't seen him since Saturday night when she left him dozing on his couch with a glass of water and two Motrin waiting for when he woke up, but she had texted him twice to check in.

"So what you're saying is we're losing smaller customers because our pricing structure is volume-based, and these offices don't have the same volume to give us as established accounts?"

"Exactly. These new offices are using our competition's products and are getting comfortable with them early in their career cycle. It's a lot easier to establish rapport and systems from day one than to try to win them back from competition five years in when they finally have the volume to get premium pricing."

"Seems like a major competitive threat."

"Agreed–it's a slow decay. We don't see the lost business because, technically, it never existed. We're setting ourselves up for a large-scale failure when these offices reach the mature stage of their business cycle and our bigger customers begin retiring."

"Have you tried escalating this to your manager?"

Jesse's face colored noticeably, and Cali wondered if there wasn't any tension with the manager she currently covered. "I explained it to her once, but I don't think I did a good enough job explaining the potential upside of the idea. I created a PowerPoint presentation, but she didn't think it was worth sending up the ladder."

"Maybe a second pair of eyes could help to fine-tune your idea. Would you mind emailing it to me? I'd like to see what you put together."

"You're not going to steal my idea, are you?" Jesse's voice rose to play off the comment as sarcasm, but Cali saw the genuine worry in her gaze.

"No!" Cali started, then calmed down. "Not at all–sometimes two pairs of eyes are better than one. When did you last look at the data?"

"About a year ago, but I can easily update it. I'll send it to you tonight."

"I appreciate you trusting me. Even if this goes nowhere."

"Thank you for listening." Jesse gave her an unguarded smile, and Cali released the breath she had unconsciously held. Inspiration might take a while, but trust was a good first step.

YOU ARE NOT FOCUSING ZAP. YOUR AIM IS MISSING HIM.
HE'S MOVING AT SUPER SPEED. YOU TRY HITTING SOMETHING MOVING AT THE SPEED OF A BULLET. IF I GO TO WIDE I'LL DESTROY HALF THE ART IN HERE.
THAT IS NO EXCUSE.
CRASH!
AVAST, YE BILGE SUCKING VILLAIN! I'LL NOT LET YE TAKE DESTROY THESE FINE WORKS OF ART. YOU'LL BE ROTTING IN THE BRIG OR I AIN'T THE FEARSOME PIRATE PRINCESS MAD MCSWIGGANS!
!

CHAPTER 11

Pulchritudinous: *(adjective) beautiful*

SIMON REVIEWED his work with a critical eye. Nothing he drew could compare with his neighbor's beauty, but he hoped he'd captured the hidden parts of her personality that slowly revealed themselves at every interaction.

Caring, clever, obsessed with words, loyal to her family, hard-working, desperately anxious, and kind. It reminded him of how artists sometimes said they discovered the artwork in a medium by peeling away layers of stone and clay. Incredibly self-centered as it sounded, he could not help but feel Cali offered him a peek of herself she didn't give to others. He was honored, and to be honest, enamored. He had a crush, and it needed to be nipped in the bud, pronto.

Dammit, Anton is right. He grumbled under his breath as he continued to work.

Inking the soft curves of Mad's face, he considered how to make her appear vulnerable and strong. Standing on a stone bench in the sculpture garden, she stared down at the villain ravaging the city's art museum to steal a ship's painting that concealed a treasure map.

"Fearsome..." He smiled down at the image when a cheerful knock on the door interrupted his work.

Simon blinked and sat up. His ankle had been slowly improving, but was still far from one hundred percent. Focusing on his artwork helped to lessen the tics that intensified his discomfort, but now that he stood, his expression contorted, the vein on his neck straining. He would pay for the hours he'd spent at his desk today.

"Hey, Zap, it's me!" Cali called from outside his door. "I brought you sustenance!"

Simon hurried to the door–as much as he could–to find Cali in a black business suit and heels, holding a plastic takeout bag.

"Zap?" he asked her.

"You call me Mad, seems only fair. Have you ever had soup dumplings?" she asked with a delighted look on her face. Where was the ill-at-ease woman he'd met two months before? The brittle smile that felt like it belonged to a game-show model had long given way to secretive grins, pursed lips, and outright belly laughs. This smile was a fall day, a vat of movie theater popcorn with melted butter, a Yankees win...

He moved aside to let her in, and she strolled inside, putting the bag on his kitchen counter. "My colleague, Jesse, introduced these to me, and I thought you might be hungry. They're also a thank-you gift for the incredibly helpful advice you gave me." She glowed at him, and his heartbeat quickened in response. Maybe it was better she was standoffish with people–who could fight those eyes?

"Thank you. That was thoughtful." He absentmindedly scratched the back of his neck. How could he get her to stay? "I know you had them for lunch, but would you like to share them with me?" He was maneuvering to the kitchen when the pain in his foot asserted itself, and he grimaced before tapping his thigh again.

"Okay..." Cali nodded her head as she appeared to take him in. "Here's what we're going to do. You will sit on that couch, and I'll heat up some food, and we can watch a movie." She raised her eyebrows in an amiable entreaty. "Sound good?"

He nodded mutely. Some men might feel embarrassed, letting her take charge like this. He called it a boon that he got to spend more time with her. It didn't occur to him to feel insecure about his tics. He didn't imagine he was anywhere in her league for one second, which took the pressure to impress off of him. This small realization provided equal parts solace and sadness.

Whatever, Peter Parker isn't with Mary Jane either, at least not on Earth-616.

"Have you ever had these before?" she called to him from the kitchen while she searched for utensils and bowls.

"The bowls are in the cabinet above the microwave." He gestured with a flick of his wrist. She nodded and took out two. "Yeah, there's a good place in Ridgewood. I'll take you there when I'm feeling better." He watched her as she made herself at home, dishing out portions for the two of them. She'd pulled her hair back in a messy bun, and the itching of his hand to remove the elastic and see those locks fall free had nothing to do with his tics but much to do with his libido.

"What should we watch?" she asked as she put the bowls down on his coffee table.

"I think you should get to choose this time." His eyebrows wagged in glee, eager to peel back another layer of the Cali onion. He pinched his chin like an amateur detective. "What kind of movie do you like, Mad?"

"Shallow, superficial...women like me are all about the rom-coms." She looked up from the bowls at his soft groan. "Don't tell me you're one of those boys who think rom-coms are lame?"

"No—that was a tic. But to answer your question, it depends on the rom-com. I certainly don't reject them on principle."

"Well, with the day I've had, I feel like the vibe is right to watch *Working Girl*."

Simon had never watched the 1980s classic. However, he found it amusing to see Harrison Ford as the romantic lead in a workplace comedy rather than a science fiction or action-adventure epic. Cali pursed her lips in appreciation when the man went topless.

I'm better looking than he is. Simon knew he was conventionally attractive, but it had been a few years since he'd had a regular girlfriend.

His last hookup had been at a comic book convention a few months earlier. In art school, he'd had a series of casual relationships and occasional hookups, but the connections felt limited. Were they like his high school girlfriend, seeing him as an unusual 'other' worthy of experimentation? Or perhaps they dated him with the painful caveat of *despite.* Ben and Kat overheard one girl he liked stating she liked Simon "despite his Tourette's"—as though she were heroic for putting up with him. Fuck that.

The Haldol tamped down his sex drive somewhat, but as a healthy young man, Cali's head on his shoulder served as an unholy temptation. He could smell the shampoo she used, but while many scents caused his body to react, the soft waft of vanilla relaxed him further. Instinctively, he picked up her hand, playing with it as he had two days before, and the contented sigh he heard from her filled him with both warmth and desire.

How would she respond if he kissed her? Would it be a welcome development or ruin a burgeoning friendship? He judged it unwise to do anything now, not until he knew if she would return his affections or if he could survive if she didn't.

"How do these soup dumplings compare to the local ones?" she asked.

"Not bad at all. I like the broth better with these than I do with Shanghai Café Deluxe." He unfortunately chose that moment to burp loudly.

Well, clearly I'm not gonna be able to make a move tonight, anyway.

"Ugh—disgusting!" Cali laughed uproariously. Simon also laughed as her face contorted in mirth. "We should change your name to the Magnificent Belch."

"Funny, am I? You're gonna pay for that one, Mad."

"I'm quaking in my pumps, Belch."

"You think so? Do me a favor and grab me the Amazon envelope by the front door."

Cali stood to retrieve it, her eyes narrowed in a look of calculated discernment. “You got nothing.”

“Go on, open it. It’s a present for your next challenge.”

She fought with the plastic seal of the blue-and-white bubble pack. “I figured these were on hold until you were a little less gimpy.”

“I’ve recruited two backups, and they are *very* excited to help.”

Cali finished wrestling out the contents, and the color drained from her face. “Oh no.”

His answering smile conveyed gleeful chaos. “Oh, yes.”

CHAPTER 12

Diaphoresis: *(noun) excessive perspiration*

"IT'S NOT THAT BAD, Cali," Sheila cajoled as Cali refused to move from their Uber. The driver gave her an impatient stare.

Of course, Sheila said that—*she* looked chic in a little black dress with her light brown hair pulled back into a high ponytail.

"I disagree—it's pretty bad," Kat countered. Kat looked boho chic with a red patterned dress that accentuated her curves and dark skin.

"He could have at least gotten me one to match my eyebrows. Blond eyebrows with a black permed wig, people are going to think I *chose* to look this way."

"I mean, that's kind of the point, right?" Sheila offered. "Awkward experience 101—the bad haircut."

"I need a cocktail. Maybe several." Cali moaned. It didn't matter that she wore her sexiest halter dress. She still looked like the victim of a first-year hairdresser tasked with giving her first perm.

"We offered to pregame with you." Kat pressed her lips together, but a smile reached her eyes. "Come on, I'll buy you a mojito."

Kat and Sheila had dragged her to Casa Enrique, a Mexican restaurant that transitioned to a nightclub after dinner hours had finished. The three women sat at a booth while Kat and Sheila ordered nachos and drinks, and Cali did everything she could to make herself as small as possible.

Most people were in their mid-to-late twenties, dressed to dance and impress. She'd been dragged to enough of these venues in college and grad school to know the drill. She would have a few drinks and occasionally get pulled out on the dance floor with a group of drunk girls while she tried to avoid the creepy guys who tried to 'dance up on' her. She knew her beauty attracted others to her orbit in these circumstances. Physical attraction replaced conversation when loud music made conversation impossible. Her girlfriends used her presence to their advantage, attracting free drinks and admirers. They insisted on her staying even as they offered crocodile tears when she departed, leaving the spoils to them.

The acrylic strands of the curly black wig made her itch, and she shrugged her shoulders to stave off the sensation and avoid bringing more attention to the hideous coiffure. The unconscious action reminded her of Simon's uncontrollable motions. She'd checked in on him before she left, allowing him to laugh at the disaster he had wrought upon her, knowing his humor came from a good place. Her cheering him up from his current state of gimpiness also motivated that particular act of generosity.

"The wig is on–what am I supposed to do now?" Cali asked Kat and Sheila, and they shrugged. "I'm still not sure why he assigned me this when my first mission was pirate cosplay."

"Oh, I forgot, he texted me!" Sheila pulled out her phone and read the message. "Cali, tonight you need to let your inner light shine. Your mission, should you choose to accept it, is to get a suitor's phone number."

"That doesn't sound hard, getting a phone number?" Cali looked at her new friends. "What am I missing?"

The two girls immediately looked at the 'fro she sported and gave her a sympathetic grimace. Cali's fingers tangled in the synthetic fibers and moaned. "This might take a while."

"Let's get you a couple of shots. I always find it easier to chat up boys and girls with a little social lubricant." Kat signaled the waiter and placed the order for Kamikaze shots.

It took four shots of various combinations and two hours before her approach morphed from coy flirtation to out-and-out warfare. The minute any man dared to make eye contact with her, their eyes flitted to the rat's nest atop her head, and they *noped* the heck out of there. Cali had never had to try to get a man's attention, leaving her both frustrated and enlightened by the night's experience. Sometimes she pretended to be snobby to keep men at a distance. If they thought her a bitch, they left her alone.

It occurred to her belatedly—*so that's hot girl syndrome. Huh.*

Cali's college boyfriend, Zach, had approached her at the beginning of her first semester, though she hadn't started dating him till the middle of the year. Star of the school's popular baseball team, Zach came with a coterie of good-looking women fawning over his attention and good-looking men hoping to catch the less selective ones on the rebound.

Zach had been a charming, attentive, and perfectly pleasant boyfriend. His interest made her social stock soar, and though that had never been her goal, getting out of dorm living and into the sorority house was a fringe benefit she didn't mind. She had a date for the Greek formals and parties. When his baseball team traveled from Arizona to Texas, she joined, decked out in Sun Devil red and yellow. It made for as predictable a college experience as any she had seen in the '80s and '90s college films she and Grace liked to watch together.

She and Zach broke up shortly after he graduated two years ahead of her. She didn't have the chance to miss him before her second college boyfriend approached. Ted lasted until she graduated a year ahead of him. She politely ended it, uninterested in a long-distance relationship, and he seemed okay with it if the images of him with his new girlfriend on Instagram four weeks later were any indication. The same thing happened in grad school with Arun from corporate finance class. She barely thought of him anymore. It wasn't that she was easily forgettable to the men she dated; it was that the men were forgettable to her.

The men she dated were fine, both physically and emotionally. But she didn't love them, and they didn't love her. They were mutually beneficial placeholders for the real thing that none of them had been ready for. As a young woman, she missed the physical affection that accompanied a monogamous relationship. She never favored casual hookups, and she didn't have the energy to enter another relationship that provided only a pantomime of what a happy couple should be.

She watched as the men's eyes slid over her without seeing her, examining the novel experience. She'd been honest when she told Simon she'd never wanted to be popular. After her mother disappeared from her life, Cali clung to anything she perceived to be ordinary. Typical moms weren't the kind to drive their daughter to school without pants on or feed her only cereal for two weeks because they were in a manic phase. She aspired to normalcy. And she had become just that—unremarkable in every way except her appearance.

And she had done it to herself! Holding herself back so they wouldn't judge her for who she was on the inside. Because if they were close enough to *know* her, their abandonment would hurt even more.

Better not to be known than to be known and discarded.

And here she sat, contemplating her lack of arsenal in attracting any man here. She grumbled and looked at her cocktail—rum and Diet Coke. A few yards away, Sheila and Kat were dancing and having the time of their lives, and she wanted to be with them.

"Forget this," she whispered. Failure might be imminent, but she could still have fun. Downing the rest of her cocktail, she joined her friends on the dance floor. Both girls threw a drunk arm around her shoulders, and they screamed and sang the lyrics to Charli XCX. The wig was warm, and a bead of sweat ran down her forehead before falling into her eyebrow. She wiped away the perspiration and saw the smear of her eye makeup on her fingers. She laughed at how she must appear to others at the moment.

"Selfie!" Sheila shouted, taking out her phone. The three mugged for the camera, with Cali giving her best effort at a seductive, kissy face.

"Can I put this on social media?" Sheila asked, thrusting the image loosely in Cali's face. Drunk herself, Sheila didn't realize the picture she showed Cali was of Ben making a muscle pose in a pair of tighty-whities.

"Why not?" How bad could it be? She could always delete it in the morning. She giggled audibly.

Whoa, how drunk am I?

Still, as the deejay switched to "Mr. Brightside" by The Killers and her voice joined those of the crowd on the dance floor, she found she didn't care about the picture at all.

It was one a.m., but Simon hadn't been sleeping. He'd been doom-scrolling through Instagram when the photo of Cali, Sheila, and Kat appeared on his feed. Cali proffered a sideways pose with puckered lips, her wig askew with black rivulets of smeared mascara pouring down her cheeks from the outer corners of her eyes. She looked both horrible and adorable in equal measure.

He considered how to comment when the pounding on his door began.

"Simoooon!" It was like the sound of some bizarre animal mating call. "Sim-on, let me in! I did it!"

There was a muffled noise, like a body falling against the wood panel, and he limped through his apartment as quickly as he could. When he opened the door, Cali literally fell into his arms. Holding her up, he looked at her elated face, inches from his own.

"I did it, Simon!"

Backing away from him, she held up the atrocious black wig. "Oops, wrong hand." She giggled and brought up her other hand, in which she had a business card. "I got a guy's phone number wearing the wig!" She did a drunk shimmy, holding the card in front of him like a trophy.

Simon bit off a grin into his hand. "Let's get you some water, and you can tell me the story."

"Oh yeah, water would be good." She fell back on his couch with a lavish whoosh. "I don't know if you can tell, but I had quite a bit to drink tonight."

"No kidding." He grabbed a bottle of water out of his fridge, then backtracked to snag the bottle of Motrin he kept in the cabinet nearby. Handing her the water and two pills, he sat on the coffee table, facing her.

"Thank you! You take such good care of me." She giggled, took a greedy gulp of water, and downed the tablets.

"So, spill–how did it happen?"

"Well, after we went dancing, the three of us were hungry. Like, starving. There was a pizza place next door, and we decided to grab a couple of slices. And this guy was there with his buddies–I think his name was Jordan? Or was it Jefferson? I don't know." She flapped her hand repeatedly like his name couldn't be important. "Anyway, we both ordered the same kind of pizza–buffalo chicken with vodka sauce–and talked about how no one possibly appreciated the combination. It was the first conversation I'd had with anyone all night–besides Kat and Sheila, of course–so I asked for his number, and he said yes!"

She lazily thrust a fist into the air. "Mission accomplished!"

Simon gnashed his teeth painfully in his mouth as she described her drunken meet-cute. He liked vodka sauce and buffalo chicken too.

"Way to go. I'm proud of you," he offered fondly and with a touch of sadness. "So, are you going to call him?"

"Call him? No way! He smokes. I could smell it all over him. Disgusting." She sat up. "Buffalo chicken and vodka sauce are not the foundation for a healthy relationship."

"Educate me–what is the foundation of a healthy relationship?"

"Dunno, maybe friendship?" She yawned hugely and looked up at him with glassy eyes covered in the remaining makeup from a fun night out.

Simon's heart squeezed painfully, and his hand patted his thigh in agitation. Cali grabbed his hand and pulled him closer to her without warning.

"Let's watch a movie," she suggested. How could he refuse? He climbed onto the couch, and she snuggled into his arms, taking a deep breath of his shirt before sleepily whispering. "Something happy–I'm in a good mood."

Simon flipped through his Roku before selecting *The Birdcage*. By the time the opening credits were done, she had fallen asleep leaning against him. Her even breaths spread like a panacea through his body, allowing him to hold her and calming his body, leaving it unusually still. She fit so well in his embrace–like a beige puzzle piece perfectly fitting into the cacophony of colors that were his many oddities. No, not beige. There was nothing beige about Cali Barton. She was champagne, soft with a subtle but entrancing glow. Placing a gentle kiss on her forehead, he turned to watch the movie, letting the beat of her heart soothe him until he, too, fell asleep.

CHAPTER 13

Refulgent: *(adjective) shining radiantly*

PING. PING. Ping. Ping. Ping. Ping

The chiming of her phone woke her. Cali's head felt swollen and expanded, as if noise and sight grew infinitely more powerful on the sensitive canvas of her senses.

Ping. Ping.

You have fifteen notifications.

Swiping up, Cali groaned at the appalling photo that greeted her. What in the world had been going through her head when she agreed to let Sheila post this picture? She looked like a demented '80s hair metal impersonator.

"Oh no..." she whispered. The comments were a mix of good-natured teasing, with one being remarkably lewd, and the roiling in her gut grew in proportion to how funny she would have found them if it had been anyone but her in the picture.

Michael: Looking good, sis! What's with the 'fro?

Victoria: Dying! This photo is everything! You need to bring the wig to my bachelorette! Kappa Kappa Gamma for life!

Ben: This photo lives rent-free in my head.

Lauren: Looks like a fun night!

Anton: Your Slash costume is missing the hat and sunglasses.

Ryan: Since you didn't let me find out in training...does the carpet match the drapes?

She moaned into her hand and heard an echoing groan behind her. Practically jumping up, she was shocked to see Simon waking up next to her—on his couch, of all places. She looked around—when had she come to Simon's apartment?

The night came back, first in drips, and then in waves. The nightclub, the dancing and singing, the social media photo, and the drunken visit to Simon's apartment, where she had fallen asleep. Her face burned as memories surfaced, both giddy and cringe. Undercutting the fun of the experience was the feeling that she'd given up her tightly held control over her actions. It had been exhilarating, and recollecting that feeling terrified her.

Overwhelmed, her imaginary Tumor, enjoying a diet of Mexican food, pizza, and alcohol, screamed in victory. Dropping the phone, she ran to Simon's bathroom and emptied the contents of her stomach in three quick retches.

"I'm such an idiot," she mumbled. Moaning pitifully, she pressed her head against the cool tile floor as Simon's plodding footfalls came up behind her.

"You okay?"

"Nope," she blurted, humiliation suffusing every fiber of her being.

"We talking standard-issue hangover, or is something else bothering you?"

"Did you see the picture Sheila posted? I look like a lunatic." She pressed her fists into the bathroom rug on his floor. The fibers felt stiff from toothpaste droppings and who knows what else, and she couldn't imagine Simon had ever washed the thing.

"That? I saw that last night. I thought it was funny."

She heard the smile in his voice.

"I'm glad you hit it off with Kat and Sheila. They're a lot of fun to hang out with." He got down close to her on the floor, then patted her back as if in solidarity with her plight.

She turned her head to look up at him, kneeling by her huddled form. He was holding her phone, studying the offending image.

"Most of these comments are harmless. The Slash costume one is my favorite." He continued reading, and his lip curled in disgust. "Who is this Ryan douchebag? Can I kick his ass for you?"

"Guy from work." She pushed herself up with a grunt and took the proffered phone from Simon's hand. "He hit on me during training, and I turned him down. I didn't realize he followed me on Instagram. And yes, he is most certainly a creep." She took the phone from Simon and blocked Ryan. "Well, that's one problem solved."

"How bothered are you by these comments?"

"I don't know. I'm more concerned I let myself get out of control to the point I let myself get posted looking like that." She leaned back to sit against the wall. Simon scooted in and joined her, his long legs in a crisscross position. "I get that's the point–I'm supposed to be putting myself out there, but..." Cali looked at Simon hopelessly.

"Can I ask you something?"

"Sure." Her thumb hovered over the image.

"If this wasn't a picture of you–if it was a picture of a friend, happy, a little inebriated, a little silly looking–what would *you* have commented on that picture?"

Cali looked at the photo with a critical eye. The girl in the picture was a hot mess, but no one could miss the fun of the moment. The girl in the photo looked utterly unselfconscious. She looked bold, confident, and happy.

"I would have said..." She looked Simon in the eye, catching the devilish glint there. He wanted her humor, her intelligence, her wit. "I would have said Weird Al Yankovic's kid sister sure looks hot."

Simon cracked up, and she laughed too, long and loud. She loved making Simon laugh. The thing in her stomach that thrived on anxiety dissipated as though their shared mirth helped to heal and drain whatever part of her had buried misery and fear deep inside her. As their amusement ebbed, she looked back at Simon in gratitude and affection.

She'd been in romantic relationships for most of her adult life. How did this man that she'd only met in the last few months become someone who understood her so well? How did she come to confide things in him that she barely acknowledged in herself? He smiled fondly at her and got to his feet before offering her his hand to help her stand.

"How about I make us some breakfast?" he offered.

"You went grocery shopping?" She followed behind him doubtfully.

"How about I order us some breakfast?" He looked back at her with a smile and a guilty glint of mischief in his eyes.

The flood of warmth that suffused her being in response to his expression felt so natural that she nearly missed her heart somersaulting in response.

Nearly.

Her gut clenched with the realization that she had a new reason to feel afraid.

CHAPTER 14

Mammer: *(verb) to hesitate*

CALI WASN'T THINKING about Simon. She wasn't thinking about the flop of dark brown hair that fell over his forehead in an errant curl. She wasn't thinking about how he held her hand or the calloused roughness of his fingers as they played upon the inside of her palm. She *definitely* wasn't thinking about how his body perfectly aligned to swallow hers in a satisfying cuddle.

What *she was* thinking about was having a *crush* on Simon. It was an entity in and of itself, taking up real estate in her brain and in her stomach, which roared like a washing machine in the middle of a spin cycle.

The treadmill was getting its money's worth. Forty-five minutes on an incline of seven came and went, and Cali kept going. Logically, she knew she couldn't outrun the knowledge that she had developed a crush—oh, and crush seemed such an inadequate word for what she knew her feelings for Simon to be—but the focus on her body kept the knowledge from becoming overwhelming.

She had never *yearned* for anyone before. The forty-five minutes at breakfast three mornings before had felt endless as she wrestled with the realization that, for the first time in her life, she wanted someone who had not wanted her first. It showed her earlier courtships were a poor facsimile of what real desire felt like. A good-looking boy asked her out. If they were acceptable on paper, kind, and reasonably interesting, she entered into an understanding with them. But she had never feared for her heart before.

Simon had determinedly broken through her barriers of politeness and bland agreeableness. He angered, entertained, and supported her all at once.

After breakfast had concluded, Cali made her escape, claiming the lingering effects of booze and a night spent on a couch. She'd been doing her level best to avoid him ever since, while she tried—and failed—to figure out what she wanted.

Grace called at minute fifty-five. *Darn it.* She was ten minutes late for their phone date.

"Hey, hon, am I calling at a bad time?" Her stepmother's voice echoed on her iPhone.

Cali focused on catching her breath, wiping away the sweat on her forehead with a nearby towel. "No, I'm sorry. I lost track of time on the treadmill." Cali immediately bit her lower lip. Grace, the detective, the mother, knew what that meant.

Grace paused, her voice dropping from curiosity to concern. "What are you running away from this time?"

"Nothing, I needed to blow off some steam."

"You act like I don't know this game, Cali. Talk to me. A mom's advice is an excellent alternative to running yourself ragged." Cali heard noise in the background. "I'll tell her, I'll tell her," Grace called out, then turned her attention back to Cali. "Your dad and Michael want to know if you're coming home for Thanksgiving," Grace paused, and Cali heard a muffled shout, "Mitch, I told you *twenty times* we won't see Cali till Christmas." Grace sounded mildly beleaguered—and maybe annoyed—with the knowledge that Cali wasn't coming home sooner.

"Tell them I say hi—oh, and ask Michael how the latest basketball game went!"

"Oh no, I haven't forgotten we're discussing your stress. Spill it."

Cali fell back on her bed, the pillowtop and comforter swallowing her, causing the fabric of her shirt to absorb the sweat that had accumulated on her skin. Grace tended to pinpoint her moods with unfailing accuracy, a quality that inspired equal bouts of frustration and closeness. Sometimes, teenage Cali wanted to keep her moodiness a secret, but Grace's uncanny ability to see the truth of her feelings made that a near impossibility. As an adult, Cali saw the interference for the act of love it always was.

"Do you remember my new friend, Simon, who I mentioned a few weeks back?"

"The neighbor? The one who draws the comic strip?" Grace spoke like someone using an unfamiliar word and couldn't be sure of the pronunciation. Was there judgment in Simon's career of choice? More likely, Grace didn't know what the job entailed.

"The graphic novelist, yes." Cali swallowed. "It turns out I've developed a teeny tiny...crush on him." Her face turned hot as she confessed to someone, finally, how she felt.

"Does he feel the same way? Is that why you're feeling upset?"

Cali paused. It hadn't even occurred to her to wonder if Simon felt the same way. She'd been too concerned about running into him, suppressing her emotions, not melting into a pile of embarrassed goo in his presence.

"I don't know." Cali longingly looked at her treadmill cooling down in the corner of her bedroom. "I don't even know if I want him to have feelings."

"You don't? But if you have a crush on him, why wouldn't you want to date him?" Grace trailed off, then another voice came across the line.

"Hey, dork." Ah, it was her younger brother. "Most people upset about a crush feel that way because they're unsure if their object of admiration feels the same way." Michael was a junior at Arizona State University, getting his degree in psychology, and he loved to show off.

"I know. I'm not, in fact, an idiot."

"Emotionally, that's debatable. Why wouldn't you want him to like you back?"

"Because he's not like anyone I've ever dated before." She almost mentioned that Simon had Tourette's, but held herself back. His tics had nothing to do with her hesitancy, did they? She didn't believe so. What she felt wasn't reticence, it was fear.

"Good—maybe he has an actual personality."

"What's that supposed to mean?" Defensiveness prickled her spine even while she remembered privately acknowledging how unremarkable her past relationships had been.

"Come on, Cali. Zach, Ted, Arun—they were the human equivalent of a baked potato. Interesting enough with all the fixings, but boring AF underneath."

"Well, I didn't date them to make you happy."

"You sure as heck weren't dating them to make yourself happy." Michael paused and spoke to Grace, who must have been squawking in his ear. "No, Mom, I mean it. She was as bored with them as we all were. Remember the night Zach spent an hour talking about the infield fly rule? I wanted to take him on Shark Tank as a cure for insomnia."

Cali had heard that lecture about the infield fly rule no less than ten times. At the time, she considered the quirk endearing, even while excusing herself to reapply her lipstick whenever Zach found a new crowd to torment. Michael wasn't wrong.

"What do you and this guy talk about?"

"Movies, board games... I took him hiking the other day." She paused. "I told him about my mom."

Michael's stunned silence felt loud all the way from Scottsdale. "Wow—you *like* this guy, don't you? No wonder you're scared shitless."

"It's not only fear. I mean, we've become good friends—and he's my upstairs neighbor. What if he doesn't feel the same? If he does feel the same, what if we're better as friends than as a couple? What if he's bad in..."

"I beg you not to finish that sentence. No brother wants to hear about his sister's sex life." Michael sighed. "You're so focused on all the stuff that can go wrong. What if he likes you, and he's an amazing boyfriend? What if his...skills are second to none? Either way, there's no reason for this to lead to a panic attack. Nothing *bad* is going to happen. Let's say he doesn't like you. Guess what–we've all been rejected and lived to tell the tale." She heard a noise in the background. "Grace says she met Dad after a nasty breakup, and it was the best thing that ever happened to her."

"How did you get so wise for twenty-one?"

"The psychology program at ASU is nationally ranked. How did you get so dumb for twenty-seven?"

"I was too busy getting my MBA to talk about my feelings," she snapped back, feeling guilty. Michael was trying to help.

"Oh, Cali, *you* should learn to talk about your feelings."

She wanted to respond that she was fine, but at that moment, the imaginary Tumor in her stomach chose to make a gurgling noise akin to a dying walrus, and her longing looks at the treadmill shifted to her bathroom instead.

"I'll call you later, Michael."

"Love you, Cali. Think about what I said. It wouldn't hurt you to date someone you enjoy for a change."

Hanging up, Cali considered her brother's words. She thought about what Michael said about rejection. Simon saw her in a way others hadn't bothered to uncover. If he rejected her, it would mean so much more. At the nightclub, she realized how much her appearance shaped her romantic life. While Simon likely found her attractive on the surface, would he want what he saw underneath? Wanting Simon and wanting to date him were two different things. Perhaps, if she tried, she could reconcile her heart and head.

CHAPTER 15

Complot: *(noun) a secret plan*

SIMON HADN'T SEEN CALI in over a week. It wasn't long in the scheme of things. After all, their friendship was relatively new, and Cali had a job and—probably—a life outside of their interactions. Maybe she was off hiking or something. Anton had tried to get her to come to a Halloween-themed game night at his home in Wayne with all the usual suspects, but she begged off, claiming she had a big work project keeping her busy. This may have been true, but Simon had the feeling Cali was avoiding him.

Had she caught on to his growing feelings for her? If she had, perhaps she'd decided to politely ghost him so as not to lead him on.

But he questioned that conclusion. Yes, he had—accidentally—slept with her on his couch, but her reactions the morning afterward appeared to be more influenced by the silly photo on social media than by his presence. He calmed her and helped her reframe what she saw as embarrassing into something amusing. He was good at that. It was why she needed him.

His mental detective work left him distracted as Anton asked him for the third time if Simon had any wool to trade for wood in their group game of Settlers of Catan. Simon looked at his cards without seeing them.

"Where are you tonight?" Ben asked, snapping his fingers in front of Simon's eyes. Simon stood abruptly, his hands fluttering against his thighs in agitation. His ankle had healed nicely, so his tics had fallen back to their normal rhythm, annoying but neither painful nor distracting.

"He wants to know why Cali didn't join tonight." Anton gave his friends a knowing look and added with a theatrical whisper, "This is Mena Jackson all over again."

"For fuck's sake, this is not Mena Jackson. Mena Jackson liked having a freaky boyfriend to mess with her parents. Cali is nothing like that."

The group of them gave him satisfied looks with arrogant smiles, and he realized, belatedly, that they had lured him into a trap.

"Called it! I so called it." Ben smacked his hands together with a thwack.

"Simon's got a cruuuuush," Kat gushed in a singsong voice.

"To be fair, I called this weeks ago." Anton claimed his share of the prize.

Kat shook her head. "Only 'cause you met her before the rest of us. No extra points for you."

"Very mature. Thanks. I'm glad you take such glee from my romantic anguish." Simon ran a hand over his face, enjoying the feeling of his fingernails scratching his forehead. In truth, it was a relief to admit his feelings, if only because now he could talk about it.

"Hey, you have our approval. She's perfect for you," Anton offered from the floor around the coffee table as he perused his resource cards. "She's smart, kind, a secret dork, and good-looking. What's not to like? Although..." Anton pursed his lips, "She did skip game night. That's a ding on her letter grade."

"She's helping her colleague, Jesse, put together a PowerPoint for a meeting on Tuesday. I should think she gets extra credit," Sheila said, and when they all stared at her, she waved off their surprise. "What? I took her to my favorite yoga class on Wednesday night, and we had a glass of wine afterward. She told me about it."

"She picked work over Settlers of Catan?" Kat asked incredulously. "Booo!" She made a thumbs-down gesture.

"Yeah, who picks work over Anton's frozen appetizers?" Ben called out.

"Did she say anything about me?" Simon asked, unashamed of his eagerness and not caring to pile on with his friends.

"No..." Sheila paused thoughtfully. "But it was like she was determined not to mention you even when you should've come up in conversation naturally."

"What does that mean?" Ben asked his girlfriend, as if he was only now discovering the hidden depths of her observational psychology skills.

"Cali's nature is one of reticence. She's an overthinker. If she didn't mention Simon, she did it on purpose. That means she's avoiding you because she either doesn't like you or she really, really does." She looked up, seemingly surprised at everyone staring at her, waiting for her to continue.

"But how do I know for sure which one?" Simon practically begged for the insight.

"I mean, you don't. Not until you talk to her. But for what it's worth, my money is on she likes you but doesn't know what to do about it."

"Because she's not sure he likes her back?" Kat asked.

Sheila shrugged. "Maybe. Or maybe she doesn't know what she wants to do about it. I don't get the sense Cali has ever had to be the romantic instigator before. She was hopeless at the bar the other night."

Kat nodded. "Oh yeah, her game had all the consistency of underdone Jell-O."

"Or maybe that was because you got her drunk," Simon posited.

"Nah, the drinking helped. It got her out of her head. I wouldn't recommend that approach for the long haul, but we had fun." Sheila looked over at Kat, who gave a begrudging nod.

"So, what do I do now?" Simon addressed the question directly to Sheila. Not only did she know Cali better than his other friends, but she also revealed a knowledge of others that he and his awkward friends had missed. Sheila could read people. "I want to see her, but I texted her this week, and she left me on read for twenty-four hours before she responded."

"Do you have any more missions for her?" Anton asked.

Simon shook his head. "No, I'm not sure if it's a good idea after the photo from the last one sent her into such a panic."

"Sheila and I had an idea for one I think could be a lot of fun—a big confidence booster as well," Kat said. "Would it be okay if we organized the next one? You could come for moral support."

Desperate for ideas and grateful for his friends' support, Simon nodded. "What did you have in mind?"

"Let me put the pieces together first. Trust me—this is right up her alley."

CHAPTER 16

Synergy: *(noun) the interaction or cooperation of two or more agents to produce a combined effect greater than the sum of their separate effects*

"I'M IMPRESSED WITH the work you two put in on this project." George Melone, Cali's boss and Jesse's boss's boss, sat back in his seat at the Panera Bread in Fair Lawn, New Jersey. A decent-looking man with light brown hair and the definition of a 'dad bod,' George was teetering on the edge of forty. He nodded definitively and rubbed his chin with his thumb. "What inspired you with this idea, Cali?"

"It wasn't me, George. This is Jesse's baby. I helped fine-tune some of the slides with a clearer formula to display potential ROI, but my contributions are minimal compared to hers." Cali gave Jesse a small smile meant to encourage her report.

Jesse's body buzzed with nervous energy, her hands clenching together, but Cali could only guess as to what caused her such anxiety. Perhaps it was because they were going over her regular manager's head. Doing so could be seen as a career risk.

"Jesse, sometimes ideas are such no-brainers you wonder why no one came up with them before. I think this falls under that category. I'll forward this to my leadership team tonight. If it works with them, I'd like you both to present it on our next area leadership call." He looked back and forth between them. "If that's acceptable with you both, of course."

Cali looked at Jesse. This was her idea, her decision.

"Yes!" Jesse paused and cleared her throat. "Yes, I'd love the opportunity." She flustered momentarily. "If you'll excuse me, I'm going to use the restroom."

George and Cali watched her go before George turned back to Cali. "I'm impressed. Inviting creativity and encouraging your team takes real leadership skills. Jesse's been working for us longer than I've been with the company. She's a quality sales rep, but I fear she's been pigeonholed in her current role for too long. Thank you for pointing that out."

"She provided me with excellent insights into how our customers perceive our organization. I think she's someone the marketing team should reach out to for field feedback."

"You took my advice after training. I can see you're doing what you can to bond with your team. How are things going with the other trainees from the program? Have you connected with them at all?"

Cali's stomach churned a bit, but she forced herself to take a deep breath. "I need to be better. I got off on the wrong foot with some of them, and I'm nervous about resetting. It's not acceptable, I know."

"Hey, stop it. I can see you're taking my feedback seriously and making strides. Baby steps. Start simple. Lauren's going on vacation next week—I'm going to volunteer you to provide her with the intel from our next call. You can't force camaraderie, but a great way to start is by offering to help someone in need."

Ugh, Lauren, great.

But Cali had to admit, Lauren had been oddly solicitous ever since the run-in at the Renaissance faire. She hadn't told anyone about Cali's pirate experiment and had made bland but supportive comments on Cali's humiliating Instagram photo. She hadn't necessarily been friendly, but Cali sensed a guarded warmth there. At the very least, she could pass along meeting notes.

Jesse, for her part, let out a cheer as she drove Cali home after their meeting.

"I want to thank you for taking my idea seriously. I admit, when I first met you, I thought you were another corporate stooge—only interested in parroting the company line instead of listening to what other people had to say."

Cali looked at her from the passenger seat and gave a begrudging smile. "You're not wrong."

"Yeah, but you changed up your approach. That takes a lot of maturity. I'm looking forward to seeing how you do here, if that doesn't sound condescending."

"Not at all. I'm touched, honestly." She paused. "And I'm looking forward to seeing how your presentation advances your career as well."

"Oh, that's nice of you, but honestly, I'm not looking to get promoted, at least not until my kids are in high school." Jesse smiled at Cali's scandalized expression. "Don't look so surprised. Not everyone's goal in life is to climb the corporate ladder."

"Then what was the point of your project?"

"So that's it? The only reason I could want to better the company is if I want to go into management?" Jesse sighed. "This company is filled with hundreds of reps who want to see our company succeed, some because they want to improve their bonuses, some because they want to get promoted, some because they believe in our company's mission."

"You're making me feel green right now." Cali laughed, not offended by Jesse's bluntness.

"You *are* green, but you know it. That means you'll learn."

As they pulled into Cali's driveway, Cali spied Simon receiving a bag from a delivery driver. Unconsciously, she smiled at him. It had been over a week since they spoke in person—though she'd responded to his humorous text messages as appropriate. He had taken to sending her funny words he came across to see how many she knew. So far, she'd known ten of twelve, but to be fair, the two she hadn't known were a metal from Marvel comics—adamantium—and a word about Tourette syndrome relating to repeating one's own words—palilalia.

"Who's the tall drink of water?" Jesse interrupted her reverie.

"Oh, he's my neighbor, Simon." Simon spotted them and leaned against his porch railing, waiting for her to get out of Jesse's car. He had a warm smile on his face. "Looks like he wants to talk to me about something."

"Uh-huh, something. Have a good night. I'll talk to you tomorrow."

Cali got out of Jesse's car and looked up at Simon. Oh, but she had *missed* him. His porch light illuminated from above, giving him a beatific aura.

"Hey, Mad, how did the meeting go?"

"You stalking me, Zap?" She smiled back at him.

"Nah, Sheila mentioned it at game night. Good luck getting a restraining order though."

"I could know a guy."

"Judging by the happy snark, I take it the meeting went well?"

"Yeah, it did." The grin on her face felt natural. She was pleased with the meeting's results and felt a surge of happiness that she could share the news with Simon before anyone else.

"You feel like celebrating over sushi? I ordered way too much." He gave her a look filled with subtle entreaty, as though he missed her too. How could she possibly refuse?

"Sure, let me change into something a little less professional."

"Kinky."

"Yes, my flannel jammies are super kinky. See you in five."

She would have preferred to wear something nicer than flannel jammies, but felt trapped by her description. Her flare leggings did more to show off her figure. Then she second-guessed herself again for obsessing about which pajamas to wear to her neighbor's apartment. Standing on the precipice of a decision, Cali saw each choice layered atop the others so that the sum of their parts compiled. It reminded her of something she learned in math class—folding a single sheet of paper in half forty-two times would make a piece of paper tall enough to reach the moon.

Lord, she was bad at this.

By the time she arrived, Simon had set out plates and various sushi options. Like with the Thai takeout, she noticed some of her favorites among them. It made her giddy, all these little things they had in common, how they fit together.

"Chirashi...yum!"

"My favorite too. I like sushi too much and always order more than I can eat. And this stuff doesn't keep well."

"What, you don't like day-old raw fish?"

Simon squinted awkwardly and involuntarily, and his hand absently patted his thigh. She knew him better now, knowing when his tics were more than usual. His regular cadence was almost invisible to her now, but when it was out of the ordinary, it prickled at her senses. Certain he felt on edge, she longed to hold his hand, to let him know he needn't be anxious with her. Unsure how to proceed, she pretended not to notice.

Sitting on his couch, she filled her plate. "So, what are we going to watch tonight?"

After some good-natured debate, they ultimately selected *When Harry Met Sally*. As the film progressed, they shifted from eating to sinking into the deep cushions of the sofa. Cali curved into the shape of him, enjoying his lanky form. She admired his long forearms and how his tendons stood out against his skin. His arms and legs had a fine dusting of hair that abraded her arms pleasantly. Like clockwork, he took her hand with his own. What had begun as a source of relief for him had become a longed-for affection for her. His ministrations typically began with gentle presses to her palm, before he intertwined their fingers. As he played with each finger, she was lulled by the sensation, as if his ministrations were a massage. She smiled in contentment and cuddled closer. His head rested on hers, and she smelled sliced ginger on his breath, his exhalations feathering against the crown of her head.

Cali's mom had introduced her to the film as the most perfect romantic comedy ever produced. Cali didn't understand half the jokes at the time but laughed along with her mother, eager to please. Grace reintroduced the film a few years after, and the more mature jokes landed. The rare memory connected her mom to Grace, the two women who shaped her into who she was today, good and bad. The realization coincided with the finale in which Harry confessed his love to Sally. Sally stared at Harry, her furrowed brow of aggravation giving way to a torrent of tears and that magical New Year's Eve kiss.

It mildly humiliated Cali to realize how the emotion of the scene had led to her eyes filling with tears. She didn't know if the tears resulted from the memories of her mom or from the heartrending scene playing out before them. She bent her head into Simon's chest, seeking reassurance from him—or maybe to keep him from seeing her tears. He held her close, and if he was surprised at her actions, he didn't betray it.

"Do you want to talk about it?" Simon asked, his hand brushing her back in soothing motions.

"It reminded me of watching this with my mom when I was a kid." She sighed, her face flushed. Could Simon feel the heat in her cheeks pressed against his chest?

"I think I was eight years old when my parents first showed me this movie," Simon commented after a while. "Way too young. I did not understand the diner scene."

Cali chuckled into his T-shirt. "You didn't understand orgasm faking at the age of eight? That's not surprising."

"But I knew my parents thought it was funny, so I kept saying, 'I'll have what she's having' after every conversation. My parents would laugh every time, even though it must have gotten old for them after the twentieth or thirtieth time I said it." Simon's chuckle reverberated in his chest.

"At least you weren't copying the fake orgasm sounds," she murmured and unburied her head from his embrace.

He looked down at her, and she noticed his touches on her hand had moved from soothing sweeps to gentle tracings meant to evoke sensation. His fingertips danced along the inside of her wrist and up the soft, smooth skin inside her arm. They were purposely arousing, and her face turned hot as she looked up at him. Slowly, he brought his free hand up to cradle her cheek.

"If I kiss you right now, will it ruin whatever it is between us?" His eyes were darker than usual, intense and earnest. She saw their need, and it reassured her that she was not alone. With Simon, only with Simon, she was never alone.

"Maybe," she whispered, and when he pulled his hand away, she pressed it close again. "But I want you to kiss me anyway. Please."

He pressed his forehead against hers, still cradling her cheek in his hand. With deliberation, he pressed kisses on the delicate skin of each cheek before finally brushing his lips against hers, the back-and-forth motion slow and careful, opening her with each pass as his tongue tasted her, the flavor of ginger lingering there. He smoothed the hand on her face back to massage the skin at the base of her neck. She gasped at the flood of arousal his slow seduction wrought, and he took the opportunity to deepen the kiss.

Simon was good at this.

He kissed her reverently, thoroughly. She had already known her feelings for him were romantic. She wanted his kiss, but this was far more erotic, more masculine than she had expected. She thought her past liaisons were men, but none had taken the time to savor these minute explorations. For Simon, kissing was akin to making love, not merely a prelude.

He continued to kiss her, pushing her gradually so they were lying together on the couch. He seemed in no rush to push boundaries, though one of his thighs rested between her legs, and the pressure of him there set her core aflame, and she writhed against him unconsciously.

He smiled against her mouth, trailing his lips down to her chin, then gliding across her face to her neck. "That good, huh?"

"Yes," she admitted, smiling in response. He placed open-mouth kisses on her neck, and she moaned helplessly, lolling her head to the side to grant him access.

"Christ, Cali, when you make those sounds..."

"What...ah...what does it make you want to do?"

"You have no idea. I've been dreaming about you this way since we met. Even before I liked you, I thought you were beautiful, but even more, you're so amazing, smart, funny, sexy when you spell those big words." He kissed her clavicle, breathing in her scent.

"You're not supposed to be *this* good at this." She gasped as he did something particularly wicked with his tongue against her neck. "You're supposed to be a nice boy, not a..." She sighed as he caressed the sensitive skin of her stomach beneath her sweater. "Not a..."

"Not a what?" His voice was bemused, and those calloused fingers tracing the skin beneath her breasts were as beguiling as she had hoped.

"Not some kind of practiced seducer..."

"Sorry to disappoint," he murmured, but she could hear the smile in his voice, and her heart melted. He was still her Simon. Granted, he was far more gifted than she had anticipated, but he was still the same man she had grown to care for.

He continued to kiss her, his hand climbing up her shirt to fondle her breasts over the fabric of her bra. Cali took a sharp breath as he gently pinched one nipple, a delightful warmth pooling between her legs. She let out a plaintive sigh, and the length of Simon twitched against her through his pants.

Simon let out a tortured groan and pulled back. "I hate what I'm about to say more than anything I've ever said." He swallowed. "But we need to slow down. I like you a lot and don't want to rush this. I want to take you out on a date. And also, I want to have sex with you." He laughed and ran a hand through his hair. "I want to have *a lot* of sex with you, but I don't only want that."

"You're making it hard for me not to want to jump you right now when you talk like that."

"Hard, huh? " He flexed his pelvis into her, and his hardness grazed against her, making them both laugh softly. Could this be what a relationship was like? Laughing even at these moments of seriousness? Self-consciousness falling away because the person you wanted made you feel perfect, even in your foibles?

"Okay, I need a moment to think about something distasteful."

"Distasteful?" He gave her a fond look, his fingers tangling with her loose blond hair, which had come undone from the hair tie she had worn when she arrived at his apartment. He savored the silkiness of her tresses, as though he'd longed to feel their strands and his wish had finally come true.

"You think men are the only ones who get epididymal hypertension?"

"Epi-what?"

She bit the inside of her cheek and grinned. "Blue balls. It's the medical name for blue balls."

Simon bit his lip as he looked at her, momentarily holding in his mirth. Soon, he failed and laughed loudly, and Cali doubled over laughing. The much-needed break in tension provided a reminder that though they were taking a step forward in their relationship, they were doing it together, just as they had started.

HOW LONG HAVE YOU BEEN IN THE GAME?
NOT IN IT NOW.
SO WHY DID YOU STOP THE ROBBERY AT THE MUSEUM?

HE WAS STEALING A MAP THAT WOULD HELP UNCOVER THE RELIC MY MOTHER DIED PROTECTING. I HAVE TO KEEP HIS HANDS FROM GETTING ON IT.
BUT HE GOT AWAY WITH IT.
AYE, AND A FALSE MAP IS ALL HE STOLE. HE'LL CARRY IT ALONG WITH THE TRACKER I PLANTED TO HIS BOSS SO I CAN BLOW THE MAN DOWN IN TIME.

CHAPTER 17

MomI'mBoardGameClub WHATS APP GROUP

TheMagnificentZap (Simon)
FYI Cali will be joining us at game night from now on.

MuppetMaster99 (Anton)
Fantastic! You guys made up?

TheMagnificentZap (Simon)
You could say that... 😘 ☺️

CruellaTheHero (Kat)
Called it! Ben, you owe Sheila and me $10.

HammerDontHurtEm (Ben)
I didn't say it wouldn't happen, I just thought it would take a few more weeks before Simon pulled his head out of his ass.

TheMagnificentZap (Simon)
Chill, chill. It's early days yet.

CruellaTheHero (Kat)
Does that mean Sheila and I have to call the next mission off?

TheMagnificentZap (Simon)
Um... why don't I talk to Cali about it?

CruellaTheHero (Kat)
It was supposed to be a surprise. We were going to kidnap her.

TheMagnificentZap (Simon)
That sounds like a horrible idea.

CruellaTheHero (Kat)
Not really kidnap her, just show up tomorrow night and take her to whereabouts unknown.

MuppetMaster99 (Anton)
Failing to see the difference...

TheMagnificentZap (Simon)
Also, our first date is tomorrow... I was going to take her to Korean BBQ in Fort Lee—she's been wanting to try it.

CruellaTheHero (Kat)
Come on, Simon. Sheila and I have been planning this for over a week now - can you take her to our surprise after dinner? I can almost guarantee she'll love it. I'd wager money on it.

HammerDontHurtEm (Ben)
Can anyone get in on this action? Cause I got $50 on Sheila and Kat. I have faith in my woman.

TheMagnificentZap (Simon)
I'll give it some thought.

CHAPTER 18

Sciolism: *(noun) a pretentious display of knowledge*

CALI HAD DELIBERATED with approximately fifty percent less care than normal when deciding on her first date outfit with Simon. On previous first dates, her attempts at appearing attractive had to walk the line between prudish and sexy, prim and proper, or party girl extraordinaire. Pink lip gloss was too childish, but red lipstick was too aggressive.

Look good, but don't try too hard.

But with Simon, well, she knew he didn't care what she wore. All she had to do was dress well for the weather. And maybe make her date sweat a little bit–in the best possible way.

She decided on a white blouse, dark blue jeans, a black moto-style leather jacket, and a jade necklace that made her green eyes shine. When Simon knocked on the door of her apartment, he complimented her appearance before giving a not-so-subtle look at her cleavage and pressing a lingering kiss near her mouth.

Mission accomplished.

Cali cleared her throat, her face heating at his regard. "Where are we off to?"

"You said you wanted to try Korean barbecue, so I made a reservation at a restaurant in Fort Lee that's been around for generations." He held her jacket for her to put on. "After, I thought we might take a walk along the Hudson River."

Cali smiled at his thoughtfulness. "That's one smooth itinerary, Zap."

"It is? How hard is it to take a girl to a place she said she wanted to go?"

"You'd be amazed how much most men mess it up."

"Well, on that note–" Simon began patting his thigh. "There's something I need to tell you–even though I'm not supposed to tell you."

Cali looked at him while she rolled up the cuffs of her jacket. "Is everything okay?"

"Sheila and Kat want me to help them kidnap you later tonight." Simon groaned, a grimace and eye roll coming in quick succession.

"Kidnap me?" She looked at him through narrow eyes and tilted her head.

"For another mission." He sighed, and his body calmed. "A couple of weeks ago, they asked if they could organize something for you, and I may have given them the go-ahead?" His voice lifted at the end of the sentence, and anxiety emanated from him in waves.

"Without talking to me first?" She gave him a concerned look, her eyebrows bent inward.

"To be fair, I don't think they would do anything to make you unhappy. I genuinely believe they want to help you. Also, at the time, I thought perhaps you were avoiding me. I hoped this might help us reconnect–if there were a reason to spend time together again."

Her smile faltered as she contemplated his statements while Simon studied her.

"You okay over there, Mad?" He stepped closer, his hands smoothing her upper arms through her jacket. "You want to share what you're feeling with the class?"

Cali took an internal inventory of her body, waiting for her stomach to tell her how she felt. It gurgled slightly but with nowhere near the familiar torrent. "I'm still processing," she said finally. "I'm not good at feeling things–I compartmentalize a lot, suppress." She looked at him. "But I'm trying to be better."

"Okay, take your time."

The sun was setting as they exited her apartment and walked to where his car was parked at the back of their row of townhouses. The cool early November air shook her from her stupor of introspection when she finally responded.

"I'm not angry, not at you, not at them." Warmth filled her chest–joy maybe, or delight? She looked at him, more confused than ever, as he clicked the unlock mechanism, and the car let out a chirp. "If anything, I'm weirdly flattered. No one has ever wanted to 'kidnap' me before." She used finger quotes to reference the planned event.

"They mean well. They understand the point of the exercise–get you out of your comfort zone."

They were quiet for a few moments while Simon entered the restaurant location into his car's GPS. Cali turned to him as they drove, her brain caught on something else he had said in her apartment.

"Why did you think I was avoiding you?"

"Weren't you?"

She nodded. "I was totally avoiding you. I had a crush on you and didn't know what to do about it."

Simon gave an arrogant smile when she confessed her feelings. "There you go."

"Will you be there? You won't drop me off and leave, will you?"

"I don't know what they have planned, but I promise I'll stay the whole time. And if *you* want to leave at any point, I'll rev the car engine and create a distraction so you can make your getaway."

"That's all I can ask."

"Don't rat me out later. I wasn't supposed to tell you about the surprise."

"I appreciate you telling me."

On her last first date, Arun Sharma had taken Cali to his favorite French fusion restaurant. Cali smiled through the amuse-bouche, salad, entrée, and cheese course. She politely declined the chocolate soufflé as the cheese wreaked havoc on her stomach—her lactose intolerance rearing its ugly head.

She dated Arun for two years and invested in lactase pills. He was good on paper, after all. But stellar resume notwithstanding, she hadn't missed him in the slightest after they broke up. When a recent Instagram post of him on a date with a friend of hers from grad school popped up, the most surprising thing was how little she cared. Serena and Arun were well-matched. She hoped they would invite her to the wedding that would undoubtedly follow in the next year or two.

Would she have the same reaction to Simon dating someone else? As she was putting her outfit together earlier, she'd wondered if she had done such a good job of compartmentalizing her emotions that falling in love would be beyond her capabilities.

Simon was as far as possible from the kind of man she usually dated. His dating resume had been unexamined. As her neighbor, he was practically a nepo baby—a date of convenience by location. But she'd looked forward to this date more than any in recent memory. In addition to his consideration about the date location, he'd been on time, looking handsome and at ease in his dark-green short-sleeved button-down shirt and dark jeans.

And she already knew his kisses made her feel giddy.

At the restaurant, he walked her through the options, and they selected a combination of their choices. The tables were covered in grill tops, and waiters and waitresses brought around platters of banchan, small Korean side dishes normally served with rice. After stuffing their faces with small plates of kimchi, stir-fried glass noodles, spicy radish, and sautéed spinach, Simon and Cali ordered a selection of rib eye, skirt steak, and pork belly.

When they deemed the first round of protein ready, Cali took a bite. The sweet and salty flavor flooded her mouth, and she closed her eyes ecstatically.

"That good, huh?" Simon asked with a tight grin when she opened her eyes.

"Did you ever see the movie *Defending Your Life*?"

Simon shook his head.

"It proposes an afterlife where you can eat whatever you want, as much as you want, and you won't gain any weight. Oh, and it all tastes incredible."

"And this is relevant because?"

"I'm pretty sure my heaven will look like Fort Lee, New Jersey."

"I take it Korean barbecue is a success?"

"I don't know if I've ever had something as delicious as beef bulgogi."

Simon took a piece for himself with his chopsticks, carefully blowing on it before indulging.

"Didn't you say something similar about Xiao long bao?" Simon asked, dipping his next piece in one of the varieties of sauces provided by the waitstaff.

"I believe I said heaven will look like Fort Lee. The soup dumpling restaurant is four blocks away. The way I see it, as long as they have a halfway decent Thai restaurant in walking distance, I might have to move here."

"Housing here is too expensive. It's better in Ridgewood. Anyway, the real secret is to come here with a crowd so you can order more dishes to try." Simon sipped at the Cass beer they'd ordered with their food. "So, tell me more about food heaven?"

"I like that, food heaven. In the movie, the characters are judged to see if they lived a life where they conquered their fears. If they've overcome their fears, they get to go to heaven. If they haven't, they must return to Earth and try again."

"Sounds surprisingly deep for a comedy."

"You don't think comedies can be deep?"

"Comedies can be deep." Simon nodded. "But conquering existential dread is deeper than most films."

Cali conceded his point. "Makes you think. Do most of us even know what our fears are to begin overcoming them?"

"And that's deep for a first date." Simon tilted his head. "Okay then, what would you say your biggest fear is?"

She shook her head. "Do we know what our biggest fears are when we are alive? Or do they reveal themselves to us at the end of our lives when we experience regret?"

"You don't think we know what we dread?"

"Maybe we have an inkling, but I think our day-to-day concerns are overarching symptoms of real anxieties. Let's say a woman is nervous going on a date with a guy or gal she likes."

Simon raised a humored eyebrow. "Go on."

"If the date goes badly, she won't see this person again. She probably won't even remember their name by the same time next year. So, what is she afraid of?"

"Being alone, being unloved?"

"Being unlovable? Makes a date a much bigger deal than a cup of coffee or a beer or..."

"Korean barbecue?"

"Exactly." Cali flattened her hands on the table, palms down.

"And yet, here we both are." Simon reached for her hand along the side of the table. He rubbed his thumb across her knuckles gently, making her blush. "Conquering our fears together. Aren't we brave?"

"And here we are in food heaven to prove it."

Simon had dated in high school and college, though recent years were more casual liaisons. Simon's looks got him attention, and in a bar, he could play off most of his tics without being obvious. Long-term relationships were another story. In more intimate and ongoing interactions, his situation became apparent, and he grew wary of being someone's object of pity or the focus of conversation. Tourette's didn't keep him from trying to date. It was more that he hadn't met a woman worth moving from the bar to the bedroom and beyond, not until Cali. She'd slipped under the radar until he couldn't imagine not wanting her in all ways.

Simon wasn't above feeling smug as he tucked Cali's hand in the crook of his elbow. The evening was cool and crisp, but the air was refreshing rather than bracing, and the city's lights reflected on the smooth water of the Hudson River. They had walked in silence for several minutes, each taking in the view, when Simon stopped them and pulled out his cell phone.

"There's something I want to show you." Simon paused. "A few weeks ago, my agent told me the publishing company I'm contracted with is considering putting marketing dollars behind my book. They don't usually do that with first-time authors, so it's a big deal that it's being discussed."

"That's amazing, Simon! What an incredible accomplishment."

Simon waved off her congratulations with a casual flip of his hand. "It's not a done thing yet. She–my agent Joanne –wanted me to speed up a new season of the webcomic to help boost interest. It comes out this weekend, and I confess some of our adventures inspired me." Simon handed her the phone with the photo album loaded. "Tomorrow, I'll introduce the world to Princess Mad McSwiggans."

The comic book character was a cartoon-stylized version of Cali in full pirate regalia. Her blond hair was pulled back in a low ponytail, falling down her back. She held a cutlass at the throat of a villain she recognized as the Fleet Bandit from previous episodes of his web comic.

Cali looked up at Simon, her jaw dropping to her chest. "You drew me into your comic," she said, looking back down as if burning the image into her memory.

"She's not you, more inspired by our adventures," Simon quickly reassured her. "But I thought you might like to see that you were my muse. I hope you don't mind."

"I can't believe you created a comic character based on Mad McSwiggans." Cali laughed. "I thought the puppet was flattering enough, but this is next-level."

"You're not angry?"

"I maybe would've liked a little more notice." She looked at the image again. "But as long as the character's secret superhero alias name isn't..."

"California Barton?"

Cali looked up at him with comically wide eyes. "How did you know? I haven't told anyone my full name in years."

"Cali from California." He looked into her eyes, which reflected the streetlamps along the waterfront. "I took a guess." He leaned against the iron bars that kept sightseers from falling over the cliff face. "Still don't know your middle name, though."

Cali swallowed, appearing to weigh how to proceed with great deliberation. "Modesto. California Modesto Barton. My mom was pretty out of it on drugs after my birth–it had been complicated. When she filled out the birth certificate, she confused the city and state spaces with the spaces set aside for first and middle names. By the time she realized her mistake, we were home from the hospital, and between a newborn baby and a penchant for the dramatic, she decided to go with it. A name like California was sure to produce an interesting child."

"You got your revenge by only being interesting in secret."

"I still can't believe you figured it out. I had it legally changed to Cali in high school."

"Why?" Simon asked. "Why not just go by Cali? Was it necessary to change your full name?"

"I was—am—*was* so obsessed with being normal. When my mom died, it was like my connection to her had been severed. Only my mom called me California, and without her in the world, it felt like I was holding the end of one of those tin can telephones with no one else on the other end of the string." Her eyes lingered on something far away, or far in the past, before flickering back to him. "Spending time with you makes me feel differently about it now. Maybe normal and unusual aren't mutually exclusive terms." Cali's brow furrowed.

"There's freedom in that, I think." Simon nodded. They were distracted by a party boat noisily transversing the Jersey side of the river by where they stood. The muted melody of "Celebration" by Kool and the Gang played on the speaker.

"I want to say this view has some special meaning to me, but when I'm here, all I think about is how this is the place that Ben and I snuck away to smoke cigars the summer after our freshman year of high school. We found a guy who would sell them to us with Ben's brother's old ID. We thought we were so cool. Spoiler alert, we weren't." Simon snorted. "And we thought we were so clever as well, until we learned something fundamental about cigars."

"They make you smell like ass?"

"They make you smell like ass." Simon nodded sagely. "I forget if it was my mom or Ben's mom who smelled it on our clothing first—either way, we were ratted out and grounded for a week."

"I tried a cigar in my freshman year of college before we went to a showing of *The Rocky Horror Picture Show*. I remember thinking someone smelled so bad, only to realize it was coming from me!" Cali laughed. "I ended up sneaking away before anyone realized it."

"Always running away from embarrassment, huh?" Simon maneuvered Cali so she faced him, her back against the railing. She shivered, and he wrapped his arms around her middle.

"Not since I met you. You've convinced me to start loving my inner geek."

"Your outer geek is pretty hot." Simon traced his lips along her cheek, and Cali shifted until her lips met his. She had taken a mint after dinner, and the cool flavor sent a chill up his spine. Kissing Cali was torture and paradise in one, and his body hardened against hers. When she moaned softly as he pressed against her core, he almost bit his lip to keep his cool.

"I'm addicted to kissing you." He smiled as he continued claiming her mouth. "Why haven't we been doing this since day one?"

"Mmm... I wanted to. Why do you think I brought my cute new neighbor cinnamon rolls?"

Simon pulled his head back and looked at her. "Yeah?"

"Yeah, but then I thought you didn't like me. And I realized I was wrong. But then, after the faire, I thought you really didn't like me..."

His forehead came to rest against hers. "How many apologies about being an idiot do you think I owe you?"

Cali gave him a cheeky grin, clearly enjoying her ability to mess with him. "None. Keep kissing me, and we'll be even."

Simon lowered his face to hers, intending to continue as she commanded, when his phone chimed three times in quick succession. He pulled his phone from his pocket to see several messages from Kat. Simon groaned.

"Let's raincheck this for the next two hours. Kat is threatening to castrate me if we don't get to Englewood in the next twenty minutes for her and Sheila's 'surprise' for you—that is, if you're still okay with going." He held out a hand to her, and she tucked her fingers between his. He pressed a soft kiss on the inside of her wrist. Cali's face flushed, and when he looked back at her, it seemed a magnetic force pulled them together as they kissed fiercely for a few more moments before leaving the river view behind.

The large banner that hung across the neon sign advertising the Craftsman Bar in Englewood read '*The Drunken Bee: Bergen County's Oldest and Drunkest Spelling Bee.*'

Cali's eyes were wide as saucers as she took in the sign at the gastropub. Simon studied her expression, a competitive craving warring with fear. What word had they learned at game night?

Accismus: a fake refusal of something you really want.

"What are you thinking, Mad?"

"I don't quite know what to say."

"Impressive, given your vocabulary." He stood before her, placing his hands gently on her shoulders, his eyes kind. "Hey, you don't have to do this."

"Hell yeah, she does!" Kat threw an arm around Cali's shoulder, who responded with an alarmed look on her face.

"You made it!" Sheila jumped in glee as Anton and Ben hovered in the background.

"Cali, I'd like to introduce you to my new, um, friend." Kat nodded shyly, and a young woman with short, bright pink hair joined their group. "This is Aoki. She organizes the Drunken Bee every other month, and you are what she's been looking for."

"I am?" Cali looked over at Simon, who shrugged in response.

"It's nice to meet you, Cali! I've been talking to Kat about how the Drunken Bee is my pet project. It's been going on for about two years, but for the last year, it's always been the same winner–Graham Jewell." Aoki couldn't contain the sneer that crossed her face as she mentioned the name. "I don't mind a good champion, but this guy is so obnoxious and condescending! He won the Scripps National Spelling Bee about fifteen years ago and goes out of his way to intimidate other competitors."

Aoki took out her phone and showed Simon and Cali a video. "These are a few clips from the last bee." As they watched, a tall, blond man paced the stage as his fellow competitors took their turn. He subtly crowded them, male and female alike. A younger man, probably in his early twenties and painfully awkward, became distracted by the man's footfalls and made an error. An older woman flinched as he walked past her. He coughed loudly during other players' turns. He moved his chair and made noises. It was unmistakable dickhead behavior.

"I need someone who can hand his ass to him, and Kat here says you might be the woman I need."

"Ahem." Kat cleared her throat.

"Chill, Kat. I meant for the bee." Aoki kissed Kat on the cheek, and Kat nodded, appeased.

"Why is this a drunken bee? What are the rules of this thing?" Cali asked with a nod of her head to the sign.

"Excellent question! At the start of the evening, contestants take a ten-word spelling test. After the tests are graded, the contestants have to decide if they want to continue. If they're in, they have to do a shot for every word they got wrong on the test. Then we go to the rounds section. Each contestant takes a shot of their choice at the beginning of each round before spelling their assigned word. If they miss the word, they're out. When we get to the final two, we stop making them drink shots between words because the last two can go on for a while, and we don't want anyone to be hospitalized. The contestant who gets the first word wrong loses."

"What's the prize for the contest, other than liver damage?" Simon asked as he mentally added up the number of shots a contestant might be asked to imbibe.

"We don't mess around here. The entrance fee is $200 each, and we cap it at twenty attendees. The winner takes the pot, so the competition gets cutthroat. And..." Aoki looked over at Kat. "Kat, Sheila, Ben, and Anton all chipped in for your entry fee!"

Simon looked over at his friends with a rush of emotion. He loved his tribe so much, but seeing their embrace of Cali made him feel his fortune in spades. That said, he wouldn't let Cali get bullied into this if she didn't want to go through with it.

"Hey guys, let me talk to Cali for a minute."

"Okay, but don't take too long. The test starts in ten minutes." Simon watched as the group filed inside, leaving them alone on the sidewalk. She bit her lip, but he couldn't tell what she was thinking.

"How are you feeling, Mad?"

"I haven't been in a spelling bee since the fourth grade." She looked from Simon to the sign above the bar. "Not since I lived with my mom."

"Can you tell me why you stopped?"

"In the fourth grade, everyone called me a freak because of my mom, because I didn't know how to dress, because I didn't brush my hair, because I didn't know how to be. And this...jerk, Luca Genna, didn't let me forget it for a second." Her face grew dark, and he watched her lip curl in remembered anger. "When I went to live with my dad and Grace, I decided I needed to put that version of myself behind me. So stupid, I know."

"You were trying to survive," Simon said softly. "But you still loved words."

"I still *love* words," she corrected him. "And I abhor, loathe, detest, despise, curse, condemn, execrate and hate bullies." She pressed her lips together and practically quivered with competitive furor. "Let's do this."

"Good turnout tonight," Simon heard Aoki murmur to Kat on his right. They were seated near the front as Aoki also served as the MC to the crowd. "We always get the biggest crowds on Saturdays."

"With a $4,000 pot, I can understand why," Sheila replied.

Aoki nodded. "We have contestants from all over the area—the city, Connecticut, and even Pennsylvania. The northeast has quite the logophile community!" She stood to take the stage. "I'm recruiting you all to help set up the shots after the test." She walked up on stage, dressed in a tartan miniskirt and knee-high boots.

"Your new girlfriend is hot, Kat," Ben whispered, and Sheila rewarded him with a smack to the back of his head. "Ow! It was a compliment!"

Simon took in the group of contestants. The contestants sat on folding chairs with candy-colored TV trays in front of them like something out of a 1950s diner. The makeup of contestants was split down the middle with men and women, with an age range that appeared to vary from early 20s to late 50s. He hoped the older crowd could take the booze. The contestants were given clipboards and a pen. Two middle-aged judges sat off to the side, ready to grade the tests.

Aoki stood on stage and recited the evening's first words. Of the first ten, he had only heard of one of them.

"Sternutation... Soushumber... Tachygraphy... Eosinic... Pulchritudinous... Moraine... Floripondio... Paduasoy... Oogonium... Paedomorph." After each word, Aoki listed the definition and language of origin before repeating the word again.

A quiet laugh echoed through the crowd, and Simon understood why. While approximately half of the contestants—Cali included—raced through the words without breaking a sweat, while the other half looked flummoxed. They'd thought this was a promise of easy money.

One contestant waited until almost the last minute before arrogantly starting to fill out the answers—Graham Jewell. Sitting with coiffed blond hair and a sweater vest, he looked like the villainous yuppie from *Pretty in Pink*.

Douchebag.

Simon wondered if he would make a good villain for the Magnificent Zap and Mad McSwiggans to vanquish. In his mind, he envisioned the scene in which the Vainglorious Villain—he needed a better name, alliteration was not *always* necessary—met his comeuppance.

But Cali looked calm, collected, and sexy as fuck up on stage. She finished her answers before the other contestants and looked around the stage, as if confused about why they were all taking so long. Her unaffected nerves caught the attention of Graham, who gave her a once-over from two rows back. Simon could see the other man sizing her up as his competition. When the spelling test portion ended, Cali walked off the stage, completely chill, and went up to her friends.

"How did it feel up there?" Sheila asked.

"You looked so aloof." Kat grasped Cali's hands.

Simon nodded in agreement. "Sexy, too." He bumped her shoulder with his own.

"That was a lot of fun." Cali nodded. "I think I got them all right. I'm certain Moraine ends with an E."

"Moraine?" Simon asked.

"Glacial debris." Cali nodded again and looked up at him with a smile.

"Word nerd." He kissed her quickly, and she raised an eyebrow. "For luck."

"Ladies and gentlemen, we have the scores." Aoki strolled onto the stage, holding a sheet of paper. "Now comes the actual test. Contestants, if you wish to continue, you will need to drink a shot for every word you get wrong. If you choose not to drink, you will forfeit your entrance fee. The following contestants–Ben, Jess, Rob, and Kristin–have ten wrong answers."

Simon watched as the contestants decided whether to continue with the competition. Anyone who got six answers wrong or more decided not to die of alcohol poisoning and left the competition gracefully. A handful of the rest continued. Cali and Graham were the only two with no incorrect answers. In the end, there were eight contestants.

"Here are our semi-finalists!" Aoki crowed to the audience's approval, and Simon saw her give Cali a wink. "Pleasure to see some new faces in the group. Will anyone be able to defeat our long-standing champion, Graham 'The Man' Jewell?"

The audience booed Graham, who played his part as villain perfectly by performing muscleman poses and kissing his bicep in arrogant glee. Aoki, with the help of Kat and Anton, laid out the shot glasses for everyone but Cali and Graham to partake in.

"What do you think, Graham? For the first time in months, one of your competitors got a perfect score on the test. Is your streak on the line?"

Graham gave Cali an oily once-over. "She's a little blond to be a threat, Aoki."

Simon considered Graham's approach. His knowledge was evident, but his real talent was fucking with up-and-comers. Simon also considered Cali's ability to don a mask, but would she be able to fight her anxiety? Her face had taken on a placid demeanor, as if the blond bimbo reference couldn't possibly be about her.

"Well, I guess we'll see what the competition brings. We all ready?" Aoki watched as a 6'5" man named Warner downed his fifth shot and looked around blearily. "The first word is for you, Warner, and it is Abscission. Shedding off, as of a leaf or a claw. Abscission."

The first few rounds sped by quicker than he had expected. It concerned him when Cali had to down her first shot and immediately followed it with a glass of water. Still, she handled it well, her jaw clenching with determination at each new word thrown her way.

The difficulty of the words combined with the alcohol required to compete made decently quick work of three of the eight remaining contestants after the first round. With each series of words, attendees got drunker, and their reactions to the requested words got more humorous. After four rounds of words, only Cali and Graham were left on stage. Simon was so focused, he barely moved. Had any baseball game with his dad ever felt as crucial as a drunken spelling bee in Englewood, New Jersey?

"Our finalists! From Ridgewood, New Jersey, we have Cali Barton!" Aoki indicated Cali with a flourish. "And in this corner, from Larchmont, New York, we have Graham Jewell!" Aoki looked at both contestants. "Now, we don't want either of you to die of alcohol poisoning, so moving forward, this is a straight spelling bee. The first contestant to misspell a word loses. Are you ready?"

Graham looked over at Cali with a sneer. "To take down Barbie? No problem."

Aoki shook her head in disdain. "Pig. And you, Cali?"

Simon watched as Cali gave Graham a glance and a brief hand wave, deciding he was not a threat. "I only hope a girl as blond as me can represent."

"Love the spirit, Cali. Your first word is cejijunto - a person who has one long, continued eyebrow."

The crowd fell silent but for the words flowing fast and furious between the contenders. Schwenkfelder, bullate, caliginous, cachinnate... Cali remained cool as a cucumber, admiring her manicure whenever Graham stood up for his turn. When Cali spoke, Graham watched and applauded as if humored by a small child learning to walk for the first time. When that didn't throw her off her game, he hovered on his feet close to her spot as if to intimidate her. He moved his folding chair along the stage, creating a prolonged scratching sound. He coughed loudly. She ignored all of it, and her poise unnerved him more than anything he had done to her. Her refusal to be browbeaten proved to be her biggest weapon. Graham's turn came once more. As he stood before the microphone, Cali noisily moved her folding chair, causing it to scratch the stage. Graham stared in fury as she sat with her legs daintily folded at her ankles, ever the lady, refusing to look at him–not out of fear, but because Graham existed beneath her notice.

"Graham, the word is lychnobite–one who works at night and sleeps during the day."

Graham looked at Aoki as if she were as guilty as Cali of the disrespect he was experiencing.

"Lychnobite. L-I-C-H-N-O-B-Y-T-E..."

"I'm afraid that is incorrect." Aoki was unable to hide the wicked gleam in her eyes. "Graham, you will sit. If Cali can spell the word correctly, she will be our new winner. If she is unable to do so, we will proceed to a new set of words."

Cali stood, calm as could be. Walking up to the microphone, she gave Graham a mock salute. "Lychnobite. L-Y-C-H-N-O-B-I-T-E, lychnobite."

"That is correct! Ladies and gentlemen, we have a new Drunken Bee champion!"

A seismometer could have measured the vibrations caused by the bar's noise, and geologists would have sworn a small earthquake had occurred at the Craftsman Bar in Englewood. Anton, Sheila, Kat, and Ben screamed and pulled Simon backward into their group hug. On stage, Aoki had her arms around Cali as she jumped up and down in a state of feminist ecstasy. An overturned chair clattered, and Graham stormed off the stage in infuriated embarrassment.

Aoki handed Cali the trophy–a metal bumblebee attached to a martini glass and a large envelope with the night's winnings. Cali took them both, looking dumbfounded by the evening's events. She looked down at Simon, calm and beaming, her joy transcending her fear. Offering her a hand, he helped her off the stage and pulled her into his arms, kissing her hard on the lips before holding her close.

Aoki insisted on a social media post featuring Cali with the trophy. Cali gave Simon a look that said, '*Oh well, can't be worse than the wig,*' but after the third guy came over to hit on his date with the excuse of congratulating her, Simon intervened. Grabbing her hand possessively, the implicit *she's with me* scared off future suitors.

"Way to go, Mad," he whispered in her ear over the din of the crowd. Well-wishers were still surrounding them, wanting to congratulate the new victor. "How did fighting those demons feel?"

"Amazing and exhausting." She pulled back. "Let's go home, Zap. You might not be able to tell, but after four shots, I'm a little drunk."

Saying goodbye to their friends, Simon channeled his inner superhero, quickly dragging an amused and tipsy Cali through the Saturday night throng before driving them back to their townhouse in Ridgewood.

CHAPTER 19

Aphrodisiac: *(noun) of, relating to, exciting, or expressing sexual attraction or desire*

CALI DOZED in the passenger seat on their short drive home but woke as they pulled into their shared driveway. Her eyes met Simon's, though her vision was glassy. In the quiet of the car, Cali let out a loud hiccup. "Simon, those last two shots did me in, I think." She hiccuped again. "I'm so sorry..."

"Why in the world are you sorry?"

"'Cause I really, really, really wanted to have sex with you tonight. But there is a much greater than zero chance I will throw up on you if we do it. 'Cause I'm drink... I'm drink... I'm d-runk. Not because of you. I want to have sex with you."

"I want to have sex with you too, but I cannot tell you how much I don't want you to throw up on me." He kissed her tenderly as he unbuckled his seatbelt. "Think you could handle an all-night spooning session with sex in the a.m.?"

Cali appeared to weigh his suggestion with excessive deliberation.

"Yes, let's do that. Spoon tonight, fork tomorrow." She cracked up at her joke before grabbing Simon's arm. "We need condoms. And a toothbrush."

"I have both condoms and a spare toothbrush."

"You're prepared. There's nothing sexier than being prepared."

"Should I dress up as a Boy Scout? Would that do it for you?"

"I'd probably let you tie me up with your merit badge sash." Cali smiled broadly.

"You can't say things like that to me when I have to wait another ten hours to see you naked." Simon groaned, dropping his head back onto the car's headrest. Even drunk, her clever wordplay still managed to catch him off guard.

"Good things come..." she said in a singsong, pausing meaningfully.

"What a way to put that! You get filthy when you're drunk."

"I'll tell you a secret," she whispered. "I'm pretty filthy when I'm sober too."

"I never would have guessed." He shook his head. Simon got out of the car and walked around to open her door as well. She sat, contemplative, as she waited for him.

"I can't believe what your friends did for me–sponsoring me in the contest."

"I might be crazy, but I think it's time you start thinking of them as your friends too."

"They wouldn't even take back their original investment." She took a deep breath. "I want to do something nice for them. Perhaps I could treat us all to a fancy dinner with the money. Do you think they would like that?"

"Four thousand dollars would get you one hell of a nice dinner. We can talk about it in the morning. In the meantime, let's get you some Advil and a gallon of water."

"Can I borrow a T-shirt to sleep in?"

"We could stop by your place and pick up your pajamas if you'd like."

"No, I want to sleep in one of your shirts. It'll smell like you."

How could he argue with that?

"I'm amazed you're so inebriated. You were so cool up there. I couldn't tell at all."

"I've always had"—she hiccuped again—"a delayed reaction to alcohol. Nothing for an hour, and then it packs a wallop. It almost got me in trouble in college my freshman year before I realized it. I'm lucky I didn't get sick—or worse." Simon opened the door to his apartment, and Cali took off her high heels. "I normally don't drink this much. Makes me nervous."

"Why is that?" Simon tossed her a T-shirt from his clean laundry pile and watched her from the coffee table. His eyes widened when she took off her blouse in front of him. She put on the shirt and performed a magic trick to remove her bra through the sleeve of her acquired "nightgown."

"People with bipolar disorder tend to self-medicate with alcohol. I get nervous with drinking—what if I'm masking something?"

"A lot of people with Tourette's do that too. That's why I limit myself to an occasional beer now and then."

"Or mead." She giggled. Simon offered her a headache pill and a tall glass of water, which she took with a grateful smile. "Kids of parents with bipolar have a ten to twenty-five percent chance of getting it themselves. What if I miss that something's wrong with me because I drink too much? Getting drunk twice in a month is anathema to me." She sighed and closed her eyes, lying back on the couch. "Sorry, I use the big words when I'm drunk."

Simon paused. He didn't know she feared inheriting her mother's bipolar disorder. He had a well of sympathy for her fears.

"You're sexy when you use those big words. I couldn't get over you on that first game night."

"Yeah?" She smiled softly, though her eyes remained closed. "I thought you didn't like me. You were so cold."

"I always liked you. I don't always like myself much." Simon admitted, quietly reflecting that perhaps she was still out of his league. Cali's breathing slowed as she teetered on the verge of sleep.

"S'okay." She softly exhaled. "I'll like you enough for the both of us then."

Simon watched her with melancholy longing before carrying her to bed.

Fingers danced along the skin of her back, tracing paths from her neck, down her spine, and up her side, where they brushed the responsive skin of her waist. Soft breaths feathered the back of her neck, lulling and arousing in equal measure. The sun's warmth filtered through the blinds of a bedroom she had never been in. On the nightstand stood a bumblebee on a drinking glass and a thick envelope of cash.

"Good morning," came Simon's voice, deep behind her. "How are you feeling?"

Unlike the night at the bar with Sheila and Kat, which came back in waves of horror, last night came back in waves of joy so potent that she struggled to process that it had happened to her. Like anxiety, the waves threatened her equilibrium, for they burned intensely. Her heart raced, her breathing quickening as the walls between her body and her emotions broke down.

"Hey, just breathe, Cali." Simon kissed her shoulder tenderly, one hand smoothing down her arm. "I won't keep you to a drunken promise if you're not ready. We can order breakfast and watch–"

Cali grabbed his hand and pulled it around her midsection. Solid and warm, she wanted to live in his embrace. His hard length pressed against her back, but the feeling didn't frighten her. She sensed Simon holding himself as still as possible, respecting her boundaries to the point of pain.

"Simon." She paused and considered what to say. "I like having my neck kissed."

"Do you?" His pleasure at her confession, her implicit permission, was evident in the relief those two words brought. "Like this?" His lips traced a path from the nape of her neck.

"Here." She touched her throat, not at all minding his initial kisses.

Simon didn't waste time; his mouth followed where her fingers touched. His kisses were open-mouthed and warm, a slight touch of his tongue followed by the pressure of his lips pulling at the flesh and setting her senses on fire. She let out a soft moan as he continued his onslaught on her sensitive skin. Removing her shirt, he rolled her onto her back to gain better access, raising on his elbows so as not to weigh on her too heavily. After many moments, his kisses stopped, and Cali looked up at him. He stared at her so seriously that her core flooded with warmth.

"Where else should I kiss, Cali?" He rolled to her side, resting on an elbow while he traced lazy patterns from her neck to her breasts and down to her slit before traveling upward again. Cali understood–he wanted her to conduct his seduction of her.

"Here..." she whispered and traced a line around her nipples with one hand. Blood rushed to her face as his darkened eyes beheld her nipples, which puckered at his attention. He didn't ask her to examine her embarrassment, too eager to fulfill their mutual desires. He closed his mouth on one breast, sweeping back and forth with the flat of his tongue while his callused fingers traced and manipulated its partner into an equal state of arousal. He switched between peaks as if ensuring both received their share of his attention. As he did so, his hard thigh came to rest between her legs as it had the other day on the couch, and she writhed against him. As she whimpered in frustration, Simon pulled back.

"Where else should I kiss you, Cali?" he asked, his desperate voice begging her to continue.

"Here." She didn't make him wait as she took his hand and placed it against her slit. "Please, kiss me here."

She swore she heard Simon mutter a relieved '*finally,*' but she couldn't be bothered double-checking as he fell upon her. Removing her panties, he opened her thighs with his hands, and he kissed the sensitive skin before exploring her with his tongue. Patiently, he licked those sensitive folds, but not the place she desperately needed him to be. He drew out her pleasure, making sure her anticipation built, layer upon layer. His kisses were languorous and fluid, taking steps toward where her body wanted him before pulling back a fraction and continuing upon the path again.

Her hands had moved from covering her eyes in embarrassment to grabbing his dark brown hair for purchase. Her sighs had become moans as she rode his tongue. Finally, his mouth found home as he suckled gently on her clit. He curled one finger into her, hitting a spot so pleasant that she wailed. At that moment, he swirled his tongue along her center, and the combination of sensations lit her on fire, and she came with a cry. Her thighs came together against his head as she twisted against him. Dedicated to her pleasure, he didn't let up until every ounce of bliss was wrung from her body.

Drowsy and limp, she watched Simon rise with a self-satisfied smirk, wiping his mouth against his forearm. His eyes watched her as he removed his shirt and boxers. She hadn't seen him naked yet and enjoyed the sight of his body, lean with a dusting of hair on his chest and arms. A small tattoo on his chest looked like an early version of Zap. Simon stood and retrieved a condom from his bedside stand.

"I like your ink."

"Is that all you like, Cali?" He unwrapped the plastic before slowly sheathing himself with it. He clenched his jaw as his hands touched his length.

"I like all of it." She held up her arms, welcoming him into her embrace. Quickly accepting her invitation, Simon claimed her mouth with a kiss. She tasted herself on him as he entered her mouth with his tongue and slowly eased inside her with his cock.

"Christ, Cali." His forehead rested against hers, and she wrapped her legs around him. Everything about making love with Simon enamored her. His smell, his taste, it all enveloped her. He was holding back, easing into her, inch by inch. "You feel so fucking good," he whispered.

"So good," she agreed, pulling him down for another kiss. She pressed her hands against the muscles of his back, wanting to feel his chest against hers. She loved being surrounded by him, not knowing where he ended and she began.

"You're so beautiful, so beautiful..." Simon crooned. He eased one hand between them, spreading her wetness back to her nub. "Please tell me you're close. I'm not certain how long I can last, Mad." His rough touch enthralled her, and she was gathering, gaining, and how could she possibly be coming again?

"Simon," she gasped and exploded while Simon groaned and followed her–their shouts mingling in the quiet morning sun of his apartment.

CHAPTER 20

Gurning: *(verb) making a face*

"I'VE NOTICED you don't tic when we have sex," Cali mentioned two weeks later. They'd entered into a pattern of spending the days apart, where Simon worked on formatting his book and creating new episodes of the web comic while Cali worked with her temporary reports, helping them to close out their sales for the year. Each night, they met up, usually at his apartment, so he could work late into the night if necessary. They would eat dinner, make love, or even enjoy the quiet of one another's company.

"It's funny, isn't it?" Simon agreed. "Anything that takes focus tends to override the urge to tic. It's when I start to relax that they get worse."

Cali nodded, as if her suspicions were confirmed. Sometimes playing with her hand helped, and sometimes it didn't. Often, he would get up and sit on the couch until he was certain she slept, so as not to disturb her. Simon knew his tics were in a quieter phase now and said so.

"It's definitely the sex," he offered sagely, making her laugh.

"I think it's also that you've had such a good response to the new season of Magnificent Zap."

Cali was right. His readers loved the dynamic between Zap and Mad, and his revenue from Webcomicz had grown decently as a result.

He'd even bought Cali a little present, though he hadn't found the right time to give it to her yet. New and old readers alike commented on how they loved the fiery wordplay between the two characters, and long-time readers said they were so glad Zap had finally met his match. Cali herself had lots to say about how he portrayed her—not as a superhero but as her secret identity, Zap's bitchy neighbor.

"Snotty hottie? Why do I feel like that's something out of real life?"

"For five minutes, I might have thought you were snotty, but I think we both know that was sexual frustration. You're not even a little snotty." He rested his head on her chest, kissing her clavicle before drifting south.

"I should make you pay for that," she murmured as he partook in a pleasurable exploration of her body.

"What sorts of services do you require, Mad?" His tongue dipped into her navel, and her foot arched against his back.

"You're the worst, Zap."

"Not what you said two nights ago."

After they made love, Simon smoothed the skin of her back with his fingers, which made Cali purr in contentment.

"I can't stop thinking about how confident you came across at the spelling bee." Simon smiled in her hair. He wanted to bottle her smell, which worked to calm and arouse him equally. "It was extremely sexy."

"Hmm..." She assented, "Confidence is sexy."

"You're going to have to explain to me—how can you both hate being the center of attention but also be such a natural at it?" He twined his fingers with hers.

"Confidence isn't the issue. I know how to fake that." Cali stretched and sat up, leaning against the bed's headboard. Simon followed her with his eyes and turned to lie face down against the pillows, propped up on his elbows.

"I'm listening," he urged her to continue. He gave her a sleepy-eyed smile and got an answering grin, which had been his intention.

"When I was trying to fit in, Grace said to me, 'You can observe a lot by just watching.'"

"That's Yogi Berra!"

"I forgot–you're a Yankees fan." Cali's eyes locked on the ceiling where a lazy fan spun in slow circles. "The point she made was that I would get a better understanding of the social stuff if, instead of focusing on how people saw me, I focused on what I could learn about them. So I watched, and to some degree, it worked. But I got so used to being the observer that I kind of lost my voice in the process."

"Sheila mentioned something about that–the way you watch the room."

"Now, Sheila is good at reading people." Cali nodded. "It's a lot easier to be the watcher and understand the inner workings of a situation when no one is paying attention to you. It's a lot harder to do when you're the one everyone is looking at. After a while, I came to associate that feeling with being..."

"Vulnerable?"

"I was going to say nervous, but that works."

Simon felt a new piece of the puzzle of Cali falling into place. "When you're watching, you have the high ground."

She nodded. "Of course, when I, um, developed, I got more attention, so I distanced myself further. I became the 'snotty hottie' without meaning to do so. But the other night when I was out with Kat and Sheila, I realized how much that sets me apart from everyone." Cali lowered herself back to the bed to look at Simon from her pillow, their faces inches apart. "What am I missing out on by being so self-protective? What if I had missed out on you?"

Simon's voice became husky with unknown emotion. "I'm glad I didn't miss out on *you*, Mad." Clearing his throat, he bypassed the seriousness of the moment with a lopsided grin. "Does that mean we can go to karaoke?"

"You do not want me to sing–I'm tone-deaf!" She laughed. "But maybe, just maybe, I'll defend my title at the Drunken Bee in two months."

"And the prize money has nothing to do with that?"

"A girl's gotta eat." She kissed him tenderly, and they might have started up again had her phone not begun to ping repeatedly. Cali groaned, grabbing it from Simon's nightstand.

"Ugh, these girls are driving me crazy."

"Who's that?"

"I have a bachelorette party in Manhattan next weekend with some of my sorority sisters from college." She rolled her eyes. "They're debating whether to have us wear T-shirts saying 'Bridal Posse' vs 'I Do Crew.'" Her eyes widened as she read through her messages. "Oh, and there's a separate chat thread debate over whether the T-shirts should be hot pink or baby blue because baby blue is our sorority color–except not all the bridesmaids are Kappa Kappa Gamma, so the Maid of Honor thinks that's a 'major deal-breaker.'"

Following the great T-shirt debate was making Simon dizzy. "Wait–who is this getting married?"

"Victoria Cooper. We were in the same pledge class." Cali typed angrily. "I don't care what color we wear. And why should it matter if Victoria's sister didn't pledge? Let the girl wear baby blue!"

"Were you close?"

"Not particularly, but we were part of the same circle. She organized all the formals but took them way too seriously. I followed her orders." Cali made a quick salute as she perused the messages. "There was this one formal–we were only told we had to wear black floor-length gowns and this one particular pair of silver shoes. One of our sisters recently had foot surgery and wasn't allowed to wear heels. Victoria made her get a doctor's note and even then, forced her into the shoes for the group photos."

"Sounds ruthless."

"Cutthroat. Hopefully, she's chilled out since college."

"You sound doubtful."

"You know what? I'm going to be optimistic. Look at how much good sex relaxed the two of us. Maybe it's done the same to Victoria."

"What if her fiancé is lousy in bed?"

"Poor Victoria."

"When did you say this party is?"

"Next Saturday, the twenty-seventh."

"I'm meeting my agent for lunch that day. Do you want to come with me? I think she'd get a kick out of meeting my muse."

"Your muse?" A blush crossed her cheeks as she looked up from her phone at his comment. He gave her a soft kiss on the lips.

"My personal Calliope."

A curvy, petite woman, what Joanne Kelly lacked in size, she made up for with sheer willpower. Cali was immediately intimidated by how she took in every detail with narrowed eyes and a calculating expression. This woman could wield her powers for good or evil, depending on which side she chose.

"Cali, it's nice to meet you." She gave Cali a firm handshake. "When I suggested Simon give his hero a girlfriend, I had no idea it would come from his personal life, but clearly, Zap and Simon are lucky for your presence in their lives."

"It's a little strange, having a character out there even somewhat based on me," Cali admitted.

"Don't fool yourself, every character everywhere is based on someone. Somewhere, a client probably wrote a story where I'm a twelve-foot-tall dragon. Stories are fanfiction of everyday lives. You're just fortunate you know it for a fact instead of guessing at it."

Cali looked at Simon. "Is this true?"

Simon shrugged. "For me, it is. I can't speak for other writers."

"It's true for every writer—some are simply more self-aware of the fact. What is writing if not working through our issues on paper? When that happens, we steal from our conflicts with the people in our lives—our parents, lovers, friends. Sometimes it means a pretty blond heroine who talks like a pirate. Sometimes it means a prince who debates with himself if he must avenge his father's murder, but there's a grain of truth to those emotions based on a conflict the author understands or experiences."

"You're getting a helping of philosophy with your soup dumplings," Simon teased.

"Yes, thank you for taking us to Din Tai Fung," Cali said, looking around at the Midtown restaurant. The famous Taiwanese chain was known for its high-quality Shanghai cuisine. Set below street level, the modern interior had been designed with beige wood and dark grey floors. A bronze statue of an anthropomorphic soup dumpling sat in one corner. The smell made her mouth water for the experience to come.

"I hate Times Square, Simon insisted. He said you liked soup dumplings, meaning you had to try the best."

Cali looked at Simon and melted at his blush and involuntary grimace. Joanne viewed Simon's tics with equanimity. Cali felt like she barely noticed them anymore unless they were upsetting him.

"So why did we need to meet, Joanne?" Simon asked after the waiter had dropped off their waters.

"To celebrate! Carson Mathers is thrilled with the latest pages *and* the new numbers from Webcomicz. Subscribers are up twenty percent! They want to make you one of their headline authors for a winter release. This involves a marketing campaign with their PR team and placement in their monthly book box for subscribers, reaching 5,000 readers. This means an automatic spot on the *Times* bestseller list."

Floored and so pleased for Simon, Cali brought her hands up to press against her cheeks. "That's amazing, Simon! What incredible support for your work!"

"Thank you, Cali," Joanne commented approvingly. "This is big–it means attention by studios. I already have Netflix poking around, asking for an advanced copy. How do you feel about Paul Mescal playing Zap in a live adaptation?"

"What...what will I have to do?"

"Nothing unusual. A regional book tour, of course. I've researched some local bookstores and comic shops to support independent businesses and, of course, a handful of Barnes & Noble locations in the northeast. Oh, and likely television interviews, podcast interviews, etcetera. March is Disability Awareness Month, so we can use that to get good media attention. Tourette's awareness month isn't until the summer, but that will give us a chance to do a second go-round with publicity before the summer beach read season."

"Joanne–this–I'm so grateful for your help, but I don't know if I can do media appearances."

"Why not?"

"Why not? Joanne, look at me. I can barely make it through a lunch without making a spectacle of myself! I can only imagine how I would respond with a camera on me."

Cali watched in dawning horror as she saw Simon's demeanor thrown into disarray. As it happened, his body reacted in a way she hadn't seen since he had hurt his ankle several weeks before. His hand hit the table in a painful rhythmic pattern that shook the silverware, making a clattering sound. His eyes blinked repeatedly, and he grimaced, sucking in air through clenched teeth. People at the neighboring tables were starting to look at them.

"Simon." Cali moved closer to Simon and spoke quietly. "Simon, would it help if you held my hand?"

Without thinking about it, Simon grabbed her hand, squeezing it harshly, and quickly used it to calm himself. He closed his eyes as the tics lost some of their initial ferocity and eventually slowed to their regular cadence.

"Thank you," he whispered to Cali. He turned back to Joanne, whose face had taken on a calculated look.

"Can you take her on tour with you? She can be your emotional support human."

Cali grew cold as she considered Joanne's quick, opportunistic shift. "That's a fairly callous thing to say."

"Here's the real deal, Holyfield, I'm here to ensure Simon's success. If he didn't want to be published, he could have stuck with Webcomicz. He'd still be working as a graphic designer and drawing in his spare time on weekends. This success will free him up to make art full-time. Isn't that what you told me you wanted months ago?"

"Yes," Simon said quietly.

"I'm not a villain. I'm a pragmatist. Do you know how many books are released in a year? Five hundred thousand to one million. And that's just traditionally published books. You can add another two to three million self-published works as well. The average US book release sells less than 1,000 copies in its lifetime. It's my job to help you break through the noise. I believe in you, Simon, and more importantly, I believe in *The Magnificent Zap*. It's well-drawn, well-written, and I've seen how important it is to its readers. But make no mistake, this is a business, and at the beginning, your talent will only get you halfway there. God willing, your next volumes won't require you to go the publicity route, but you're a new writer, and there are dues you must pay."

She paused. "And you're *lucky*. Most writers would be thanking me right now. I understand why you're upset and stressed, and I'm here to help. We can do media training. We can attempt to have the interviews pre-recorded. We can ensure your well-being as much as possible, but if you want your story out there–and I hope you do–we must fight this battle together." Joanne looked at both of them as she said this. As part of this team now, the Tumor in her stomach rejoiced at having something new to feed upon.

"I'll...I'll think about it," Simon finally said. "And I do appreciate your help, Joanne."

"I know you do, Simon. Let's put this away for now. This restaurant makes black truffle soup dumplings, and if I'm having a working lunch on a Saturday, then my expense account is going to pay for it."

As if responding to the angst of their meeting, the weather had turned from a kind late fall to a bitter early winter over the course of their lunch with Simon's agent. The wind whipped through the tall buildings of Midtown as they made their way to Hudson Yards, where Cali was meeting up with the other bachelorette party attendees. Simon walked quickly, with his head down and hands stuffed in his pockets, while Cali rushed to keep up.

"Simon..." She couldn't tell whether he didn't hear her or needed a moment to himself. "Simon!"

"Yes?" He stopped and looked at her. His eyes were wide, flustered, as if he was momentarily disoriented.

"We missed my street. I'm going this way." She indicated West Thirty-Third Street. "Why don't you let me head the rest of the way alone? I know lunch stressed you out."

"No! I said I'd walk with you." He took her hand with his own, his grasp fierce, surprising them both. Realizing what he'd done, he dropped her hand with a horrified look.

"Hey, hey." She put her other hand on his shoulder. "I know you have a lot on your mind. I'm here for you."

Simon looked at her as if he were emerging from a trance, his eyes softening as he focused on her. "I know." His breathing slowed. "I know you are." He bent down to kiss her on the top of her head, pulling her into a tight hug. "I have a lot to think about."

"Do you want me to skip the bachelorette party tonight?" She wanted him to say yes. Not just because she worried about him, but also because she had no desire to go.

"No, it's important you spend time with your friends. I'll see you tomorrow night, right?"

"Of course, " she reassured him.

A small smile broke through. and he kissed her ardently, his hands clasping her face. "I don't know how I got so lucky you moved downstairs from me, Mad."

Cali flushed at Simon's words. Lost in his embrace, it took a few seconds longer than it should to realize someone called her name.

"Cali! Is that you?" Cali and Simon both turned at the sound and were immediately assaulted by three women. Two of the women wore identical tight jeans, jackets, and the "I Do Crew" T-shirts Cali had complained about a few days prior. The last woman wore a white sequin top and a "Bride" sash.

"*Cali*!" the three women screamed. Their fingers spread as they shook their hands in a similar welcome gesture that harkened back to their days together at Kappa Kappa Gamma.

"Hey, guys!" Cali gave a forced smile and turned back to Simon. "Simon, these are my sorority sisters, Marisa, Lorraine, and of course, the bride-to-be, Victoria! Girls, this is my...this is Simon." She and Simon had not gone so far as to define their relationship, and she was not about to have that conversation on a city street in front of half the bridal party.

"Nice to meet you, Simon." Victoria gave him an assessing look from top to bottom when Simon went to shake her hand, and instead, he did a highly accurate physical copy of the women's excited greeting with one another.

On the busy streets of Manhattan, Cali swore she could hear a pin drop. She didn't know whose expression was the most shocked. No, that wasn't true. It was Simon's. Simon looked mortified.

She took his hand quickly. "Simon and I met because we're neighbors, can you believe it? He made quite the first impression on me too."

"I'm so sorry," Simon said quickly. "I have Tourette's, and sometimes my body doesn't cooperate with me."

"Oh...oh! No worries." Lorraine waved it away with her hand, though Marisa looked torn and Victoria still a bit miffed. "My cousin's husband has Tourette's. It's nice to meet you!" She offered a hand to Simon, who took it gratefully. The initial awkwardness passed, and the other two girls properly introduced themselves to Simon, though Victoria's sneer seemed permanently etched onto her face.

"All right, I'm going to get going. I'll see you tomorrow night?" Simon looked at Cali and bent down to kiss her on the cheek.

"Tomorrow..." she whispered, watching him leave before returning to her girlfriends. "So where is this hotel where I can change into my T-shirt?"

The rest of the bridal party, along with other friends of the bride, were waiting for them in one of the three suites Marisa had arranged for them for the night. The sumptuous room featured a spacious living area with plush couches and tables stocked with snacks and drinks. The view overlooked the Hudson River, and Cali thought she could see the area on the New Jersey side where she and Simon had walked along on their first date not so long ago. Why did it feel as though they'd been together so much longer? She smiled, remembering their trip to the Renaissance faire less than three months prior. Perhaps their relationship had been a courtship all along.

It reminded Cali of that summer after her first year in grad school. She'd gone home to visit her family and picked out a bikini from the closet. But even though she hadn't grown in the past ten months, it fit strangely. Her favorite piece no longer hung on her frame in quite the same way. Her friendships with her sorority sisters felt that way now. Slipping into her college persona felt like putting on that ill-fitting swimsuit.

"How are you doing, Cali? They have you and me rooming together." Lorraine smiled and handed Cali a glass of prosecco. Cali had always liked Lorraine. Tall and gorgeous, Lorraine was one of the few sisters who took school as seriously as she did. After most of their sisters had gone to party, Lorraine and Cali would work in their sorority house's study room. Lorraine studied for the LSAT while Cali prepared for the GMAT. They had lost touch after college when Lorraine took a year off to travel.

"I'm doing well, thank you. Living in Jersey now. I got a job working for Marcus & Meyers." Cali indicated the Jersey side of the river with a tilt of her head.

"That's a great company. I'm in downtown Brooklyn, attending the law school there." Lorraine blushed, but Cali could see the pride in her accomplishments.

"Congratulations! What year?"

"Third year. Only ten months, then the bar exam looms." Lorraine shook her head in dread at the suggestion of the horror of that exam.

"You'll kill it. You always did so well in college."

"Thank you!"

The warm moment between the women was interrupted by a loud voice calling for everyone's attention.

Marisa held a glass of prosecco and hit the side with a knife to get everyone's attention. "Ladies! We're here tonight to celebrate Victoria's upcoming wedding!"

A dozen women screamed excitedly, including Cali, who knew how these parties worked.

"I'm the maid of honor, Marisa Crane, and the master of ceremonies for tonight. I hope you all got your beauty sleep last night, because we're going big tonight, ladies!"

"Soon, we will enjoy an in-room beauty treatment, complete with hair blowouts and makeup, followed by dinner at Nobu and VIP tables at Litchi. Tomorrow morning, we'll have massages at the Prendy Hotel spa, accompanied by a champagne brunch."

In her mind, Cali added up the cost of the activities, glad for the extra $4,000 in her checking account. So much for the new Peloton she'd been eyeing.

"But first, the entertainment will be a little...spicy!"

A man dressed as a chef broke through the doors of one of the adjoining bedrooms, wearing a chef's hat, apron, and nothing else. The tell-tale chords of "Relax" by Frankie Goes to Hollywood played on Marisa's iPhone, and the girls screamed in ecstatic joy.

"Great, a stripper." Cali sighed. "Got any singles?" Cali's eyes met Lorraine's. They both shrugged with a smile and went to join the others.

"That stripper was remarkably talented, given the third leg he has to carry," Lorraine joked as she and Cali enjoyed mimosas after completing their respective beauty treatments. Relaxed, but not quite tipsy, Cali wanted to keep closer to sober tonight after two drunken forays in the previous month.

"I feel bad for his girlfriend or boyfriend. It looked like a lot to handle." Cali smirked into her glass. The chef had been remarkably well-endowed, and the crowd of women had been both titillated and amused by his routine.

"Speaking of 'handling' things, how long have you and Simon been dating?"

Cali blushed to think of how their relationship had evolved. "We were friends first, so it's hard to say. We only became romantic recently."

"He seems like a great guy."

"He is. He's sweet and funny and smart."

"Good for you. Are you bringing him to the wedding? Victoria told me she's inviting us all with plus-ones."

Cali was saved from responding–as she didn't know–when another party member approached the two women.

"I know you!" the spiky-haired brunette said. She looked to be in her early twenties. "Oh my God! I do know you! I was at the Craftsman like two, three weeks ago when you beat Graham Jewell at the Drunken Bee!" The girl sat down to join them. "You're my hero! Cali, right?"

"What's the Drunken Bee?" Lorraine asked, amused.

The girl, Victoria's baby sister, Julia, walked Lorraine through the event's details while Cali felt her face flush red. She never thought anyone outside her new friends would know about the event. I mean, who attended adult spelling bees? Then she realized *she had won an adult spelling bee* and was in no place to judge.

"This girl here outspelled the biggest douchebag in Bergen County."

"He was quite a douchebag," Cali agreed with a nod. Lorraine looked impressed with Cali's quirky talent. Maybe, *maybe* this event wouldn't be so bad. Maybe she had misjudged her sorority sisters.

"Oops! Out of prosecco," Lorraine said.

"I'll get us some. I want to hit up the ladies' room anyway." Cali stood while Lorraine and Julia continued to speak, then headed to the suite's main bedroom. As she finished using the bathroom, Victoria and Marisa entered mid-conversation.

"Ugh, I can't have him at my wedding. He'll probably scream curse words as I walk down the aisle."

Marisa laughed with a discordant snort. "I agree, it would ruin the whole day. What is Cali thinking, dating him?"

"But what am I going to do?" Victoria's voice listed in a petulant whine, like a teenager who had been told she couldn't borrow her mom's car.

"Don't invite Cali with a guest. It's not like they've been dating that long. She hasn't even posted any pictures of him on Instagram."

"Yeah, but have you seen what she *has* posted? The photo of her in the wig with those two losers?" Victoria scoffed. "Anyway, I told the other girls they could bring a plus-one. She'll know something's up if I invite her solo."

"Tell the other girls you had to change your plans. It's your day, Victoria. It's not your fault Cali decided to date a freak."

"Ugh—this is so going to mess up my aesthetic." Victoria paused. "I almost cracked up when he made that face on the street. How does Cali bear being with him? So much for Miss High-and-Mighty. Her social stock is plum-met-ing..." Victoria's voice sang the last word, betraying a pleasure at what she perceived as Cali's decline in popularity.

I never wanted to be popular.

The roar of pain in her stomach hit so suddenly she swore she heard it as a rush in her ears.

'You see, Cali, this is what you get for hanging out with weirdos.' Her Phantom Tumor's voice gurgled insidiously and brought forth waves of anger aimed at Victoria and Marisa, but mostly at herself because she knew she might have judged Simon in that way even one year ago. Not out of cruelty—she wasn't a cruel person—but because she had an unhealthy terror of being seen as different. She would've avoided him. She would've crossed the campus and been swallowed into her own bubble.

In high school, in college, in grad school, she would've fallen back into the pattern of making herself smaller, of being the proxy for what people expected her to be.

The Phantom Tumor was telling her she needed to do just that—to stop this regimen of self-exploration because otherwise, she would be the class freak and...what if that happened again?

A soft buzz from her phone indicated a text message, and an image of Simon wearing his tricorn hat filled her phone's screen. The simple message let her know he missed her and wanted her to have fun with her friends, but it worked like a tonic, a soothing balm against the Phantom Tumor's ire. The anxiety in her stomach changed shape—it burned hotter, with less churn and more fire. How dare anyone reduce Simon to this one fact? Simon was so much more, and these women were idiots for not seeing that. She stood in the bathroom for a full minute, her head pressed against the marble wall as the two selves within her argued.

When she stepped into the bedroom, she leveled both women with a cool, steady gaze.

"Cali..." Victoria hesitated, clearly unsure of how much Cali had heard. "I...uh..."

"Thank you, Victoria. I can't tell you how much I didn't want to stay for the party, and you've given me the best excuse ever to head home."

"Go? You can't go..." Marisa whined, but Cali held up her hand.

"I can. I suppose you'll have to absorb the extra cost of this ridiculously overdone bachelorette party."

"We...shouldn't have said those things. I'm sorry," Marissa sputtered inelegantly.

"Listen. Of course, you can bring your boyfriend to the wedding. It's just, Cali, we're worried about you. It's not like you to date someone so..."

"So what?" Cali felt cold and annoyed, morbidly curious as to how Victoria would finish the sentence.

"So weird," Victoria finished lamely.

'Cause that's what you are, California—a freak!

"Well, I guess I'm weird too. Because I'd rather be with him than spend another second here."

Forcing down the screaming in her stomach, Cali mused that it was more than Zap that struggled with a parasite. On her way out of Victoria's suite, Cali took a bottle of prosecco, handing it to Lorraine before she left. "My plus-one got rescinded because my boyfriend has Tourette's, so I'm going to leave. Julia, it was cool meeting you. You're nicer than your sister. Lorraine, if you weren't fake, tonight was fun. Text me, and we can meet up."

And she stormed off before either woman could respond beyond raised eyebrows and shocked expressions.

CHAPTER 21

Neophilia: *(noun) love of or enthusiasm for what is new or novel*

"I CAN'T TELL HIM."

"Of course, you can tell him, and you should tell him," Kat responded. Cali didn't know where to go when the bachelorette party spectacularly imploded. If she got home early, Simon would know something was wrong, and after Simon's lunch with his agent, she didn't want to pile on to an already stressful day. She called Sheila and Kat and decided to crash at Kat's apartment.

"I don't want him to feel like he's responsible for my friendships going down the toilet."

"Cali, I was there when he was a kid. Simon's been through worse than your bitchy sorority sisters, and he knows more than anyone how people suck. Moreover, he wouldn't appreciate it if you kept things from him. It's not your job to protect him any more than it's his job to protect you." She put a hand on Cali's shoulder. "You're not his mom. You're his girlfriend."

"You wouldn't want him to keep things from you, would you?" Aoki added.

"No, I wouldn't," Cali admitted. "He just–" Cali sighed. "Earlier in the day, we met with his agent. They want to do a media push for his book, and I think Simon is feeling a little conflicted about being front and center with his ticcing."

"That's incredible that they want to market his book," Aoki said with an impressed nod. "That's quite rare. I work for a publishing house. What an accomplishment for a debut author!"

Kat sat with her hands folded before her mouth, contemplating Cali's words.

"What are you thinking, Kat?"

"Simon had a hard time of it growing up. He was a loner in middle school. We didn't become friends until high school. There was this bully, Adam Higgins, who used to abuse him mercilessly. Adam made it his mission to make Simon feel as small as possible. Of course, with Tourette's, the more someone draws attention to your tics, the more likely you are to do so."

Cali nodded, recalling Simon saying something similar in their conversations.

"I wasn't friends with Simon yet, but I knew him, or rather, I knew of him. We had a couple of classes together. It was toward the end of freshman year, and Simon was this guy who kept to himself and tried to stay out of the way. And I was trying to survive myself. Higgins liked to make fun of me too. I heard it all—on my race, on my sexuality. So I didn't go out of my way to make pals with the grade weirdo. I didn't need any more spotlight on myself. One day, Higgins was fucking with him in the cafeteria, and Simon must have had enough because he finally talked back to him. I watched it all go down. Here was this skinny, awkward dude who kept making weird faces and could barely control his body, standing up to this bully twice his size. I remember being so proud of him for doing that."

Kat's eyes welled up. "Higgins went on the attack. He shoved Simon to the ground and was about to kick him in the gut when Anton, Ben, and I came between them. Bear in mind, none of us were friends yet, but we had all been victims of Higgins's taunts. That dude could have wiped the floor with any of us, but together, we protected Simon. Higgins backed off. Afterwards, we were all gathered around Simon. He was so incredibly frustrated. He tried to play it off, and we all let him. I remember feeling so guilty that I had let this sweet guy be destroyed daily because I was too cowardly to befriend him. That incident proved to be the tipping point. After that day, we were a foursome."

Cali rubbed her eyes, startled to find that she'd started crying. "You all saved him," she said with a wet voice. "He told me about Higgins, about how dark his life was before he found you. I always assumed he was the hero for some reason, but it was the three of you."

"He was the hero! If he hadn't stood up for himself that day, we never would have had the courage to do the same. And it wasn't just that day. He came to all our defenses at some point or another over the next three years. Not only with Higgins, but because teenagers can be assholes, and we were all trying to survive. Thanks to Simon, Ben, and Anton, my high school experience didn't suck. We had a lot of fun together and still do, as you know. I tell you this because Simon doesn't want to be seen as an object of ridicule or pity. And I think that's probably giving him pause with the book appearances—putting him in a place where all he'll be seen as is his diagnosis."

"Then maybe I shouldn't tell him about the bachelorette party. It's just going to provide a confirmation bias."

"May I share my opinion?" Aoki asked.

Kat and Cali nodded.

"He's got to get over high school. No one survives youth unscathed. Yes, his was worse than most, but it wasn't fun being a Japanese immigrant—and lesbian to boot—when I moved here at age twelve. Your bubble protected you all in your youth, but Simon's an adult now. There's probably a nine-year-old kid out there with Tourette's who will be thrilled to have a superhero to look up to." She paused thoughtfully. "Representation is important for a reason."

Kat looked over at her girlfriend with raised eyebrows and a smile. "Hard to argue with that logic."

Privately, Cali agreed with Aoki and Kat, but how to convince Simon? And more importantly, should she even try?

Mad McSwiggans looked fierce, her cutlass aimed at Mirror Zap—a dark version of the Magnificent Zap, determined to take over the planet. Simon needed to work on the villain's name. It could be stronger. Behind her, Zap called upon a lightning strike, using Mad's sword to focus his powers. The joint efforts of the two heroes succeeded in defeating their foe, where alone, they would have failed.

It was a little on the nose, but Joanne said she wanted a romantic superhero partnership to attract both comic and romance fans. His experience with romance might have been limited to a handful of shorter relationships and one-night stands, but with Cali, he felt a strange optimism. Indeed, he'd never included a romantic partner in his artwork, although his friends had long featured among other characters in the series.

With the image done, he'd completed the eighth episode. The first four were published in bulk two weeks prior, and the fan comments were almost universally positive. It was as good a result as he could have hoped for, but the conversation with Joanne had echoed in his brain over the past twenty-four hours. Media tour? Book tour? Who was he kidding? How could he make it through even one meeting without making a spectacle of himself? And if he did, wouldn't that take away from what he created? Art should speak for itself—it shouldn't need his voice to succeed.

A knock on his door broke him out of his reverie. He looked at the clock—eleven a.m.

"Hey, Simon, it's me!" Cali's voice called out from the landing to his apartment.

"You're back early," Simon commented when Cali greeted him with a kiss on the cheek. "Wasn't expecting you back for another few hours."

Cali paused, as if unsure how to respond. "The other girls were hungover from last night, and we all decided to skip the champagne brunch, so I caught an early train."

"Did you have fun?"

"I had fun catching up with Lorraine. She texted me on the way home–we'll meet for brunch in a few weeks."

"I liked her. She seemed unaffected." Simon didn't add that the other girls set off his bitch radar. He barely knew them, and it wasn't fair to judge Cali's friends without getting to know them. That attitude had almost cost him the opportunity to get to know his neighbor.

Cali sat on the couch, and Simon joined her, taking her hand in his. As he played with her fingers, she cuddled inward. It amused and comforted him how they had created a physical language of affection. He craved her touch as she craved his embrace. Never had Simon understood people who depended on touch as their love language, but with Cali, the pieces fit together.

"How are you feeling? I worried about you all night."

"I'm feeling..." Simon groaned and ran a hand through his hair, pulling up on the skin of his forehead. "I'm feeling like a failure, to be honest. I spent the last three months telling you how happy I am with myself, and now that I have an opportunity to go out there and share my...story...my work, I'm running away with my tail between my legs." He looked over at Cali, surprised at her confused expression.

"I admit, I'm a little surprised by your reaction. After your pirate act at the faire, I didn't think you were the self-conscious type. Can you tell me why you're so hesitant? Is it because you're scared you'll tic on television?"

"Growing up in Arizona, did you ever attend a bar mitzvah?"

Cali shook her head, perplexed by the turn in the conversation.

"A sweet sixteen?"

"Oh yes, those were popular. Quinceañeras, as well."

"Well, I want you to imagine that, but for all Jewish kids. A bar mitzvah is supposed to be a significant ceremony welcoming a thirteen-year-old to adulthood, at which time they read from the Torah in front of their family and friends—and there is that. Still, it's also an excuse for families to throw lavish parties with DJs and insane party favors at fancy country clubs, nightclubs, or catering halls. Most bar mitzvahs in my town were easily $50,000."

"That's more than most weddings!"

"There's a lot of keeping up with the Joneses—or Weinbergs."

Cali gave him a blank look.

"Sorry, bad joke. You'll catch on the more time you spend in Bergen County." He paused. "For my mom and dad, well, they saw it as an opportunity to redefine me socially, and I may have given them some pushing in that direction. I'm one of the oldest in my grade, so I figured it could be a good way to create a cache about who I was instead of letting my tics define me. I remember what you said—if I'd had a pill to cure my tics, would I have taken it? By the time I was thirteen, I was past wishing for something like that, but I still wanted to fit in. My bar mitzvah seemed like a way to stake my flag." Simon got up and walked to a bookshelf, picking out a thin leather-bound album. He flipped to the first photograph of his younger self, wearing a navy-blue suit with a yarmulke on his head, holding a large bundle wrapped in blue velvet with embroidered Hebrew lettering.

"I spent six months memorizing my portions for the big day. The good thing about Tourette's is that, for me, focusing tends to diminish tics, and I knew I would be focused during my portions of the ceremony, which were the only times I'd be up there. I was determined this one thing would be as normal a thirteen-year-old experience for me as possible."

"My parents were in full support. The theme of my party was baseball, which was extremely unoriginal. Still, my father had contacts with the Yankees through his cardiology practice, and we had CC Sabathia scheduled to sign baseballs and take photos with the attending kids and parents. We had a batting cage, a carnival ball throwing game, and the giveaways were slick—Nikes, iPod minis, game day tickets..."

"It sounds like something out of that MTV show—"

"*My Super Sweet Sixteen*? Yeah, I think my mom studied it for tips. It was disgusting. I see that now."

"What happened?"

"On the big day, everything started great. I recited my haftorah and Torah portion, and even my speech, thanking my parents, my rabbi, and my cantor for their help preparing me for the big day. I felt good, and my tics were at a minimum. Everything was done. My mom cried, she was so proud. Even my dad was choked up. The kids looked bored, but how many kids cared about the ceremony? They only want to go to the party afterwards. I had to get through maybe ten minutes more, and then we would take the bus to the party venue for four hours of partying."

"And then Rabbi Eisenberger got up..." Simon's face took on a pained grimace, and his hand came up in a gesture of ancient frustration that had not yet found relief. "After all these years, I try to tell myself the man meant well, but he was so fucking clueless. He threw a brotherly arm around me and talked about the trials and tribulations God put upon me. He called me a modern-day Job, when I was just some putzy kid in a yarmulke trying to buy his popularity in the seventh grade. He went on and on for ten excruciating minutes, talking about how my tics would come on me during Torah practice and what a shining example of Jewish manhood I was for members in our congregation."

"He took your moment..."

"I'm certain he thought he was making it more meaningful, but like, I wanted *one* thing to be normal, outside the lens of my Tourette's syndrome. One thing. One stupid teenage moment where people could make fun of me for my voice cracking because of puberty instead of hitting my thighs, clearing my throat, or making faces. And of course, the minute that schmuck brought attention to me, my focus dropped, and my tics went crazy. I remember looking at my parents, and they were horrified at the rabbi. My sister gave him a death glare. Later, my parents canceled their sponsorship of the synagogue, much to the frustration of the head of the endowment. And while she denies it, I think my sister

Rebecca egged Rabbi Eisenberger's car the following Sabbath so that he couldn't get it cleaned for another day."

"Your sister sounds amazing." Cali looked at the photos of his family. Simon appeared adorably dorky as a thirteen-year-old, but his older sister looked chic with straightened dark hair and a fuchsia cocktail dress.

"Yeah, she is."

"What happened after that?" Cali turned her gaze from the album to look at him.

"I stormed off the stage the minute I could do so. I spent the reception in the venue's bridal suite. My parents didn't even try to get me to come downstairs because I was ticcing so badly. It was my welcome into manhood, but I felt like a child, self-pitying and beating myself up—both figuratively and literally."

Simon looked over his shoulder at Cali. She'd been making soothing passes down his arms as he lay against her. Sitting up, he turned and took her hands in his, kissing them tenderly. She was masking her emotions from him again, but he knew.

"You pity me, but you shouldn't. I was a spoiled brat who didn't get his way."

"You were a struggling kid grasping at straws. I...pity the boy you were, not the man you've become." She kissed his cheeks and lips, but they were chaste and loving rather than passionate. "And who am I to judge? I, who buried anything remarkably unique under the veneer of the pretty blond girl."

She leaned against his chest, and he took her hands in his, their eyes inches apart.

"It turns out, Cali, I'm not that different from you. I'm thrilled I don't have to go into an office anymore; that I don't have to suffer those stares from my well-meaning coworkers every time I do anything slightly unusual, whether it relates to my tics or not. My friends and family are the only ones who see me as a complete person and not a person with an asterisk next to their name." He looked down at her. "Them, and you."

He stroked her palm absentmindedly. "My comic is something I've worked on for years to make it what it is today. If a stupid speech by an inconsiderate rabbi could ruin that day for me, couldn't a stupid reporter do the same thing? What if that interview is about the inspiring story of a young man with Tourette's? I don't want my work to be diminished, and then, if it is, what if I'm unable to control myself on national television? There's no winning–it's only different ways of losing." Simon sank into the couch, his face scrunching repeatedly. "I don't want to be inspiration porn; I want to be like any artist presenting his work."

Cali sat up, and he could feel her eyes on him. "Can I tell you what I think?"

"Of course," he said, but he didn't open his eyes.

"You need to reframe the narrative. There are jerks out there that will comment on your ticcing, either because they pity you or judge you. But there's a whole other audience out there rooting for you. Not just me, Anton, your other friends, or your family, but wouldn't you have liked seeing someone like you on the news as a kid? Someone who could have made your journey a little more bearable?"

"More inspiration porn." Simon scoffed.

"No, inspiration porn is the objectification of disabled people for the benefit of non-disabled people. I googled it." She nodded decisively. "I'm talking about for the benefit of people like you, like me, like Anton and Kat. People who had a rough go of it when they were growing up, who need to know they'll find their tribes, their calling in this life. Change the story away from you and make it about them. Make Zap matter to them because they need to remember they can be heroes too."

"You make me out to be a hero as opposed to a dorky kid who needed an escape."

"There are lots of kids out there who need an escape; your graphic novel can be a way to help them find one." She paused as if parsing out how to proceed next. "But I think you should take this step by step."

"How do you mean?"

"Simon, when was the last time you tried to present yourself to new people without worrying about being the man with the asterisk next to his name?"

"I mean, it's not like I'm a shut-in. You've seen me at bars and restaurants."

"But perhaps it might be worth trying to put yourself in a situation that feels less familiar, less friendly. Perhaps it would be worthwhile to conduct a test run. You took me on a few adventures; perhaps you might try doing the same. Let's take you out of your comfort zone for a change."

"As someone once said to me, I like my comfort zone. It's comfortable for a reason."

"I recall that didn't stop you from encouraging me to challenge myself."

Simon considered her point, amazed at how they'd come full circle in such a short time. "What did you have in mind?"

"I got an email from my manager last night. The leadership call went quite well. They're moving forward with Jesse's idea. Marcus & Meyers's CEO, James Russell, purchased three tables at the Robin Hood Foundation's annual gala this December, and Jesse and I have both been invited, along with guests, to attend. Would you want to come as my date?"

"To a fancy-ass gala?"

"It will probably be boring, but it's for a good cause. The Robin Hood Foundation raises money for poverty initiatives in New York City. You'll have the opportunity to interact with new faces. Perhaps experimenting with meeting new people might help break down some of what's holding you back."

"I'm going to have to rent a tux, aren't I? Like some demented adult prom?" He gave her an aggrieved look.

"I'll put out in your dad's SUV afterward," she joked, harkening back to his high school story.

"You make it tempting." He looked at her. "Can I think about it? I'm not sure..." He paused, taking a deep breath as his free hand patted rhythmically against his thigh. A fancy black-tie event? What if he made a scene in front of her coworkers? Would she decide he wasn't worth the trouble to be with? Or if he chose not to attend, would she grow frustrated by his inability to get out of his own way?

"Of course, it's not until December. Take whatever time you need."

"Thank you." He closed his eyes while his body calmed. "Any chance I could get a taste of the post-party SUV activities?" He trailed his fingers up her thigh and gave her a suggestive look.

"Thought you'd never ask." Cali's eyebrows arched playfully in response. She looked so adorable in her mock seductive pose that he couldn't resist.

Simon bent low over her but held off on kissing her, letting his nose trace along her face and neck before placing small open-mouth kisses between her breasts, pulling down the V of her T-shirt to nuzzle her gently. Simon pulled back after a few moments of light kisses.

"Simon?" She looked at him from where she lay on his couch.

"Something's missing," he mused. "I know." Standing quickly, he went to his drawing table and brought back a small box. "I saw something that reminded me of you." Feeling shy, he handed her the box.

Cali looked at the small black leather box with a half smile on her face. She didn't seem to be in a rush to open it.

"Is there something wrong?" he asked, ill at ease with her hesitancy.

"No, not at all. I'm absorbing this. It's a lovely moment." Her gaze flickered from the box to his eyes.

"Making a memory?" he asked.

"Yes, exactly." Her eyes crinkled as she slowly opened the box and gasped.

"You can return it if you like–if it's not your style."

"I wouldn't dream of it." The gold bumblebee pendant was covered with alternating white and black stones to emulate stripes. She took the pendant and its gold chain out of the box and admired as it glistened against the light seeping in through the glass doors of Simon's porch. "This is..." Her smile became a firm press of her lips as her chin wrinkled. "This is so thoughtful; I love it so much." She worked her fingers to undo the clasp. "Help me put it on!"

"You want to wear it now?"

"I believe you said something was missing." There was a genuine smile in her voice, and it made him feel about one thousand feet tall. She turned around and let him fasten it around her neck. The pendant rested between her clavicles in the space above her breasts.

Simon brushed her hair aside and watched as Cali played with the pendant. Kissing along her neck and shoulder, he wrapped his fingers around her waist and pulled her closer.

"Is this when you take advantage of my gratitude for a beautiful piece of jewelry?" Her head lolled to the side, granting him access to her neck. He was already lifting the hem of her T-shirt, impatient to feel her skin against his.

"I would never presume to equate gifts with sex, but if you're feeling properly inspired..." He smiled against her shoulder. Her hands rested on his fingers and helped him lift off the garment, separating him from her skin.

The apartment must have been chilly, for Cali shivered as her shirt and bra were removed in quick succession.

"Cold?" he asked, feeling the texture of goosebumps along the back of her arms.

"A little," she admitted, but he heard the smile in her voice. Simon removed his shirt and turned her so their lips met.

Every time they made love, Simon felt a profound sense of belonging. The way she opened to him with equal parts passion and trust humbled him. He remembered how cynically he had initially considered her and felt vaguely ashamed at his inability to see deeper into this woman. Body and soul, he'd never known a woman as beautiful as Cali.

Her fingers were tangled in his hair, as if savoring the texture of his dark brown locks. He brushed his thumbs back and forth across her cheeks, and she smiled up at him as he paused his kisses.

"I love the feel of your fingers," she admitted. Turning her head to kiss his palm, she said, "I like how rough they are; it makes me feel like you're sculpting me."

"I've always preferred the pen to clay, but..." He moved his fingers south to her breasts. Ever responsive to his touch, she keened as he massaged the soft pillows of flesh before tracing lines back and forth across her nipples, causing them to gather into tight buds. "With you, I like pretending I discovered or imagined you into being, that you were made just for me. It's incredibly self-important of me, but you're my fantasies brought to life."

"Galatea to your Pygmalion." She smiled at him fondly before moaning when his fingers drifted further down. Her eyes closed momentarily as his touch became firmer.

"Tell me I'm not alone. Please tell me you feel it too–this connection between us." His voice grew husky as her body grew rosy from his ministrations.

"I..." She rolled her eyes as his fingers pressed pleasantly against her core. "For the first time, I don't feel wanted only because of my appearance. I feel wanted because you *know* me. I could look any other way, and you would still care for me, desire me." Simon brushed his thumb back and forth in a rhythm designed to drive her crazy. Her core was warm and silky, a texture he could happily dwell within for the rest of his days. "You make me feel so good."

"I want you to cum on my fingers...and on my cock. Do you think you can do that for me, Mad?"

"Don't stop, please." She reached down and held his hand in place while her body chased its pleasure, riding the waves of sensation as he slipped two fingers inside her and flattened his palm against her clit. Simon loved watching her face flush, her thighs tighten, her breasts swell as he took her from arousal to orgasm. Laser-focused, her expressions, her pleasure washed over him like a validation of his ability to be a good partner, a good lover, someone who could live up to what she needed and wanted.

When she came down, limp and floppy in his arms, he gathered her close. Kissing her forehead, he could taste the salty flavor of the sweat beading there. Though painfully confined in his pants, Simon enjoyed her sated form snuggled in his arms. She mewled, or perhaps purred, as she floated back into herself and ran her fingers through the sprinkling of hair on his forearms.

"Simon, you are the sexiest man I've ever known." She paused. "It's never been like this for me."

Simon had to press his lips together to keep himself from laughing. Not because her comment amused him, but because the joy she gave him couldn't be contained in just a smile.

"Am I being doubted?" She gave him an impish look, her nose wrinkling in amusement.

"Never." His lips brushed hers, opening them with his, his tongue sliding inside. She wrapped her arms around his neck lazily. He settled beside her as he worked to remove his pants while continuing to press kisses on her face, lips, and jaw. "As much as it pains me to pause, I'll need to go grab a condom from my nightstand."

"That's fine." She continued to kiss him. "But you should know I got tested and I'm on the pill. Unless you have other concerns, we can forego the condom if you like."

In response, Simon claimed her mouth. "I'm clean," he muttered between kisses, feeling her smile against his lips. He searched her body again with his fingers, seeking to ready her and finding her soaked. When he slid inside her, they both gasped. He only hoped she felt the same completion he did. He would ask her later. Insecure, he needed to know their coupling meant as much to her as it did to him.

He was falling in love with Cali Barton and needed to know if she felt the same. He closed his eyes, overwhelmed by sensations both physical and emotional. He focused on the sounds she made as she grew closer to her peak, the rhythm keeping his body in check.

"Cali, Cali, Cali," he whispered repeatedly, like a prayer. He needed her to come before he let himself go. "Baby, you feel so good. You're so tight, I need you to come for me, please..."

"Simon..." Her barely audible pants told him she was close. He danced his fingers along her clit, soft touches using the pattern of pressure he knew she adored. When her body quickened, he could no longer hold back. He seized her lips almost violently, needing to be connected in every way possible. Her body grasped his cock as they rode out their climax together. Nothing had ever felt so perfect.

A small pain twinged in his ribs as they came down from wherever they had been. He looked down to see that her bee pendant had pressed into the skin of his chest, leaving a small imprint of its shape. His entire body replete, the charm had branded him as surely as she had left her mark indelible upon his person—mind, body, and soul.

CHAPTER 22

Whānau: *(noun) Maori word for immediate and extended family as well as close friends*

"I'VE BEEN THINKING about how to use the money I won at the Drunken Bee." Cali and Simon lay together in his bed, and he traced his fingers in a line down her shoulder to her arm. The afternoon sun lay low in the sky, casting long shadows through the window of Simon's bedroom.

"Are you still considering buying a Peloton?"

"I was, but I thought about my family. I haven't seen them since May. I know I'm seeing them over Christmas, but they're sad not to see me over Thanksgiving. Maybe I could use the money to fly them out here and put them up in a hotel for the holiday." She intertwined her fingers with Simon's as they reached her wrist. "My place isn't fit for hosting, but we could go out to a nice dinner, and I could take them to see all the holiday sights in Manhattan." She looked up at Simon. "What do you think?"

"I think it's a brilliant idea. I know how much you miss your family. Only, I don't think you should waste your money on a hotel. My parents are in Florida for the winter. I can ask them if your family could crash at their place. And we can cook a proper Thanksgiving dinner there. We can even invite some of our friends."

"Your...your parents would do that for me?"

"They don't know about you yet, to be honest, but they've been lamenting my single state for so long that I can't imagine them saying no to the request. I think the biggest concern is that they'd want to be included. Fortunately, they're flying to Texas to see my older sister for Thanksgiving."

"I think it's a great idea. Thank you. Are you okay meeting my parents?"

"More than okay, Mad. I want to know every part of you." He gathered her into his arms, so her head rested on his chest.

"Simon?" she whispered.

"Hmm?" He kissed the crown of her head distractedly.

"Are you my boyfriend?" In truth, it hadn't occurred to her to ask before now. They had been spending so much time together that she'd just assumed the title. But Cali didn't take things for granted.

Simon stilled, his arms tensing as he held her close. She tensed in his arms in response as she waited several beats for his answer. "I sure as hell would like to be your boyfriend. Would you want that?"

"I do."

"Well, that's settled then."

Cali's parents and brother were thrilled at the invitation and touched that she had gone to the trouble of looking at and arranging flights once they'd agreed. Booking tickets from Phoenix to Newark with only three weeks before the holiday had been a costly endeavor, and Cali was thrilled when Simon's parents gladly volunteered their home for her family's use. It had amused her to learn they would be subjecting Simon to an unusual wintertime visit in January solely to meet her, but she felt flattered all the same.

Simon's time leading up to her family's visit was severely tried by the looming book deadline and the weekly issues of *The Magnificent Zap* that needed to be created. Friday night game nights were officially on hiatus until early December, when Simon would deliver the final pages to Carson Mathers. Busy with work, Cali gave him the space he needed, but almost every night, she climbed the stairs to his apartment, where they would share dinner. She often brought her laptop and caught up on work while he knuckled down to complete his opus. Sometimes he would stay up late to finish his day's endeavors, but eventually, he slid into bed with her. Usually, they made love, unless his fatigue proved too much. Cali enjoyed taking the lead when his exhaustion got the better of him. She thrilled in giving him pleasure when his body needed an escape from the stress, and he always fell asleep more easily after they had made love.

Studying Simon, understanding him, became a fulfilling part of their relationship. Cali knew when his exhaustion had segued into physical discomfort by how his shoulders tensed and his facial grimaces surfaced. She never commented on his tics, wary of making him feel dissected, but she would order his favorite takeout, hold his hand, and do small things that helped him to disconnect at the end of the day. Sometimes her efforts helped, but even when they didn't, she tried to provide a calming presence and even offered to head back to her apartment if she sensed he would benefit from some privacy. He always refused. She understood—being together felt better than being apart.

While their relationship proved a source of joy, there were still moments when doubt took over. Her stomach pained her less, but whenever she felt particularly happy or excited, a feeling of dread inexplicably followed, waiting for the other shoe to drop. Her Phantom Tumor would gurgle under the surface, like the scenes in shark films when a fin would appear, gliding silently to an unsuspecting swimmer. She had experience in relationships, but not with love. In high school, college, and even grad school, she had exchanged emotional connections with friends and partners for proximity to multiple acquaintances. By design, those relationships had not been meaningful by correlation; it made losing them meaningless.

Zach, Ted, Arun—even her sorority sisters—had been place fillers. She felt guilty but sensed they had used her as she had used them. There was a vulnerability in substantial relationships. Sometimes, it made her nervous to contemplate all she risked.

The memory of her mother tickled at her consideration. That relationship had been most important and, therefore, the most consequential when Cali had gone to live with her father. It meant something, that disconnection from her mom, but whenever her mind threatened to dwell on that fact, she pushed it down, ensuring the Phantom Tumor in her stomach remained well-fed on a regular diet of suppression and denial. Her treadmill still got plenty of use.

Her parents and Michael were set to arrive on the Wednesday before Thanksgiving, and Cali was picking them up from Newark Airport. Meanwhile, Simon took a break from his overloaded work schedule to pick up the groceries Cali had preordered for both the holiday meal and for her family to enjoy throughout their stay. In addition to her family, Kat and Aoki would join for Thanksgiving, as Kat's parents were going to the Caribbean and Aoki's parents lived in Washington.

When Cali went off to grad school in Chicago, her father and Grace had traveled with her to help her move into her new apartment. Like most parents and children, it was easy to fall back into a youthful pattern when interacting as a young adult. Everyone in their family, including her father, would kowtow to Grace's direction, having come to rely on her organizational acumen. She booked flights, hotels, and car services. She packed snacks and ensured everyone had their boarding pass and gate number. She researched weather patterns to ensure everyone had the proper clothing. She made sure iPads were charged and first aid kits were organized. All emergencies had contingent responses that were well-thought-out. They arrived at the airport precisely two hours before domestic flights and three hours before international flights. Everyone else relaxed because of Grace's inability to do so.

The first time she took a trip with her dad and Grace, Cali was amazed by how detail-oriented the journey was. Where her mother's idea of fun came from chaos, Grace's idea was disciplined. At the age of nine, she didn't know which she found more enjoyable, but she knew for certain which she found less frightening.

As she waited for her family to emerge from the terminal, Cali wondered if Grace enjoyed being the family workhorse. Did she feel satisfaction from taking on the mental labor, or did she resent being tasked as the family tour guide? This week, Cali aimed to give her stepmother a break. Cali had booked the flights, ensuring each family member had the type of seat they wanted–aisle for Grace, window for her dad, and at least three rows away from his parents for Michael. She arranged the car service to take them to the airport. Cali took the day off from work to help them settle in and run out to the store if they needed anything else.

As her family walked through the terminal's sliding doors, luggage in hand, Cali couldn't resist the smile that broke across her face. There they were, the people she loved the most, different and yet the same as she had seen them last. Grace's soft ginger hair caught her attention first; it was immediately recognizable, like a beacon welcoming Cali home. Her stepmother wore a sweater set and slacks along with what appeared to be a parka of some sort. They would need to talk. They were in New Jersey, not the Arctic Circle. Her father wore jeans, a golf shirt, and a winter coat with an inflatable pillow around his neck that bounced against the back of his quickly balding head. At twenty-one years old, Michael had officially passed the middle ground between childhood and adulthood. He looked taller than he did in her memories, though he had probably not grown at all since she'd seen him last. Despite his maturity, he dressed in sweats, a T-shirt, and a hoodie. When the cool air hit him, he grimaced, and she could tell he regretted his lack of winter attire.

Maybe Simon could loan her brother a coat.

"Hey, over here!" she called and waved to them. All three paused when they saw her, as if confused, before their smiles were as brilliant as hers, making her wonder what they saw when they looked at her. Did she look markedly different from the last time she had seen them?

Michael reached her first and lifted her off the ground in a giant bear hug.

"Hey, squirt!"

"It's not fair that you're taller than me," Cali muttered into the fabric of his hoodie before ruffling his hair. "After all, you're the baby of the family."

"It is so good to see you!" Grace embraced her next, her eyes suspiciously wet.

"Are you okay?" Cali asked, alarmed.

"I'm fine. I just–I'm so glad we're all together!" She embraced Michael and Cali at once before turning to her husband. "Mitch, get in here! This is a group hug."

"Hey, Dad!" Cali muttered from the center of the embrace while her father joined, giving her a kiss on the cheek.

"Hey, Cali, you made our holiday when we got the call about this."

Cali parted from the group hug while her father touched her cheek, giving her a thorough once-over.

"You look good. Relaxed, I mean."

"Yeah, well, we'd better haul out of here because the cops monitoring the pickup line aren't going to be too happy if we don't make room for the other cars."

As they made their way to Simon's family home, Cali asked about the flight.

"Mom indulged in a glass of wine!" Michael offered.

"You did?" Cali looked at Grace through the rearview mirror.

"Well, you made this trip too easy for me, honey. I figured I would take advantage of it."

"Oh! I should stop by the liquor store later and get a few bottles for dinner and the weekend. Simon is picking up the groceries now."

"I can't wait to meet this young man of yours, hon," Dad said. "Michael and I have been reading his comic online."

"Yeah–anything you want to tell us about Mad McSwiggans?" Michael kicked the seat in front of him where Cali drove. Cali sighed. Little brothers were always going to be little brothers, even if they weren't so little anymore.

"Do not make this weird, guys. I like Simon. Please do not make this weird."

She leveled them all with stern stares. Michael smirked in response to her frustration until Grace smacked him on the shoulder. "You heard her. Save the weirdness for Arizona, Michael."

"I swear, I've never seen Cali get rattled. Miss Calm-and-Collected usually has a stick up her butt with the guys she dates. This weekend is going to be a lot more fun than I thought."

"And this is the opposite of not making it weird."

Her dad came to the rescue by filling Cali in on the latest gossip on the home front–how his accounting firm was doing and who had won the latest pickleball tournament. Grace chimed in with which kids from Cali's graduating class were already home after their first marriages ended in divorce. Her parents' running commentary calmed her until they arrived in Wayne. Simon's parents lived in the Hill section, a wealthier enclave in the town.

Cali and her family became silent as they pulled onto his street. These weren't 'nice' homes. These were mansions. Behind an extensive grey brick wall and wrought iron gate was a farmhouse-style estate on at least a full acre of land. The home's walls were cream with a slate grey roof, and all around were meticulously landscaped gardens and topiaries.

"Cali, permission to make it weird?" Michael whispered. Cali nodded dumbly.

Simon emerged from the front door, his hands clasped together, looking excited as he watched Cali's ten-year-old Honda Accord pull up along the large curved driveway.

Simon had been equally terrified and excited to meet Cali's family. Would his tics behave, or would he come off like something out of a medical drama's worst version of the stereotypical Tourette's patient? As he took in their wide-eyed impression of his family's home, he realized he needn't have worried.

Loose handshakes with her father–"Call me, Mitch" –brother–"Nice digs, bro" –and a warm hug from Grace –"It's so lovely to meet you!" –followed, and Simon showed them inside, directing them to the guest rooms and facilities. Cali made a beeline for the kitchen, and he found her there a few minutes later, reviewing and sorting the items against her grocery list.

"You could have told me what we were walking into!" Cali whispered, and Simon smiled to himself.

Simon knew he came from money, but it didn't belong to him—it belonged to his parents. Yes, they sent him to art school and initially helped support some of his efforts, but it wasn't his information to share.

"I told you my parents have a pool."

"Yes, but you neglected to mention the sauna, jacuzzi, tennis court, and putting green." She indicated the spacious backyard with a broad sweep of her hand toward the bay-style kitchen windows, which overlooked the more impressive aspects of the property. "You forgot to mention the twelve-seat movie theater with reclining chairs. I think my parents will want to forego the day trip to the city on Saturday to appreciate the hotel-quality amenities in your parents' home."

"Mi casa es su casa—or my parents' casa, anyway."

"You should be aware I intend to send your parents one heck of a gift basket after the holiday."

"They'll eat that up." Simon wrapped his arms around Cali, and she sank into his embrace.

"Grace raised me right."

"Well, that's a relief." Grace entered the kitchen, smiling at the two of them. Simon stepped back, unsure of how affectionate Cali would want to be with her parents around.

"What size bird did you get for dinner tomorrow? Are we roasting or frying?"

"I got a..." Cali looked at the list. Her eyes widened, and her mouth made an O shape like something out of a 1920s cartoon. "Oh my God. I forgot to order a turkey." She looked up at Simon and Grace. "I'm such an idiot. I got everything we needed but forgot to order the stupid turkey!" She held up the list. "Look at this. I remembered to order autumn-themed paper napkins and table runners, but I *forgot the turkey.*"

Simon looked at Cali, who was clearly furious at herself and working herself into a panic.

Grace was offering calming words of, "It's not too late, the stores are still open," when Simon's eyes met Cali's. He tilted his head and pressed his lips together to stop himself from breaking into laughter. Cali stopped in the middle of her metaphorical self-flagellation, and her mouth turned into an involuntary smile.

"Stop it, Simon. It's not funny!" But she was holding back laughter, and he could no longer hold in his own.

"You! Forgot! The turkey!" He laughed so hard, his eyes watered, and Cali joined him. And then Grace joined them as well.

"Who forgets to buy the turkey for Thanksgiving?" she agreed. Whenever the three of them tried to pull themselves together, they would catch another person's eyes in the room and start laughing again.

"What's going on in here?" Cali's father looked around the room, puzzled.

"I'll tell him. You guys head back to the store." Grace patted Mitchell on the shoulder. Cali grabbed her keys and waved for Simon to come with her. As he moved to follow, he looked back at Grace and Mitchell, who looked at Cali with bewildered but happy glances.

The Stop & Shop on Franklin Avenue was packed with shoppers picking up the items needed for their family feasts. Simon looked at the crowds and groaned.

"Do you want to wait in the car?" Cali offered.

"No, it's okay. I'll brave the crowds with you." Simon took a deep breath and rolled his shoulders back.

The weather was unaccountably kind for late November, the sun warm on Cali's face.

As they perused the turkeys, she calculated how big a bird they would need. "One and a half pounds per person times seven people equals ten and a half pounds," she calculated under her breath. "So twelve pounds would be more than enough."

"Sounds good," Simon agreed, then his phone rang. "Shit, it's Joanne. Let me grab this real quick." He walked away with a finger in one ear to hear his agent's words.

Cali turned back to the turkey selection, which seemed to be of birds no lighter than twenty pounds. "This won't work," she muttered. Seeing the meat manager, she grabbed his attention. He appeared to be in his late twenties and had a friendly, if overworked, smile. "Thank you for your help. I need a turkey..."

"Well, you've come to the right place." He gave a broad smile, and Cali responded in kind.

"I'm glad to hear it. I need something around eleven to twelve pounds, but everything here is over twenty pounds. Do you have anything smaller in the back?"

"Yeah, the seniors tend to pick out the smaller birds early in the day. Let me see what we've got. I'll be right back."

While Cali waited patiently, Simon rejoined her, stuffing his phone back in his pocket. "All done. Kept her lecture to less than three minutes. She must be buzzed from the holiday already. What are we waiting on?"

"Turkey—the manager is looking in the back for something that won't take me seven hours to roast."

"Seven hours is excessive." Simon nodded.

"Well, Miss, it's your lucky day. The meat delivery truck just came in, and I was able to wrangle a twelve-and-a-half-pound bird for you!" The man looked up at Cali, and his eyes slid to rest on Simon. "Simon Goldberg, holy shit!"

Simon froze, his eyes widening at the man proffering the frozen turkey to her. Cali's eyes flitted back and forth between the two of them before flicking to the name tag on the man's jacket.

Adam Higgins, Meat Department Manager.

Oh, no.

"Simon," Adam Higgins whispered, his jaw on the ground. "I...it's good to see you, man." Adam put the turkey in Cali's cart.

"Adam." Simon nodded, his eyes widening in horror, or maybe in shock. Cali couldn't tell, as her eyes felt like saucers in her skull.

"I... I've wanted to reach out to you for a while now." Adam took a step closer, his voice lowering. Simon took a half step back but stood taller as his childhood bully approached him.

Simon recovered enough from his shock to respond. "Was there some way you forgot to torture me in high school?"

"No, I... Shit." Adam Higgins ran a hand through his hair. "I'm about eleven years too late with the world's biggest apology, and I wish we weren't at the local Stop & Shop." Adam took out a circular bronze coin. "I've been sober for two years. I wasn't drinking in high school, but my dad used to knock me around a lot. It was easier to mess with other kids than to think about how he treated me. After high school, I got low."

Adam appeared to be biting the inside of his cheek, taking a deep breath through his nose. "I wanted to call you, take you out for coffee, a steak dinner, or something not in the freezer section. Fuck." He blew out a quick breath. "I got myself some help. Therapy, meetings–you know how it goes. I want to make amends–not just for the people I hurt while drinking, but for the people I hurt when I was hurting. You're right there near the top of the list." Adam ran a hand through his dark blond hair.

Simon stood quietly, watching as the man metaphorically groveled at his feet. "You're right, it's no excuse..." Simon sighed. "But I appreciate it." But the words were clipped. He hadn't forgiven Adam. It was like he couldn't commit to that act of generosity. Not yet, anyway.

Higgins nodded. "Thank you. Can I give you my card?" He took a small white card out of his pocket. "I'd like to take you out to dinner one night, to apologize truly. I can't undo what I did, but I'd like to offer what peace I can." Adam handed Simon a small business card, which Simon regarded with dull horror.

Higgins looked at Cali and nodded gratefully. "Wishing you both a happy Thanksgiving."

As Higgins turned around, Simon snapped out of whatever trance the interaction had put him in.

"Adam," he called out.

Higgins turned around, looking hopeful and miserable at the same time. "You should also add Anton, Kat, and Ben to your list. I know they would appreciate hearing an apology from you as well."

Higgins nodded thoughtfully and retreated behind the doors of the meat department. Simon looked at Cali, sliding the business card into his pocket.

"Let's get going," he muttered, and they headed to the checkout.

They checked out of the grocery store in relative silence while Simon processed Adam's confession, and Cali drove them back to his parents' home after. For so long, Adam had been the boogeyman out of his nightmares. Alternately, Simon had fantasized about beating him up, playing a prank, and giving him the verbal thrashing he so clearly deserved. He took those daydreams and turned them into the villains Zap faced regularly—only Zap won in those scenarios.

A full-throated, sincere apology had never entered his flights of fancy. It had never occurred to him to feel sorry for the person who made him feel so small for so much of his youth.

Cali had taken on driving, understanding without asking if he needed quiet to consider the interaction. Later, when he had replayed it in his mind and made it a less traumatic occurrence, he would text Anton, Ben, and Kat to share the conversation. He needed their feedback. They were an almost physical connection to the time before he had his life together. They were *there* during the abuse, the times when Simon's thoughts were dark enough to scare him. Thoughts of retribution dissipated once he had friends he could rely on, but Simon sometimes thought of the lost kid he used to be, and the recollections were both sad and frightening.

"I still want to be angry at him." He looked at Cali in the driver's seat, who nodded in response. "I appreciated his apology, but I don't want to forgive him."

"Can't say I blame you. From what you've told me, he went out of his way to be hurtful to you and the people you care about."

"Sounds like he had it rough." Simon groaned and patted his thigh until it hurt. "Fuck, Cali, I *want* to be the kind of man who forgives him, but I don't know if I am." Simon leaned on the window, gnawing at his thumb. The window's cool glass was soothing against his forehead, and he closed his eyes.

"Have I ever told you my favorite word?"

"Hmm?" Simon looked over at her.

"My favorite word. I love many words, but my favorite is sonder–S-O-N-D-E-R. I learned it when I was sixteen. John Koenig coined the term in 2012–he likes to make up new words. Sonder is the profound feeling of realizing everyone, from our friends to our mail carriers to the guy who runs the meat department at the grocery store, has a life as complex as our own." She looked over at Simon. "It's probably a lot easier to remember Higgins as he was in high school–cruel and hurtful to you and the people you love."

"How does that help?"

"You had your villain, and he had his. Maybe if you start thinking about him in the context of a young boy abused by his father, as the man who drank to overcome the trauma of that experience, it will help you to want to forgive him. Not because you *need* to forgive him–it's not your responsibility to forgive someone who abused you. But maybe it will give *you* peace."

Simon thought about what she said. Wasn't that why he created Zap in the first place? To give a rich inner life to someone defined by such a small part of what made them who they are. And Adam Higgins probably needed a hero as much, if not more, than Simon had at the same age.

"But where will I get the villains for Zap to fight?" Simon smiled as the tension in his chest melted.

"Well, there are a lot of jerks out there who haven't made apologies yet. Maybe you can make one of them into your next villain."

Simon considered Cali's suggestions. He'd given his villains interesting, even sympathetic back stories, but he had never made them repentant. Their feelings of betrayal superseded any self-examination. In his mind, this fact separated heroes and villains. What did it mean when a villain made amends, seeking forgiveness in his own life? Could Adam Higgins be the hero in someone else's story? If so, why did it make him vaguely uncomfortable to see Adam in that light?

It showed Adam had grown up, left his childhood behind, and conquered his childhood nightmares. As Simon considered his fears of TV and podcast interviews and book signings, he felt vaguely embarrassed.

"What's the date of that gala event again? I need to rent a tux."

Cali looked at him with a smile that made his earlier hesitancy feel shameful. "December thirteenth. Though I thought a rich boy from high school would own one from his senior prom."

"One, even as skinny as I am, I've put on a few pounds in the last decade, and this counterculture warrior went to the prom in purple so..."

"Tux rental it is."

HA
THANK
GRRR
BURP

PY
IVING
CHOMP
CHOMP

CHAPTER 23

Novercal: *(adjective) pertaining to a stepmother*

THE THANKSGIVING GODS smiled favorably upon their dinner once the adventure of the forgotten turkey was resolved—and after the incredibly awkward meat section run-in. Simon had stayed up late the night before to finish his scheduled work on the comic before the holiday, but Cali woke up early on Thanksgiving morning to prepare the food with Grace. As his tasks were accomplished, he could spend Thanksgiving without the burden of unfinished labor hanging overhead.

Everyone got along remarkably well. Simon wondered if Cali had trained her family regarding his Tourette's or whether a simple warning of his diagnosis had done the trick. Regardless, they paid him no mind when he grunted or made strange faces. At one point, Michael made a punching motion at the TV during a particularly stirring moment of the Cardinals game, and when Simon repeated the motion three times in a row, Michael simply shrugged and returned his attention to the game.

After the early game, Aoki and Kat managed to steal Michael and Mitch away for a round of Ticket To Ride before Cali and Grace served the meal in the dining room. By the sounds of the game, Cali's father had a fantastic case of beginner's luck, and Simon and Cali shared a grin as they set the table in the elegant dining room that remained unused ninety-nine percent of the time. Simon had gotten a call from his mother the week before, insisting their guests use her fancy dishware. When he reminded her that she couldn't possibly know if they used it, she commented, "Oh, I'll know."

As Grace, Cali, and Aoki oohed and aahed over the porcelain plates, he admitted that his mom had been correct in her assessment. He made a mental note to thank her for the dishes and for recommending he purchase flowers for the table's centerpiece, which had also been greeted with great acclaim. Girls were weird about stuff like that.

Throughout the day, Simon watched as Cali interacted with her family. She bickered good-naturedly with Grace about the cornflake stuffing. She teased her brother about the state of his hair. She sat calmly with her father as he shared stories about their hometown in Arizona. He kept thinking back to the hike they had shared two months prior and the assumptions he had made about her family then. If nothing else, it was clear Cali and her family cared for one another.

It struck him how Cali didn't watch them as intently as she did with others. He hadn't picked up on it before because there had been no basis for comparison. With Grace, Cali would talk while peeling apples, folding napkins, and mashing potatoes without looking at her step-mother. When they were with others, she had a tendency to observe, not with interest, but with an almost intense need to analyze the group atmosphere.

But with her family, she relaxed—less needful of inspecting every statement for emotional veracity. While some people saw holidays with family as an emotional trial, Cali appeared to be in her element.

After dessert, Mitchell announced, per family tradition, that it was time to watch *It's a Wonderful Life*. Simon recommended the in-house movie theater for the event, but Mitchell insisted that only a couch would suffice. Within fifteen minutes of the film's opening credits, Cali, Mitchell, and Michael were dozing under throw blankets on the sectional sofa.

"Right on schedule." Grace shook her head with a fond smile. "Come on, you can help me clean up a bit." Simon nodded and followed her to the kitchen. As she set up to scrub dishes that he would dry and put away, they shared a companionable silence.

"Thank you again for hosting us at your family home."

"It was my pleasure." Simon shrugged, embarrassed at the praise. "I figured it would make Cali happier than visiting you at the local Courtyard Marriott."

"You even played our porter!" Grace smiled, referring to how Simon had brought their bags to their rooms.

"Sorry for the lack of turndown service."

"Oh, you!" Grace said, sounding every bit the middle-aged mom from Arizona.

"You don't like *It's a Wonderful Life?*" Simon indicated the movie room with a tilt of his head while he helped dry the fine porcelain his mother insisted they use that was not dishwasher safe.

"I used to. But after Winifred—that's Cali's mom—died, the idea of watching George Bailey contemplate suicide lost its charm."

"I'm surprised Cali is okay with it." He looked over at the living room with a furrowed brow.

"I'm not sure if she's ever seen it. The combination of turkey, stuffing, and apple pie tends to put them all in a food coma. They usually wake up around the scene when George Bailey decides he wants to live again and Clarence the angel earns his wings." Grace laughed fondly. "Then they start to tear up."

"Were you close with Cali's mom?"

Grace thought about it and eventually nodded. "Not until Cali came to live with us. I wanted to keep them connected so Winifred wouldn't feel like she was missing out on her daughter's life. We would send emails back and forth every week. She'd send neutral emails to Cali and, in separate messages, let me know how she was doing so we could set appropriate expectations. When you talk so plainly with someone, you tend to get close, whether you plan to or not. I would send pictures and reassure her that Cali was safe and loved. Sometimes I wonder if I gave her a reason to give up because she knew her daughter was secure." Grace shook her head as she lathered up a particularly caked-on dish. "Those feelings are not fun."

Simon tried to imagine the line Grace had to walk between being Cali's stepmother and Winifred's confidante. "It must've been hard on all of you when she died."

"Yes, it was quite sad." Her hands slowed as she washed a plate, staring off into the dark picture window overlooking the property. "We all tried to help Winifred, but in the end, her demons were too strong."

Seeking the opening he had hoped for, Simon asked, "What was Cali like when she came to live with you?"

Grace hemmed as she likely considered how much to share with her daughter's new boyfriend. "You're the first boyfriend of hers who's asked."

"I'm sorry if I'm invading..."

"No, it's okay. I think it might be a good sign that you're curious." A series of emotions flickered across her face, and Simon tried to decipher them. Her eyes landed on sadness. She slowed her efforts at the sink, as if looking back across a vast chasm of regret.

"She was extremely withdrawn that first month. Without Winifred, she didn't know who she was anymore." She looked over at Simon. "It was all we could do to get her to eat or to say when she needed something. We couldn't send her to school until the next year because we were so scared of what would happen to her there."

Simon nodded. "Cali mentioned that. She told me she'd been behind in school."

Grace considered Simon's statement. "To some degree, that's true, but we could've supplemented with tutors if need be. It made me anxious to send her when she was in such a vulnerable state, and Mitch and I decided to keep her home while she acclimated. She only missed the last few months of that year, and we sent her again in the fall."

"She mentioned to me you helped her fit in."

"Is that what she said?" Grace nodded her head half-heartedly in agreement. "I guess that's true. Some of it was about implementing the rules of our household. I'm sure you had rules—chores you had to do. Brush your teeth twice a day, etcetera. When she finally confided in me, I learned about the bullying she had experienced at her old school. She didn't know how to be herself without her mom, and it terrified her to be seen as a..."

"Freak," Simon mumbled.

"Yes, exactly. I tried to reassure her, tell her how she should be herself, but she insisted she'd never fit in. So I gave her advice and she..." Grace shook her head mournfully. "She ran with it."

"What tips did you give her?"

"Oh, there's a lot of looking your best to help you feel your best, standing up straight, don't over-apologize, be cooperative with your classmates, think before you speak. Honestly, it's a lot of platitudes, but Cali internalized them because they worked for her. Of course, there's a difference between fitting in and being yourself, and that's where I failed her as a parent."

"Why do you say that?"

"I think somewhere in between trying to fit in, she forgot you don't *need* to fit in to be happy. At one point, I could've stepped in and helped her see she was enough without hiding behind a bland smile. In high school, she couldn't offer an opinion on anything for fear she'd piss someone off. That's not a healthy way to live. I'm sure you've seen the stomachaches she gets when she's upset?"

Simon thought back to the morning she threw up after seeing the Instagram post. He had chalked it up to a hangover. He nodded at Grace to continue.

"By the time I realized how bad it had gotten, she wouldn't change her approach. It worked for her, after all. Cheerleading, homecoming court, good grades—no one looking from the outside could see anything but what she wanted them to see—except her dad, Michael, and me. Never mind going to therapy; she completely shut that down." Grace swiped her hand in a motion of finality. "And we didn't want to alienate her, so we didn't push." Grace puffed her cheeks and let out a long exhale. "At least at home, she could be free. Out in the world was the problem."

"At least you gave her a safe space to land," Simon said, surprising himself when he realized how sincere he felt. His original perceptions of Grace as trying to mold Cali into an automaton were falling apart with the acknowledgment that this woman loved his girlfriend as much as any mother he had ever seen.

"Mitchell and I were talking last night after you left. I don't know what's happened out here these last few months, but it's the most comfortable I've seen Cali in a long time. She smiles now, and it's not that tight-lipped, nervous, polite smile. There's warmth there. I can only imagine you played a role in bringing that to pass, so thank you."

"It's strange you mention that. I was thinking the same thing about you. She...she doesn't watch her family like she *needs* to watch others."

Grace nodded. "What is that word my therapist told me?" She snapped her fingers. "Hypervigilant. When she's stressed or nervous, Cali gets hypervigilant." She smiled at Simon. "But she's not like that around you either."

"Which is amusing if you think about it, considering how many stares I accumulate regularly." And as if on cue, he grimaced and gave Grace a lopsided smile.

"I think it's your good looks. Now, don't go breaking her heart." Grace gave him a stern look.

"Frankly, I think it's more likely she'll break mine."

"Or maybe neither of your hearts will break. Maybe this is the first of fifty Thanksgivings together. And you can give me grandbabies!"

Simon coughed involuntarily, swallowing saliva down the wrong pipe.

"I'm sorry, forget I said that. I'm the worst sort of meddler!" Grace's face turned bright red as she slapped Simon on the back. After he got control of the cough, she handed him a glass of water.

"Please don't dump her because of me!" Grace implored with a pleading, half-joking voice, clasping together dish-soap-covered gloves that had no doubt left a palm print on the back of his shirt.

Simon laughed and refocused his attention on the dishes that needed drying.

CHAPTER 24

Nemesis: *(noun) the inescapable agent of someone's or something's downfall*

SIMON COULD TELL that Cali was faking. She sat ramrod straight in the seat of their Uber, attempting to stave off wrinkles in her floor-length strapless black gown. She was wearing the bumblebee pendant he had given her, twisting it between her thumb and forefinger. He grabbed her hand, and she smiled at his attempt to ground her. At least, she gave him the imitation of a reassuring smile.

He wasn't fooled. "Walk me through it again. Who is going to be here tonight?"

"I mean, a few thousand of New York's glitterati and a few hundred locally based corporations that want to look good to the public."

"What I mean is, who will you know there?"

"My company bought three tables at a cool $125K each, so I guess the thirty people at those tables. I know my coworker Jesse will be there with her husband. And my boss, George, with his wife, and the CEO, James Russell, probably with his wife." She counted the names off on her fingers. "There will probably be a few others I haven't met."

"Wait, did you say a few thousand people are attending?" He had no idea the event was so well attended.

"The Robin Hood Foundation Gala is hosted at the Javits Center. It's the world's largest single-night fundraiser. Last year, they raised over $65 million for area causes."

"Damn... That's something else." Simon looked over at her again and wondered about the cause of her nerves. Was it the high-ranking colleagues in attendance? Was she afraid Simon would embarrass her? Was it because she wanted him to enjoy her efforts on his behalf?

Not wanting to make it worse by putting her on the spot, he decided to wait before bringing it up. But not knowing the cause of her anxiety further rankled his own.

"This year, it's being hosted by one of the Weekend Update anchors from *Saturday Night Live*, and the musical guest is U2," she whispered with a hint of excitement as they crossed over the George Washington Bridge into northern Manhattan. The city's lights set off against the dark cloud cover and the light pollution that blocked any hopes of starlight shining through.

"My dad told me he and my mom attended a few of these events before they moved to Florida. They want me to text them a photo of us together at the party." Simon had been pressed to make the promise after a lot of hemming and hawing. His mom reminded him of her kindness toward Cali's family over the holiday and asked if she at least deserved to see her son happy with his new girlfriend. His mom had only been further excited by the relationship when she received gifts and thank-you cards from Grace and Cali. His girlfriend and her mother had been deemed 'classy,' the highest compliment ever in his mother's book.

"That's very sweet. Do I look okay?" She bit her lip, and Simon kissed her hand, still held by his. She had gotten her hair done, and it hung down her back in golden waves. He had long decided his attraction to Cali went beyond physical, but the accompanying ache when he looked at her in that dress came from somewhere further south than his heart.

"You could show up in yoga pants and that sorority hoodie of yours, and you'd still be the most beautiful woman there, but when I first saw you in that dress tonight, you took my breath away."

"You are too smooth." She poked him in the chest with a manicured fingernail, and he jokingly feigned injury. But his words had their desired effect, and Cali's stick-straight posture relaxed marginally. "Thank you for coming with me. It means a lot to me. I know things like this aren't always easy for you."

"But you made a good point, and in an event with so many people, I'm unlikely to do anything to draw that much attention to myself. It's a good beginning to breaking down some of my barriers to success. Joanne said she's starting me on media training next week."

"She must be thrilled you've decided to move ahead."

"Cautiously optimistic. She's used to temperamental artists, I think, but at least she's no longer nagging me nonstop. She thinks I agreed to it all to get her off my back."

"If only she knew." Cali quieted while her eyes drifted over the approaching cityscape.

Simon had looked at Adam's business card a half-dozen times since that fateful Thanksgiving run-in at the grocery store. He hadn't made any contact, but in his head, he had written and deleted several different emails ranging from a full-throated rage-fueled missive on how painful Adam had made his youth, to a kind appreciation for the apology Adam had offered, to something that walked the line in between. And now, Simon took steps toward a new stage of adulthood that felt fueled by a perverted competition with his childhood bully.

He knew he was doing the right thing, but was he doing it for the right reason?

The Javits Center on Manhattan's West Side had been lit in blue and gold for the night's event. The exterior and interior were designed to look like the city's skyline. Simon had attended New York City's Comic-Con at the Javits Center, so he was familiar with its vast outline, but he had never seen it set up for glamour. Gone were the vendor booths highlighting obscure comics and paraphernalia; instead, there were large round-top tables festooned with tall centerpieces composed of roses and other types of flowers he couldn't identify. Hundreds of waiters and waitresses circled the room, holding glasses of champagne for guests to enjoy.

"And I thought Victoria's sorority shindigs were over the top," Cali said, grasping Simon's hand tighter than usual. "We're at table ninety-seven. We're going to need a map to find our seats."

Simon pointed her to a standing board that provided the info, and before long, they were examining the place cards at their table.

"Oh, shit."

Simon gave her an alert glance. Cali never cursed. He'd never asked her why she kept her language so squeaky clean, though he assumed it was because she had better words to use than four-letter ones. Her expletive use indicated a problem.

"What's wrong?" he asked, instantly alert.

"Ryan Connolly." She looked dismayed at the name on the place card in front of her. "He's this...guy from my training cohort. He made a pass at me during training, and I turned him down. He's quite unpleasant." She groaned. "He's a pig."

Something tickled at the back of Simon's brain.

Does the carpet match the drapes?

"Wait–I remember this guy. Was he the one who made that gross comment on your Instagram a few weeks back?"

"The same." Cali sighed. "I can't believe I'm going to have to spend the next few hours making small talk with him. Ugh."

Without thinking about his sanity, Simon immediately switched his and Cali's place cards so Simon would be sitting between the two of them.

"You're my hero, Zap." Cali smiled warmly before standing on the tips of her heels and pressing an ardent kiss to Simon's lips.

"Hey, get a room, you two," a voice called from behind them, and Simon turned as a petite woman with short curly hair joined them. She wore a forest-green gown with a double strand of pearls around her neck.

She looked vaguely familiar before Simon realized he recognized her from the Renaissance faire back in September.

"Hi, Lauren," Cali offered with a friendly smile. Lauren gave Cali a casual hug. "I like your gown. Green is a nice color on you."

"Thank you. I like yours as well. Are we the first to arrive?"

"Yes, but it looks like the others are starting to file in now."

They were quickly joined by Jesse and her husband, Cali's boss George and his wife, and Ryan, who attended solo. The last two spots were empty, but the place cards indicated they belonged to the organization's CEO and his wife.

"No pressure," Cali whispered to Simon.

"They probably won't even show," Lauren suggested. "These corporate bigwigs buy tickets to all these events and half the time decide not to attend. It's not a big deal to them."

"I don't know that I'll ever be a big enough deal to miss out on a U2 concert," George joked, and they all chuckled.

"Forget U2–I heard that the *Sports Illustrated* swimsuit cover model is in attendance tonight." Ryan drank liberally from his cocktail and glared at Cali, who studiously ignored him. Simon needed to figure out a way to survive the night without decking this guy.

"Simon, I like your tie. It looks familiar, but I can't quite place it," Lauren said as they mingled before being called to take their seats for the formal start of the festivities.

"Thank you. My mom had it made for me."

"Your mom!" Ryan guffawed, interrupting Simon.

"As I was saying, my mom had it made for me. It's the symbol of the superhero character I created."

"Yes! I recognize it now! It's from *The Magnificent Zap*!" Unabashedly, Lauren took the tie in her hands to admire the pattern of artistic Zs woven into the silk. "You created *The Magnificent Zap*? I love that comic!" Lauren looked over at Cali with a wide grin. "Your boyfriend is one of my favorite comic artists ever!"

"Thank you. I appreciate that." Simon didn't mind the flattery in light of his aims to be out in the open.

"I'm a fan myself." Cali smiled, taking Simon's hand. No one missed the subtle issuance of *hands-off, he's mine,* but neither woman showed animosity, and in fact, the warmth he sensed came from both sides.

"I'm enjoying your latest episodes. Will we see more of...wait...Mad McSwiggans! Of course! Is Cali the inspiration for your new character?"

Both Simon and Cali blushed. "What can I say? She's my muse."

"Your own personal Calliope," Cali teased.

"So you're telling me," Ryan interrupted, the fingers on his free hand pointing to Simon with finger guns that emphasized every other word, "you draw comics for a living? Does that come with a 401(k) and health coverage?"

Unfortunately, Simon's brain couldn't resist the obnoxious motion. His right hand immediately copied Ryan's finger guns in a manner that came off as either mocking or just plain strange. Simon leaned into mocking.

"What I'm saying," Simon responded, "is that my comics provide enough income to pay for health insurance *and* a decent retirement plan."

"And Simon has a publishing deal for his back episodes going live in a couple of months. He's incredibly talented." Cali's cool voice left no doubt that anyone who messed with Simon also messed with her.

Before Ryan could respond with another insufferable comment, the overhead announcements called everyone to their seats to begin the evening's event. The Chairman of the Robin Hood Foundation took to the podium to present a video showcasing the foundation's accomplishments for the community over the preceding twelve months. By the time the footage had gone through interviews with previously homeless veterans and single mothers trying to make ends meet for their children, there wasn't a dry eye in the house.

“I can see why this event is so effective at raising money,” Cali said, teary-eyed. “I have a feeling my checking account will be at least $200 less by the time we leave tonight.”

“You and me both.” Simon looked at her, and she smiled back. He hadn’t let go of her hand yet, but she wasn’t complaining.

“Wait till you see the live auction,” Jesse added. “I’ve never been, but my neighbor went last year, and the top-ticket item went for $2.7 million.”

“What you’re saying is we shouldn’t plan to bid on anything.” Lauren laughed, holding up the auction pamphlet. “The *starting* bid for this Bulgari necklace is $5,000.”

“Lots of time to run to the restroom,” Simon suggested, making the three women laugh.

“So does that mean you won’t be buying me,” she looked down at the pamphlet, “a month at a chateau in southern France?”

“No, but there are lots of handsome billionaires here tonight. Perhaps you could ask one of them.”

“Nah, I think I’ll stick with you.” Cali quickly kissed him on the cheek, and he blushed, smiling fondly in response.

“Speaking of the restroom, I think I will make a trip before the line gets too long.” Lauren stood, grabbing her purse.

“I should go as well,” Cali said. “You okay over here?”

Simon waved her off, refocusing his attention on the presentations on stage.

Lauren cornered Cali on the way back from the restroom.

“Cali, I’m about three months late with this apology. Back at training, you overheard me saying something that wasn’t only mean, it was untrue. It was born of jealousy and insecurity, and...you have no reason to forgive me, but I want you to know that when I realized you overheard what I said, it forced me to look long and hard at myself, and I didn't like what I saw." Lauren's eyes were earnest and wide open, and she was fidgeting with her hands before she clenched them into small fists she held by her side.

Touched, Cali considered Lauren's sincerity. Her colleague had been unexpectedly kind over the past few months, so the apology didn't come off as surprising, but the regret and angst emanating from her were. "What you said hurt," Cali admitted. "But to be honest, it forced me to look at myself too, at what I showed the world. So even though it hurt, I'm glad I heard you."

Lauren nodded, relieved. "I'm an awkward person," she confessed. "I've always been clever, but more often than not, I get my big foot stuck in my even bigger mouth. I was jealous of you because, well, you come off so calm and collected. I've never been able to pull off that look." Lauren wrung her hands nervously as she continued. "In middle school, the kids called me Lauren 'Piss me offski' instead of Lauren Polski because of my lack of filter."

"I'm sorry, that's incredibly cruel."

Lauren shrugged. "They were mean, but they weren't entirely wrong. There are consequences for not thinking before you speak, and those were mine. Anyway, for whatever my opinion is worth, I don't think you're shallow or standoffish. You're funny, intelligent, and thoughtful. The company is lucky to have you, and I admire what you've accomplished with the New Jersey team."

"Thank you, I appreciate that, and...if you'd like, I'd be willing to start over." She smiled. "Hi, I'm California Barton. You can call me Cali."

"California? Huh. How about that." Lauren shook her head.

"If you tell anyone, I'll have to kill you."

"Your secret is safe with me."

Lauren and Cali shared a complicit smile, and Cali thought she might like to be friends with Lauren. It felt like they were halfway there already.

"Do you want to go get a drink from the bar?"

"Yes, please. I can't afford these auction prizes anyway."

Cali and Lauren made their way to one of the dozen bars set around the perimeter of the ballroom, where other guests waited out the duration of the live auction. The C-level executives and celebrities bid wantonly on yacht trips around the Mediterranean and Knicks season ticket floor seats. Simon stood near the bar, sipping from a glass of red wine, and Cali walked up to him with a happy smile.

"What are you doing out here?"

"If I had to listen to your douchebag colleague going on one more minute, I was going to do something that would be the opposite of good for your career." Simon shook his head with a sneer. "He spent the last ten minutes guessing which women were going commando to avoid panty lines."

"Ryan? That guy is the worst," Lauren agreed. "Some of the stuff he says... Just stay away from him. He's not a good person."

Cali nodded sagely.

"Simon, tell me about Zap—where do you get your ideas? Any spoilers you can give me?" Lauren brought her hands together in a gesture of supplication, clasped as if in prayer, and, of course, Simon immediately copied the gesture.

"Sorry, it's your..."

"Your Tourette's, yeah, I know." Lauren waved it off as old news. "I worked in sales, calling on neurologists at my last job, so I've seen it before. I could tell by the way you copied Ryan earlier, and of course, there's Zap's superpowers."

"Oh, cool," Simon said, relieved to be moving on.

"Tourette's? Does your boyfriend have Tourette's, Cali? That's fucking hilarious!" The three turned at the raucous comment.

"He's like Bloody fucking Mary," Cali heard Lauren whisper under her breath before her colleague put on a phony smile that looked more like a grimace. "Say his name three times, and he appears."

"I'd rather come face-to-face with Bloody Mary than Ryan," Cali whispered back.

"Tourette's—so does that mean you start shouting curse words in public and shit?" Ryan seemed utterly pleased with this knowledge at his disposal.

"No, Ryan, that's coprolalia, and it's more common in TV shows than in real life. But even if it were, that's not something to joke about." Cali looked at him as if he were a particularly nasty bug.

"If you don't curse, what do you do? Or are you faking?"

"Ryan, you're being obnoxious," Lauren said baldly. "Pick a new topic of conversation."

"What's the big deal? I'm curious. It's not every day I get to talk to someone with a screw loose." Ryan cackled at his nasty joke, and Cali could take it no longer.

"What do you mean by that, Ryan?" she asked after his laughter had abated slightly.

"Huh?" Ryan looked confused at the pause in the momentum of his cruelty.

"What does it mean that he has a screw loose?" Cali put on her 'dumb blond' expression, tilting her head like a puppy hearing a strange sound.

"You know." He made a waving motion with his hand. "His brain doesn't work right."

"I didn't know that." She looked over at Simon. "Your brain doesn't work right?"

"Not that I ever noticed." Simon gave her a look of understanding, his eyebrows raising and lips twitching in the way he did when he tried not to laugh. Cali bit the inside of her cheeks to keep from smiling.

"But Ryan says you have a screw loose." She pursed her lips. "Is something loose in your brain? Like a wire?"

"It means your boyfriend is a retard. You're dating some loser who can't control himself." Ryan got closer and louder, and Cali could smell the alcohol on his breath. "I'm glad we never dated if this is the kind of twitchy freak you shack up with."

Ryan had been provoked to the ultimate cruelty, and Cali looked at him with a vicious smile. "I'd 'shack up' with Simon if he had polka dots, stripes, and smelled like a swamp over you any day of the week, Ryan. Please remove yourself from this conversation."

"You're a fucking whore who–"

It was hard to say what happened first. Simon had his fist pulled back, but before he could let the punch swing that would likely get him arrested, Lauren pulled back on Simon's arm, while Cali threw her glass of red wine all over Ryan's pristine white dress shirt.

"You fucking bitch!" Ryan roared, jumping back as the wine spilled down his face and chest, leaving a purple mark in its wake. "You'll pay for that. I'll get you fired. I'll get you arrested for assault."

"What is the meaning of this?" a booming voice asked as their manager, George, arrived, along with a late-middle-aged couple dressed in a tuxedo and a long navy dress. "Why are my trainees acting like teenagers on prom night?"

"She..." Ryan pointed at Cali with fingers dripping with the remnants of her drink. "She threw her glass of wine at me. She assaulted me! I'm going to HR."

"That's not what happened," Simon interjected loudly, his body tensing up in response to the stress. He slapped his thighs repeatedly with increasing volume and ferocity, grimacing at the anxiety he was no doubt feeling. Cali grabbed his hand and shook her head, indicating he should keep quiet.

"George–that's not what happened," Lauren stated calmly. "Ryan has been sexually harassing Cali since training. Not only has he come on to her, but I heard him say he thought her recent success came at the cost of providing certain favors to you. His exact words were, 'The only hard work Cali has been doing has been on her knees.' Cali was upset at his behavior and accidentally tripped–that's why her wine is all over him."

Cali fought her instinct to drop her jaw at that news and to appear as though she had known this all along. She had no idea Ryan had been eviscerating her professionalism to such a depraved extent. She wished she'd spilled two glasses of wine on him instead of one.

"And if we watched the videos, would they confirm this record of events?" George asked with a raised brow and folded arms.

"Absolutely, they would," Lauren bluffed. "And I can provide evidence from other reps who have seen and heard Ryan's behavior."

"And you, young man, is there a reason you look so upset?" George Melone looked at Simon, whose eyes widened before storming away.

Cali looked after him miserably, but she couldn't leave without it seeming as though she was admitting to wrongdoing. "For goodness' sake, he has Tourette's. It's not a big deal. He's stressed because he didn't like seeing me get insulted." Cali finally opened her mouth, letting her anger and anxiety shine through.

"Regardless of how insulting Mr. Connolly has been, spilling wine on him is not the example we want to set as representatives of Marcus & Meyers." George sighed, his hand running through his hair. "And this is not how I wanted to introduce my best and brightest to our CEO and his wife. Forgive me, Jim."

Of course, the man who controlled their professional lives stood there with wide eyes while his wife looked ready to eat popcorn.

"And you thought this event would be boring, dear." She patted her husband on the shoulder.

"Now, Gina, I'd rather have a boring evening than see my next generation of executives acting like this." Jim Russell seemed overwhelmed by the sight of three professionals standing there like surly teenagers.

"Like you didn't get carried away back in the day." Gina Russell gave her husband a sardonic side-eye.

James Russell looked at his wife with a bemused smile on his face. "A fair point. George, I have faith you'll handle this admirably. I'll meet you back at the table."

"Yes, sir–scotch on the rocks and a Chardonnay for your wife?"

"Please."

George turned back to the three of them. The muscle in Ryan's jaw jutted out, his nostrils flaring as he peeled his soaked shirt away from his chest. Lauren and Cali stood silently, though Cali noticed Lauren standing closer to her, ready to battle as a team.

"This is quite upsetting. Cali, throwing your glass of wine is unacceptable. We will discuss this with HR on Monday, but I anticipate that it will be noted on your record, and they will expect you to complete an online course on conflict remediation and codes of conduct."

"Wait–she's not going to face any real consequences for what she's done? That bitch destroyed a $300 shirt." Ryan threw his hand in Cali's direction, the lines in his face etched with vitriol at the perceived injustice of Cali keeping her job.

George's face remained impassive, but that use of the word 'bitch' caused his eyebrows to raise. "You may submit the bill for the shirt with your final expense report."

"Final expense report?" Ryan's jaw dropped, agog at George's pronouncement.

"You forget, Ryan, your first six months are a probationary period, and I am permitted to terminate your employment at will during that time frame. I now have evidence from two female employees that you've been making sexually harassing comments. I plan to call some of your other colleagues as well–what will they tell me, I wonder?"

"Matt Watkins from Buffalo and Sandy Johnson from Chicago were there for some of these comments, George. And I have screenshots from a text thread between Ryan, Matt, and me," Lauren volunteered.

"You know what? Forget this. You can take this job and shove it!" Ryan stormed off, still dripping on the carpeted floor.

"Well, that statement there saves the need for a severance package." George smiled. "Thank you, Lauren. Moving forward, you and I will need to discuss when it is appropriate to address hostile situations before they escalate into something out of a bad soap opera. You should have both come to me sooner." He ran a hand through his hair. "As it stands,

I think the entire team would benefit from a refresher on company policy relating to sexual harassment."

"I'm sorry, George," Cali offered. "He called Simon a retard and then called me a whore..."

George paled as Cali explained what had happened. "Yes, well, maybe that HR training can avoid the comment on your record. I'd have liked to witness his comeuppance myself. Why don't you go see after your date?"

"Yes, thank you." Cali excused herself as she tried to find where Simon had gone. In the vastness of the convention center, a successful search seemed an impossibility, so she picked up her cell phone and called him. When it went to voicemail, she sent off a quick message.

Where are you? Please tell me you're okay.

CHAPTER 25

Scarper: *(verb) to run away, typically from a dangerous situation*

SIMON RAN.

By his judgment, he had about five minutes to find a quiet, unobtrusive spot, somewhere out of the way of prying eyes, where he wouldn't make a spectacle of himself to Manhattan's elite.

Bumping into a couple about to kiss, Simon didn't waste time apologizing. The feeling of lightning wormed its way from his extremities, from the tips of his fingers to his elbows, and from his ankles to his knees, searing its way up his spine to the base of his skull, where it bled freely into the space behind his eyes.

The premonitory urges—the feeling that preceded every tic but became a claxon of increasing volume and intensity before a tic attack—were upon him.

Four minutes to go, more or less.

Reaching into his suit pocket, he pulled out a cannabis gummy. While not quite the cyanide pill of a tic attack he'd like it to be, in the past, it had ensured a quicker turnaround than any other treatment. Anyone who doubted the medicinal purposes of marijuana had never been in the shoes of a Tourette's patient about to spend anywhere from five minutes to five hours in a state of physical incapacitation.

Vague memories of Comic-Con three years prior filled his brain. The bathroom lounge in the River Pavilion had a carpeted floor. With the event primarily focused on the lower floors of the Javits Center, it would provide a much-needed respite from the crowd. He hoped no one was using it for a quickie.

With what he judged as about a minute to go, he slammed open the bathroom door, relieved to see they hadn't locked it and there was a wide-open space. Sitting down on the floor, he focused on his breathing. His hands slapped his upper thighs painfully–oh, there would be bruises tomorrow. His typical gentle patting became wild slaps, and he moaned at the discomfort as his mouth grimaced.

Tic attacks could last minutes or hours. His longest lasted two hours and twenty minutes in middle school. He'd felt it coming on and gone to the nurse's office. His mom arrived and sat with him while the nurse complained they needed him to leave, as 3 p.m. had come and gone. Like he could move with his body in full tic mode? He could barely communicate, let alone walk to his mother's car. His mother, God bless her, had given the nurse a verbal smackdown and encouraged her to do her research and keep her mouth shut.

He should have seen tonight coming and taken a gummy earlier. The attacks were rare, but when they happened, they coincided with an anxiety-inducing event. Being here with Cali, meeting her colleagues, feeling the need to be his best for her sake–he'd been so stupid not to consider what might happen. Thank God he brought the gummies with him.

Recalling the look on that douchebag's face had him gritting his teeth. He would've loved to punch Ryan, but Simon was relieved Cali's colleague had stopped him. No good would have come from physical violence, and Cali could take care of herself. She took care of him as well. He took a deep breath and then another. His body moved of its own accord as he tried to escape within himself. Earlier therapists recommended grounding techniques, such as finding something blue or naming something you hear. Tonight, he went into his brain and mentally tried to paint Cali. Not Mad McSwiggans—not the comic-book version. In art school, he'd studied portrait painting and found it soothing and satisfying. He imagined holding a paintbrush and finding the exact color of gold for her hair, the combination of yellow and green that would make up the color of her eyes. In the twenty minutes he laid on the floor, he created a portrait of her as she looked that day she took him hiking. There she stood, with her chin on her arms, at peace, looking over the fall vistas while he stared at her.

Divorced from his body, he painted half a dozen portraits in his mind. One of her standing with his friends after the spelling bee filled him with warmth. Another of their hands clasped as they watched *The Birdcage*. In time, his body calmed, and when he opened his eyes, he saw his right hand bent as if holding a paintbrush. The glitching had calmed like lightning seen in the distance after a storm swept out to sea. He looked at his phone. This one had been blessedly brief, lasting only thirty minutes.

Sitting up, he took stock of his body. Tomorrow was going to suck. There would be bruises and aches, a hangover of sorts, and he still had the rest of the night to get through. His phone buzzed in his pocket, lighting up with messages and missed calls.

Please tell me you're okay.

Where are you? I'll come to you.

Did you go back to NJ? I'm worried about you.

Simon typed in a quick response, so she knew he was safe.

I'm okay. I need a few minutes.

Simon looked at his reflection in the mirror. His hair was askew, and he ran his hands under the water to slick it back into something resembling order. Running his hands under the water again, he washed away the sweat and spittle that had gathered on his face and neck. He wanted to go home and take a shower, watch a movie with Cali, and order takeout.

The thumping bass from downstairs indicated U2 had taken the stage. Groaning, he tucked his shirt back in and straightened his jacket. How had this night gone so far off the rails? Was he out of his mind to even try to make these efforts? For so long, he had found security in his routines. He'd last experienced a tic attack over two years ago, when he had been traveling for his job. The past few months had been a vacation by comparison. The people he surrounded himself with knew what to expect of him, so his body had shifted into a relatively quiet mode. Even meeting Cali's family hadn't brought any significant stress.

But tonight's implosion raised the question of whether he should move forward into new consideration. What would this mean for Joanne's efforts on his behalf? Would he lose it on national television?

He could leave this event right now. He hadn't wanted to do this. If he hadn't come to this self-congratulatory, glad-handing fest of the wealthy, he would've been on his couch eating Chinese takeout and watching *Daredevil*. He could leave this gala and tell Joanne that no amount of professional success was worth subjecting himself to mockery, pity, and the kind of physical incapacitation a media tour would surely entail.

Still, he'd made his way back to the gala. Cali's outline was illuminated by the reflected glow of the stage's glittering lights. He could turn now, go home, and text her that he'd gotten sick. He could disappear from her in degrees so infinitesimal that she wouldn't notice until she chose to end things, and he would feel relieved with minimal guilt.

He could run.

Cali turned to look at him, the fake smile she'd given to the middle-aged lady married to her CEO breaking into a genuine one of relief. She released a gulping breath, as if she'd been holding it until he reappeared. He watched her disengage from her companion to join him in the shadows outside the dance floor.

The crease between her eyebrows evened out as he approached.

"You're going to get wrinkles if you keep making that face." He touched the space above her nose with his pointer finger.

"I get the pricey stuff from Sephora, remember?" She took his hands in hers, intertwining their fingers. "Are you okay? Where did you run off to?"

"I'll tell you later." He looked around, taking stock of the other members of their party. "Did everything calm down?"

Cali's grin became one of the shit-eating variety. "In a manner of speaking. Ryan got fired."

"No way!" The news distracted Simon enough for him to offer a relieved half smile.

Cali clapped her hands together. "Score one for the good guys."

"Man, that would have lived rent-free in my brain for months. Can you give me the play-by-play?"

"I can do you one better. Lauren had her phone recording the audio. It's not a camera, but if you listen closely, I swear you can hear him have an aneurysm."

Without realizing it, Simon had begun using her hand as his personal worry stone. Cali had a dreamy look on her face. Bono sang "All I Want Is You" as if on cue.

"Would you like to dance?" Cali asked, looking at the couples pairing off. Simon watched them coalesce into slowly moving silhouettes.

Still, longing to join couldn't overcome his fear and exhaustion. "Not tonight. Another time." He smiled, imploring her with his eyes not to take it personally. He couldn't bear holding her in his arms right now. Even being in this public setting brought back the urge to tic.

Briefly, her smile faltered, but she shook it off quickly. What was going through her head? He couldn't decipher it in his exhausted state, and Cali brought her hand up to cradle his cheek, taking in the weariness of his mien. "Should we go? We've stayed long enough, and no one would fault us."

She was doing it for him, offering him a lifeline. Guilt for letting her down warred with relief. If they hurried, they could be back in Ridgewood before Mr. Wok stopped delivering. He could pretend the whole night had never happened. He shouldn't do that to her. He should shake his head and gallantly lead her out on the dance floor to sway with her to Bono's words of lifelong love.

"I'll...I'll order the Uber," he said finally, feeling small and weak as he did. Cali's smile had an artificial brightness. He couldn't tell if it was hiding frustration or simply offering a sign of support.

Or perhaps none of the above. The night had been trying for her as well.

"Good idea. Let me say goodbye to my colleagues." She kissed Simon on the cheek and untangled their hands, leaving him bereft as she made her goodbyes. He watched her explain their departure and saw her colleagues, Lauren and Jesse, look back at him, but he couldn't decipher their expressions.

They want to know what she's doing with a loser like me.

They want to know why she puts up with someone who can't go to a party without freaking out.

They want to know...

"Are you ready?"

If he measured the veracity of her interactions with him by the warmth of her smile, he deemed this one sincere.

"I can't wait to take off these heels. It's enough to wear them during the week. Nighttime is comfy slipper time."

"I can't argue with you there, Mad," he added glumly as she took his hand, and they left to find their car.

In art school, Simon postponed taking art history class as long as possible, thinking it would bore him. When he finally took the class, he became enamored with what came before and grew insecure about his inability to measure up artistically. Holding Cali reminded him of the sculpture *The Kiss* by Constantin Brancusi. The statue featured lovers embracing abstractly, with no separation between them. They were matched parts to a whole, puzzle pieces pressed together for eternity. He didn't like to think of these artistic creations because his work felt cheap and amateurish by comparison, but the art's soul felt so much more real when Cali curled within him in the back seat of the black Toyota Prius driving them to New Jersey.

They rode home in silence. Was Cali upset with him for forcing them to leave? He pressed his thumb into her palm in a pattern meant to reassure. She sat there passively, a willing victim of his insecurities. When a tear dropped from his eyes and fell on her head, she looked up in surprise and cupped his cheek.

"Hey, hey, it's okay, Simon. You did great tonight. I'm proud of you."

He pulled her close, and she soothingly caressed his back. One tear became two, a quiet torrent caught in her blond tresses.

Cali had years of practice hiding behind a mask of banal pleasantries. When Ryan hit on her, she pleasantly deferred his advances by pretending not to understand his propositions. When he had hounded her into a blatant request for a kiss, only then had she put him off with a refusal.

"I don't believe in dating coworkers, Ryan."

"Who said anything about dating? Let's have some fun while at training."

It sent a curl of disgust up her spine as she had gently but firmly refused him. After that, she hid in her hotel room, ordering takeout and room service instead of developing relationships with her colleagues.

She was good at hiding.

She didn't hide as much with Simon. Yes, she had held off on telling him about her obnoxious sorority sisters, but that was a delay, not a permanent decision. When he was in a stronger place emotionally, she would share that information. But in that moment when he said no to the dance, she felt, oh, not disappointed, but perhaps nervous that Simon's experience tonight would be one step back instead of the two steps forward they intended. Looking into his eyes, she recognized that whatever social battery had spurred him thus far had depleted. She understood that feeling well, and Simon didn't have the practice at building social walls that she did. Maybe he never would. Maybe that was okay.

She and Simon understood each other. These past three months of pulling back layers of herself to expose her heart had not redefined her; instead, they helped her find meaning. She cared deeply, but only when she felt safe to do so. Her mother's abandonment had made caring a risky endeavor. Simon made love feel safe again.

She would tell him, though not now. If she told him now, it would look like pity. She would tell him in a way he would understand when it came from a place of joy, not sadness.

Absorbing his quiet tears during the ride back to their shared townhouse, Cali let him vent his emotional exhaustion while simultaneously feeling honored that he felt safe enough to open up to her and fearful that her support would not be enough for him. She so wanted to be that person for him. The man who had at times infuriated her with his judgmental behavior became the man who took the time to understand, value, and trust her.

Loving, funny, and scared–with so much to love. She only hoped he could see in himself what she perceived in him. She *would* help him. She had failed her mother, but she would *not* fail him.

She held his hand as he walked in an almost zombie-like state into his apartment.

"I need to take a shower," he muttered, pulling at his suit jacket.

"Of course. Would you like me to order dinner?"

"Yes... Thank you," he whispered, his voice hoarse.

When he emerged sometime later, clean and with the smell of his shampoo and soap redolent on his skin, she'd changed into a pair of pajamas she had stored in his bedroom. He looked gratified to see her in her comfy clothes, as if reassured she hadn't faded away into the girl in the black gown. He pulled her close, exploring the texture of her flannel pajamas.

"Why do you look even sexier now than you did at that stupid party?"

"'Cause I took my bra off," she teased, pressing herself against him. He huffed a laugh, which reassured her. "What happened tonight, Simon?"

"I underestimated how stressed this event would make me. In addition to exposing myself in an unfamiliar formal setting, being there for you made me nervous. I wanted to make a good impression on your colleagues for your sake." Simon sat on the edge of the sofa, pulling her close, his head pressed against her stomach. Cali smoothed her hand through his hair, and Simon groaned pleasurably. "That feels nice, thank you."

"I didn't realize you would take it in this way. I knew it would stress you–that was the point, right? To help you be comfortable in new situations. But I didn't realize you were concerned for my sake."

"I wish I'd confided in you. After your douchey coworker–"

"Former coworker," she reminded him.

Simon nodded. "After he made those comments, calling me a 'twitchy freak' and 'retard,' the pressure built up. I felt a tic attack coming on. I had to escape, or I could have collapsed. I hid in an upstairs bathroom until it passed." Simon pulled up his shorts to reveal a pair of spectacular bruises blooming in shades of red and purple on his thighs.

"Oh, Simon." She exhaled, appalled at the injuries he had inflicted upon himself. She knelt, her fingers tracing the border of the bruises.

"Guess I should be grateful my go-to tic is slapping my thigh instead of my face."

Cali pressed her lips to the bruises. "Simon," she whispered, continuing her trail of kisses. Looking up, she gave him a glance she hoped conveyed seduction. "Lie back."

Simon's eyes widened as he made out her intent and laid back on the chaise. Cali proceeded to press kisses up his legs, starting at his ankles. She followed the path her lips took with her hands, enjoying the feeling of the hair on his calves and thighs. She kept her touch exquisitely gentle, listening for any sounds of distress from Simon, fearful of irritating the area he had inflamed.

As she reached his waist, she helped him divest his shorts and underwear while he removed his T-shirt. Lying there, she allowed herself a lengthy examination of his body. She kissed his stomach, tracing a line around his belly button with her tongue before placing small kisses on his cock. Simon took a quick breath as she took him in her mouth.

No stranger to the act, Cali had always considered it merely a reciprocation of similar efforts by former boyfriends. Giving had not provided her pleasure–it was simply a task to be accomplished. But as Simon relaxed under her ministrations, a warm arousal suffused her being. Loose and willing in her grasp, Simon's trust stirred her to continue.

"Cali, you're so beautiful, so sexy–oh God." Simon moaned, one hand loosely tangled in her hair. "That feels so good. You're going to make me explode," he rasped out, shifting his hand from her hair to her face, indicating she should pause. "I need to be inside you, please."

"Are you sure you're up for that?" She eyed his bruises skeptically.

"Thanks to you, it appears I'm up for...well..." He gave her a lopsided grin from the couch cushions.

Cali slid off her pajamas and climbed over him, careful not to touch the worst of his injuries. Lowering herself on top of him, they let out a shared gasp as he entered her, long and hard. They were both ready for this.

"I can't believe I get to see you riding me, Mad. This is every fantasy I've ever had come to life." Simon caressed her arms, and she rested her hands on his stomach as she got used to him inside her at this new angle. "Are you okay?"

"Yes, yes...just, I'm not used to this position." She took a deep breath and arched, causing them both to moan.

"Oh, baby, just like that." Simon's hands grasped her ass, guiding her into a rhythm. Cali's core pressed against the bristled hairs on his abdomen, and the thrill from the texture and pressure made her yelp in pleasured surprise. "Do you like that, Mad? Show me how you want to ride me."

Cali repeated the motion, bending low against Simon so her breasts hung above him. Simon moved one hand to caress her breasts while the other continued to guide her. He rubbed her nipples liberally between one thumb and forefinger, and Cali mewled in response. Hard as a rock inside her, Simon moaned.

"Mad, I don't know if I can hold on much longer." He drifted his fingers from her breasts to her clit, collecting the liberal fluid that had gathered there to rub the area above where they were joined. He slid his knuckles against her, and Cali found herself rubbing wantonly against him, riding him up and down. Her eyes met his, barely open with the force of the pleasure overwhelming her. Simon's eyes were replete even before they exploded together.

Just as they unfolded with one another at the end of every day, this shared pleasure connected them further. The moment stretched out. Cali wanted to live inside it—not only for the sake of the pleasure, though she screamed so loudly, she certainly would have heard the cries had she been at home in her downstairs apartment. Sex and love combined as she fell forward against his chest. Simon held her close. He kissed her repeatedly on her head, face, and lips, only disentangling when the Chinese food arrived some time later.

CHAPTER 26

Furtive: *(adjective) attempting to avoid notice, typically because of the belief that discovery would lead to trouble*

THREE DAYS LATER, Simon was struggling to put the events of the gala behind him. As if considering two columns, pro and con, he tallied the night's occurrences. In the pro column, he met a Zap fan, got a compliment on his necktie, and contributed to Ryan's justified firing. In the con category, the tic attack loomed large, dwarfing everything good that had preceded it.

While his emotions hadn't settled yet, his body was healing. The aches and bruises were a visceral and daily reminder of the self-inflicted violence he had experienced. The following day, Cali sucked in a breath in sympathetic pain when she saw the bruises had turned from purple to black. The pain of the bruises further fueled his brain's reaction to the soreness there, and he continued to slap the area every so often. Cali held his hand whenever possible and tossed him a new egg of Silly Putty to keep his hands busy when she showered. Today, the additional urge to touch the area had largely faded.

Earlier in the day, he'd gone to his first media training session with Joanne and her colleague, Alex. Alex was a forty-something-year-old man dressed in a red flannel shirt and jeans. With his five o'clock shadow, he looked like he'd stepped off the set of a Hallmark Christmas movie. They reviewed talking points for more than two hours, selected appropriate anecdotes for morning television, and practiced techniques for handling questions he didn't want to answer. Alex had created a mock studio setup to help evoke the sensations of being on camera. When Simon ticced, they brainstormed appropriate responses should the interviewers highlight them.

"Ideally, these interviews will all be prerecorded, but we also don't want to capture something on camera that might embarrass you later," Alex said.

"Wait, they could be live interviews?"

"It's possible. Most programs that film entertainment interviews in advance do so to air them later or at a more convenient time. Sometimes, they'll replay interviews for shows airing on national holidays."

"Unless we get you on *Good Day USA*—that interview would be live," Joanne added. "We should be so lucky—that show pulls great numbers."

The idea distressed Simon. Live interviews sounded like an immediate deal-breaker, but he kept his silence—in part because Joanne had been working her butt off to get him these opportunities and partly because he *needed* to climb this hill. His mind flitted to Adam Higgins, who had made efforts to move his life forward. Simon recognized that the only demons that required conquering lay within.

If his reasons for doing so were motivated by fear and spite, well, whatever got him out of bed in the morning.

"We'll also have a session on podcast interviews and TikTok. BookTok is the go-to for fiction. If we can get a twenty-something with five million followers to read and review your book, it'll open a huge audience."

"Does that group even read graphic novels? I feel like Cali said they focus on morally grey romances featuring stalkers that are somehow able to have a happily ever after with the woman they love, even though the man is constantly disrespecting the woman's boundaries."

"The heart wants what it wants, Simon," Joanne scolded, burying a blush that indicated her romance novel preferences. "But yes, that is usually their book of choice; however, with the success of the Hades and Persephone webcomic, the rules of BookTok are in flux. We can make a go of getting you some attention there."

Alex provided positive feedback on their initial efforts. "I can't speak for what you'll be like on the air, but you have a natural charisma."

"It's not my charisma I'm worried about." Simon patted his thigh again and winced, a reminder of how bad things could get if they went off the rails.

"That's why we practice. Let's start again." Alex adjusted the lights and began the faux interview process while Simon wished for the first time in many years that he could be a normal kid.

The exhaustion of the media training sank in as Simon dragged himself to Cali's. They had planned to go out for dinner with Anton, but hours under the spotlight had drained him. His body and emotions had hit a metaphorical wall. Between months of a grueling work schedule, the trauma of the gala's events, and potential forced public exposure, he regretted his efforts.

And resented them.

Less than two weeks away, Christmas would allow him a few weeks off to relax. Aside from fine-tuning the season finale of *The Magnificent Zap*, his workload had returned to normal. This would give him a chance for a necessary reset. Cali would visit her family in Arizona on the nineteenth but planned to return before New Year's Eve. Simon bought tickets to visit his parents in Florida around the same time. He looked forward to spending time with them but would miss Cali. He would miss their quiet when they were each other's world.

They had agreed to meet at her apartment before heading to dinner, as she ran late in getting ready. He let himself in and poured a soda, then saw the invitation on her kitchen counter.

'You are cordially invited to the wedding of our daughter, Victoria Layla...'

The invitation to her sorority sister's wedding was for a New Year's Eve event. Cali exited the bathroom, pulling her hair back into a sleek ponytail.

"New Year's Eve wedding, huh?" Simon rifled through numerous high-quality velum and woven sheets of wedding-related information, including rehearsal dinner details, hotel accommodations, and post-wedding brunch plans. "This girl goes big, huh?"

"Yeah, Victoria's good at making major holidays about herself. She's probably only doing it to make a big deal about her anniversary every year."

"Is this going to be my second outing into unfamiliar territory?" He knew Cali wanted him to continue their adventures, but he had asked her to hold off for a few days.

"Uh, no, I'm skipping this one, which she knows, so she only sent me this as a gift grab." Cali was putting on her earrings. She looked as pretty as always, wearing dark blue jeans and a short-sleeved white blouse with black piping.

"Why is that? You'll be back by New Year's, right?"

"You know, I didn't have as much fun at the bachelorette party as I thought I would. I'm not invited with a guest, and I don't feel like fighting off drunk groomsmen all night."

"Isn't it strange that a big shindig like this wouldn't invite you with a plus-one? They know you have a boyfriend." Hardly an expert at these things, Simon had still witnessed enough of it growing up in a wealthier suburb. At that moment, he looked at Cali, and her mask slipped, revealing a look of guilt. "You know something, Mad?"

"No, not at all." She turned around, making a show of trying to engage the lock on a tricky hoop earring.

She was lying to him. He could tell.

"Cali." He stood in front of her, forcing her to face him. "Cali, what's going on?"

Cali sighed, her shoulders falling. She touched Simon's shoulder as he leaned against the kitchen island. "The truth is, Victoria made an obnoxious comment at the bachelorette party, and...it doesn't bear repeating. That's why she can shove her wedding invitation up her—"

Simon knew. "She said something about me then?" He knew by the way Cali wouldn't voice the offensive comment. He knew by the way her sorority sisters looked at him that day in Manhattan as if he were an inconvenience. He knew by the way Cali couldn't meet his eyes.

"What did she say about me, Mad?" He repeated the question, boring through her discomfort with a need for the truth.

"She was worried you would make a scene at the wedding," Cali whispered and looked up pleadingly. "But I stood up for you! I swear I did. And my wedding gift to her is a book on etiquette." Her mouth had formed a firm line, as if a book on the rules of etiquette extended the ultimate middle finger to her bitchy sorority sister.

"But why didn't you *tell* me? Help me understand why I had to pull this out of you." He stood tall in front of her, blocking her from moving from his line of sight and hiding whatever she felt.

"I didn't want to upset you. You've got this big media tour coming up, and I didn't want you to worry about someone who isn't important. Victoria is a grade-A jerk, like Ryan. I didn't want you to base your decisions about your future on troglodytes like them."

"You didn't trust me to make my own decision? You decided to keep this from me?" Simon heard the note of accusation in his voice but did nothing to tamp it down. Dismayed at her betrayal, she appeared as a stranger before him.

"I wasn't going to keep it from you. I planned to tell you after the Robin Hood gala, but you were so upset that night. It seemed prudent to wait until things had settled."

"Prudent? So, you were keeping this quiet to manipulate me?"

"No, not like that." She held her hands up in a gesture of supplication. "I didn't want to upset you. I didn't want this to derail your efforts. You're so close to making your dreams a reality, and I didn't want their stupidity to get in your way."

"And my success is extremely important to you, isn't it? Is this perhaps your way of showing those sorority sisters of yours that your boyfriend isn't such a freak after all?"

She winced at his use of the forbidden F word–freak. "What are you talking about? I want to help you achieve your dream. Why do you think I care what they think?"

"Isn't that what you do? Hiding behind that fake smile? All you do is care what people think. It's why you keep yourself so small."

Cali took a step back as if he had slapped her. Her mouth opened and closed as she considered his cruelty. "That's what you think of me?"

"But I'm an extension of you now, aren't I? God, I should have known. You're so phony. You're not trying to help me break out of my bubble. You're just trying to make me an acceptable boyfriend."

"That isn't true! I want to support you like you supported me."

"You're like everyone else, thinking I'm a freak. You're trying to make me into something I'm not!" For once, the moment's emotion didn't cause his tics to go crazy. Focused on her expressions, the buzzing behind his eyes was a mere nuisance. He flicked his hand as if to brush those instincts away.

She stared at him, her face pale, her mouth agape in a state of shock. How could she have lied to him?

"But guess what? I'm a freak. I've accepted that about myself. I thought you had accepted it too."

Cali froze, her mouth turned down, puckering her chin. "Please stop using that word. You know I hate it. You're not a freak."

"You wish I weren't one. Trying to make me interesting instead of what I am. You put me in that ridiculous monkey suit to parade me in front of your coworkers."

"What exactly are you accusing me of?

"I think you regret having a boyfriend like me. It's exhausting, isn't it? Having to make sure I'm okay all the time."

"Simon, let me make something perfectly clear. I'm with you because you make me happy. I'm with you because I can be myself around you. I'm with you because I care about you," she pleaded, loosely grabbing his T-shirt.

He lifted his arms and backed away from her. "And what if all you'll get out of me is what I am right now? What if I can't attend black-tie events, interviews, concerts, or... Am I going to be enough for you if I'm some loser hiding away in his crappy apartment?"

"You're asking me if I need you to grow? To change? I don't need you to change who you are, but don't you want to grow? To evolve? To move past that thirteen-year-old boy who missed out on the party?" Cali shook her head, confused. "I want you to choose yourself and your dreams over your fears. What's that saying–perfect is the enemy of good. If you're sacrificing very good because it's not perfect, then...well, my mom chose her disease over me." Her voice became clipped, bitter. She looked at him with narrow eyes. "Is it too much to ask you to choose what you want over what you've accepted?"

Simon ran a hand through his hair. It was greasy with the sweat from the earlier lights. Her bold question temporarily quieted him. "And if I can't grow? What if this is all I am?"

Her eyes widened in response to his question, and she looked down. At her uncharacteristic silence, Simon realized he had instigated this stupid fight so she would reassure him. He wanted her to tell him she wanted him and would be there for him even if he took the coward's way out. He could still ask her now, and she might say it. She might use the exact words he needed to hear, but her smile–that forced smile–would give her away. He wouldn't accept it. He refused.

Her eyes were growing moist, and she hugged her stomach, a sign of her terror.

She had the gall to get upset? She had lied to him to get him to do what she wanted. She would never accept him. He would always be too weak, too weird, too pitiable for someone like her.

"I think I need some space tonight. I'm tired from the last few days." Simon grabbed Cali around the back of her neck and pressed a quick kiss on her forehead. "I'll call you tomorrow."

As he turned to go, her fingers ghosted at the hem of his shirt. If she whispered a response, he disappeared before she spoke it.

CHAPTER 27

Drapetomania: *(noun) an incredible urge to run away from home*

THE SAND UNDER HIS FEET shifted as Simon walked in front of his parents' beachfront condo. They'd purchased the Delray Beach condo shortly after he graduated from college when they'd decided New Jersey winters were no longer worth suffering through. Like many families from the New York metropolitan area, they became snowbirds, pairing increasingly thin skin with Tommy Bahama-sourced wardrobes and a love of outdoor concerts featuring classic rock cover bands. In the week he had been there, they had already gone to see Buffet to Go, a Jimmy Buffet cover band, and Petty Bitches—an all-female Tom Petty cover band.

True to his words, he had called Cali the next day after their argument. When the call went to voicemail—he had intentionally scheduled his call for her weekly conference call time slot—he informed her he would be spending the next three weeks in Florida visiting his family.

If he was going to be utterly chickenshit, at least he was going the full Monty.

Cali hadn't responded—an act of indifference that first relieved and now rankled him. He wanted her to yell at him. He wanted her to beg for forgiveness, but for what? He wanted her to need him enough to forgive his immature and petulant behavior. He wanted to fly back to New Jersey and take her in his arms.

But...he was chickenshit, and his anger found its proper source pointed inward.

"Simon, come on in! Lunch is ready!" his mom called from the deck of their home. "Your dad got latkes at Poppy's Deli for Hanukkah."

"What night is tonight?" he asked as he took his sandals off on his parents' porch and entered through the screen door.

"Night three."

"Does that mean I'm getting socks?"

"No one wears socks in Florida. I got you SPF 50 sunscreen so you don't burn. Melanoma can be easily avoided with a little bit of self-care." His mom, Susan, would never stop looking out for him. Parenting him was her full-time project whenever he visited.

"Simon doesn't need sunscreen; he's made his obligatory trip to the beach. He'll spend the rest of the time in air conditioning like he does every visit." Simon's older sister Rebecca had arrived that morning with her two-year-old, Emerson, in tow. Rebecca's husband planned to join the following week when his company went on holiday break.

"I told Emmie I would help her build a sandcastle later, so that sunscreen might come in handy after all."

"Wow, two beach trips in one day. Almost like you're trying to avoid thinking about something."

"Or someone," his father said from behind the pages of *The New York Times*. "Where's my shiksa future daughter-in-law? Why didn't you bring her with you?"

"We so want to meet her," his mom added. "The gift basket of wine and chocolates she sent after Thanksgiving was incredibly thoughtful, and Anton said she is delightful."

While Simon doubted Anton had used the word 'delightful,' he was sure Anton had done enough legitimate sharing that a conversation would need to be had about keeping his dating life away from his parents. There were consequences when your parents knew your friend group since high school. "Probably in Arizona, visiting her family by this point. We haven't talked."

"How did you fuck it up?" Rebecca asked, looking up from her plate of deli offerings.

"Should you be talking like that in front of your daughter?" He indicated Emerson, who fed herself bits of cut-up latke and applesauce while watching something engrossing on her iPad.

"She can't hear me. She's watching Elmo. That little red Muppet is the toddler hypnotist." As if on cue, Emerson burst out laughing at the antics on screen. Rebecca ruffled her daughter's hair. "Seriously, how did you fuck it up?"

"What makes you think it was me?"

"Tell me what happened, and I'll tell you if you're wrong." Three years older than Simon, Rebecca was both friend and adversary. She never hesitated to call him on his bullshit, and he delivered as good as he got.

"She's out of my league. She's never going to be satisfied being the girlfriend of a guy who can't even go out to a party without having a freakout."

"Did she say this to you?" Rebecca looked offended on his behalf.

"No, but she kept pushing me, and she hid things from me. Like how her sorority sisters talked shit about me. She kept that a secret from me as if I were a child."

"To clarify, your issue with her is that she didn't tell you someone said something cruel about you?" Rebecca raised a quizzical brow at Simon's responding scowl; she held up her hands in defense. "I want to be sure I understand."

"I don't want to date someone who can't be honest with me." He looked at his family, who looked unsure of how to respond.

"Oh, how dare she!" Rebecca finally spoke. "How dare she avoid hurting your feelings with unkind words from people you don't know and don't care about!"

"She should have told me," Simon insisted. He heard the obstinance in his voice and cringed.

"Why? So you can feel bad about yourself?" his dad added, setting the paper down. "It's like the famous radio host Bernard Meltzer used to say, 'Is it true? Is it kind? Is it necessary?' Why did she need to tell you some people were assholes? What good would it have done you to know this?"

"True, but she did it to manipulate me."

"Simon." His mother spoke in a low voice, trying to defray the tension in the room. "How did she manipulate you?"

"By forcing me to do the media tour for my book."

"Did you tell her you didn't want to do the media tour? Was she trying to get you to do something you didn't want to do?"

"No. I told her I wanted to do it, but she knew. She knows I'm nervous about doing it."

"Let's get this straight. Your girlfriend encouraged you to take a step that would help advance your career, as you had expressed a desire to do." Rebecca considered the statement, and at Simon's glower, she self-corrected. "I mean, that bitch! How dare she!"

"Is she still friends with the mean girls who said unkind things about you?" his mother asked, trying to find some justification for his anger.

Simon thought about what Cali had said about not attending the wedding. "No. I think she cut ties with them."

"I like this girl. She has a spine." His dad returned to his newspaper. "Do you guys want to see a movie tonight? There's a good review for the new Jordan Peele movie."

"We would need a babysitter for Emmie," Rebecca replied. His mother commented that they could call their long-time housekeeper for help, but Simon ceased listening.

They let Simon linger in the emotional tempest of his creation. His family had helped him see that his reaction to Cali's secrecy had been an overreaction. The obvious solution was to call her, text her, fly across the country to see her. Cowardice and longing pulled at his equilibrium with equal ferocity before he left to barricade himself in the room his parents had reserved for his use.

Where was Cali now? Was she thinking about him? Would he ever be able to stop thinking about her?

"Hi, sorry I missed you. I wanted to let you know I'm catching a flight down to Florida to see my parents. I've finished formatting the book, and I need a break. Have a Merry Christmas with your family."

A break? What did that mean? A break from her?

The call came in at 4:04 p.m., right as her weekly team call began. Coincidence? She doubted it.

There was no promise of a future call, only a perfunctory wish for her to have a safe trip to visit her family in Arizona.

The Phantom Tumor in her stomach was living its best life. Roaring in glee at her dread, leaving her alternately running on the treadmill or sitting on the floor in her bathroom. It made the pain after corporate training feel like Day Five menstrual cramps by comparison. This was a kidney stone. This was 9 centimeters dilated in labor. This was an aortic aneurysm.

Simon had abandoned her. No, he hadn't ended things...yet. But he had a foot out the door. The connection they had forged had felt so implacable, but he was severing it, and she would let him. Better to cut the cord quickly and cleanly than to let it linger in the place of what-ifs.

Ugh. *Why* did she get involved with her next-door neighbor? Cali thought about his accusations, his anger, the look in his eyes when he suspected she couldn't care for him. Were there sinister motives behind her efforts to help him? Had his assessment been correct?

It didn't matter. She couldn't be with him anymore. The risk was too significant. He wanted to languish in a cage of his own making. She'd seen that path. She'd experienced it as her mother pushed her further away until all that remained were promises her mother had no intention of keeping. How many planned visits were put off because her mother wanted to wait until she felt better? In the end, Cali stopped trying to make those meetings happen so that she wouldn't be disappointed.

Then, when her mother died... Well, she'd barely survived her mother's death. She couldn't be part of that dynamic again.

She longed for something to numb the anxiety. Exercise worked to a point, but even her body had its limits. She wasn't the kind to call her friends to analyze emotional play-by-plays, but even a cup of coffee felt like too much effort when her brain swirled with longing and hurt. After evening Pilates, Sheila tried to tempt her with frozen yogurt or a glass of wine, but Cali feigned a headache and went home, ignoring her friend's furrowed brow. When Kat called, she let it go to voicemail and responded by text. She buried herself in work, traveling with each of her team members in turn until her flight home to Arizona. With her manager's permission, she extended her travels through the first of the year. She would fly directly to San Diego for the national sales meeting in January, giving her an extended stay with her parents and brother, who knew how to walk the line between pleasant distraction and emotional space.

Her brother greeted her with a bear hug at the airport, and she ignored the look of confusion he gave her as he observed her admittedly half-hearted response.

"You excited to be home? It's been almost six months."

"Yeah, the weather has been getting dark so early in New Jersey. I think the sunshine will feel good for a few weeks."

"A few weeks?" Michael gave her an alert look. "You're staying that long?"

"Yeah, our national sales meeting is in San Diego. I'm going to fly there on the ninth instead of heading back to New Jersey first."

"Oh." Michael nodded to himself, his hands almost imperceptibly tightening on the steering wheel of his late-model Camry. "Well, it'll be good to have you around."

It didn't escape her notice that he didn't ask about Simon.

But 'around' was a good descriptor. Cali spent the next few days being busy without doing anything. She accompanied Grace on shopping trips to the grocery store and mall, where they acquired last-minute holiday gifts for friends and family. Cali had finished her shopping weeks before, and the gifts arrived in neatly wrapped gift boxes from different online vendors. She thought of the gift she'd planned to order for Simon, still in her Amazon cart.

She tried cleaning out her childhood bedroom before getting tired just thinking about the emotional and physical toll of the task. She started and put down three books on her to-be-read list before giving up and watching TikTok videos. She looked up recipes she might want to try over the holidays before making a grocery list that she never completed.

She was antsy, as if her skin was ill-fitting, but she didn't want to explore those feelings with her family or with herself. It harkened back to the dark days after her mother's illness sent her to Arizona and took up a large portion of her headspace before she developed the armor to keep the feelings at bay.

Her dad and Grace instigated game night, and Cali went through the motions, uninterested in anything more than a few rounds of Battleship, happy when she lost so she could go back into her cocoon of self-preservation. She ignored the looks of concern on her parents' faces. When Grace asked about Simon, she waved her off and made an excuse about some end-of-quarter reports that needed to be done.

Grace didn't ask again.

On December twenty-second, Michael stormed into her room. She'd been buried under blankets with the blinds drawn. Michael pulled the cord on her shades, letting bright sunlight into the room, and Cali yelped at the painful glare.

"What are you doing?" Cali asked in the tone she reserved for her younger brother when he bothered her.

"I need your help. I don't know what to get my girlfriend for Christmas. Come shopping with me."

The demand and the entrance broke her out of her stupor.

"You have a girlfriend? Since when?" And why didn't Cali know this? How bad had her pity party gotten? "And you haven't gotten her a gift yet?"

"It's new. I still have two days. Put on your shoes. We're going to Biltmore."

The Biltmore was a large open-air mall in Phoenix offering a wide selection of stores, ranging from moderately priced to high-end. With three days to go before Christmas, the crowds were sure to be enormous, and Cali groaned at the forthcoming throng.

"Can't you get her a gift card at Walgreens? The Biltmore is going to be crazy."

"How would you feel if Simon got you a gift card for Christmas?"

Cali bit the inside of her cheek and ignored the gurgle in her gut. "Fabulous. I'd love it," she deadpanned with a heretofore unknown level of mean-spirited sarcasm.

Michael ignored it and threw a hoodie at her. The weather was warmer than in New Jersey but still changeable.

"Fine. Give me ten minutes to brush my teeth."

Twenty minutes later, Michael had them on the road to Phoenix. She looked out the window at Camelback Mountain, which defined the horizon as Michael observed her from the driver's seat.

"What do you think I should get her?" Michael asked her after they had been driving for a few miles.

"Who?"

"My girlfriend."

"I'm going to need a little more information than the fact that she's interested in you for some bizarre reason."

"She's kind, funny, artistic..."

"Artistic?"

"Yes, she loves to draw."

"Did you meet in art class?" she asked smartly, turning to face him. Michael didn't respond, and she looked back at the window. "So why aren't we going to Michael's to get her art supplies?"

"She's thoughtful. She brings out the best in me. I can relax around her. She makes me laugh." There was a ghost of a smile on her brother's lips as he described this unnamed girl who had stolen his heart. "She likes board games," Michael added.

Cali looked at him, arrested. Michael had found someone special. It made her heart hurt to think of Simon, thousands of miles away, effectively shut off from her. She could call him. She could text him. But what if he didn't call back? And what did it matter when he had made it clear how incompatible they were?

"I'm glad you've found someone who makes you so happy," Cali said, not looking at Michael. How nice that her emotionally generous younger brother had found someone worthy of his affection. He deserved a girl who would see that and not just the handsome undergraduate. How often did she feel the same—that no one saw her—not until she met Simon?

Simon.

She closed her eyes and rested her forehead on the cool glass of the window. The pain in her stomach migrated to her head, no, to her face. The pain burned in her nose, in the space between her eyes. She pinched her nose at the bridge as the burning increased. When her hands came back wet, she realized she had started crying. Horrified, she pinched the bridge of her nose harder, squeezing her eyelids shut as if she could keep the tears inside, reabsorb them in some insane version of reverse osmosis.

"Do you remember Mr. Fletcher in AP History? He told us this insane story in eleventh grade about Spartan society. These guys would train their sons from infancy to be badass soldiers. They would make them stand at attention for hours, and if you moved, you got beaten.

"There was a kid who captured a baby fox and decided to keep it as a pet. He would feed the fox, but the soldiers weren't exactly providing these kids with a healthy diet, and the fox was starving. One day, the general called all the kids to attention, and the boy stuffed the fox in his shirt and waited to be allowed to go back to his bunk. Only the fox was so hungry that he took bites out of the kid. Hours passed, and the kid had to stand there at attention while this fox ate away at his insides. Finally, when they were relieved from standing at attention, the boy collapsed. The fox had eaten him to death."

"Does this story have a point?" she asked through quiet sobs. She wiped her eyes on the sleeve of her hoodie.

Michael pulled over in the parking lot of an In-N-Out Burger off the highway. He pressed his hand warmly on her shoulder.

"The Spartans thought that story was the epitome of manliness," Michael said. "But what I'm getting at is that suppressing your feelings doesn't make them go away. It just makes them more dangerous when you finally get around to processing them when they come out, which they will." He paused. "Which they have?"

Cali looked over at her brother, his empathetic expression making her smile, and she cried harder. He pulled her into a hug and let her cry noisily into his ASU hoodie.

"You're such a know-it-all," she complained, rolling her eyes. "Do you even have a girlfriend?"

"No. Do you still have a boyfriend?"

"I don't know. Probably not."

"Can you tell me what happened?"

Cali looked forward. Her eyes stared back at her from the rearview mirror, the green bright in their red-rimmed sea. The sun gleamed off the roof of the burger place they'd parked in front of. She tilted her head toward the burger joint, opening for early patrons.

"Let's go get a soda. I'll tell you everything."

In-N-Out Burger was one of the few Arizona landmarks Cali missed now that she resided in New Jersey. Sure, Shake Shack and Smashburger were halfway decent, but nothing beat the caramelized exterior and Russian dressing-style spread on an In-N-Out burger with fries. But even the tempting carnivore creation couldn't break through the fear gurgling in her gut. Michael devoured a three-patty tower while Cali considered her meal disinterestedly. Ever since Simon had left town, her appetite had taken a nosedive.

"I want to be sure I understand everything that happened. Simon is preparing for interviews to promote his new book, and it's causing him to panic. He asked you if you would still want to be with him if he..."

"Gave up on his dreams–spent the rest of his days hiding away."

"And how did you respond?"

"I told him he should want to grow, to evolve." Cali looked at her brother's shocked expression. "That probably sounds callous to you, but you didn't grow up with a mom who took to her bed the better part of your adolescence. It wasn't my mom's fault she was sick..."

"It sounds like you still blame her for it," Michael commented, sipping at his orange soda.

"I do. She sent me away so she could get better, but then she didn't make the effort to do so. She quit on herself. She quit on me!" Cali smacked the small table, making it wobble.

"If she had sent you away because she had cancer and died from cancer, would you still be upset with her?"

"Of course not, that's ridiculous."

"And yet...bipolar has been shown to have a physiological cause."

"But there are treatments. I'd be angry if she had cancer and left it untreated too."

"I can't tell you if what you're feeling is right or wrong. That's not my place. But Simon is not your mom. He had a moment of doubt. Haven't you ever doubted yourself? It's not fair for you to hold him to the standards set by what happened with your mom."

"Then I should be with him and watch him bury himself away?"

"You should give him a chance because I think you love him and because he deserves someone who will partner with him even when he's second-guessing himself." Michael punctuated the point by rolling up his burger wrapper into a ball. "But if you can't, maybe you shouldn't be with him. He should be with someone who can accept him the way he is, doubts and all." Michael swallowed the last of his soda. "And you can go back to dating boring douchey dudes whose most interesting characteristic is their love of French cheese and baseball."

"You're being unfair."

"No, you're being unfair. You're talking to someone who saw how happy Simon makes you. Were you under the misapprehension that couples don't hit roadblocks? Don't you think our parents have their ups and downs?"

"So what should I do? He left me one message to let me know he left town, and I've heard nothing since then."

"Have you reached out to him at all?"

"No. What if he doesn't respond?"

"What if he does?"

"What if he doesn't?"

"Why do you think rejection is the worst thing that can happen? Let's say you reach out, and he doesn't respond. Well, that will give you an answer. At least you can grieve instead of walking around in a frightened fog like you've done for the last three days." Michael seemed relieved to be getting through to her. "But first and foremost, you need to decide if you're willing to support him through ups and downs. If you're not, let him off the hook. But if you love him, like I'm certain you do, then do something about it. Shit or get off the pot, Cali."

"Shit or get off the pot?" She gave him a bemused look. "Ninety percent of the time, you sound like a therapist, and then you say something like that and remind me you're still in college."

"My point is valid even if I say stupid shit."

Cali looked at the remaining half of her burger and lifted it, taking a hearty bite. With the emotional confession came a return of her appetite. Michael looked longingly at her french fries, and she pulled them closer to her with a narrowed gaze.

As if awakened from some miserable trance, she realized how much she missed Simon. Michael was right; she'd been unfair to him. She'd let her emotional baggage sabotage the most meaningful relationship she'd ever had. Maybe Simon would be better off without her.

No. No more self-pity. No more burying her feelings underneath her anxiety. She loved Simon. If their relationship was over, it wouldn't be for her lack of trying.

"You look like you've come to a decision," Michael said, smiling at her and surreptitiously stealing a fry.

"I need you to drive me to Home Depot. There's something I need to get."

CHAPTER 28

Shchekotiki: *(noun) the feeling you get when you finally figure something out*

THE PACKAGE ARRIVED on Christmas Eve, the eighth night of Hanukkah.

"What's in the box? What's in the box?" Simon's mother yelled theatrically to blank stares from Simon and Rebecca alike. "You know? From the movie *Seven*?"

Simon and Rebecca looked at her as if she had grown three heads.

"What? I like horror movies and Morgan Freeman." She shrugged. "But seriously, who's the package for?"

"Simon." Rebecca lifted her pointer finger in a motion that reminded Simon of any time his sister tattled on him until Simon taught her snitches got stitches–or noogies, if he was being specific. "Who's it from?"

Simon recognized Cali's handwriting on the return label. His hand patted his thigh in quick, nervous motions.

"I'm going to go open this in private." He lifted the box and headed to his bedroom. As he walked up the stairs, he heard his mom ask his sister if the shiksa had sent the package.

Approximately the size of a shoebox, was there a letter inside? A present? A glitter bomb? Tomorrow was Christmas. He hadn't gotten around to getting her a gift before he left for Florida and had been unwilling to venture out since he'd arrived, fearful he would be making a purchase that would be returned out of hand by his recipient. In the ten days since they had last spoken, Simon had composed more than twenty text messages that he'd promptly deleted. He placed the box on the bed and walked around it, as if doing so would grant him clarity.

After ten minutes of pacing, Simon became embarrassed at his indecisiveness and tore at the brown paper that wrapped the package. The box underneath was printed with holiday symbols–trees, snowmen, and the like. Lifting the lid, he rustled through the tissue paper, feeling something smooth and cool before lifting it from its carefully packaged prison.

Simon let out a bark of laughter as he lifted the plaster cast of Cali's hand from the box. Holding the model of her palm and fingers in his own, he lifted it like he imagined Prince Charming lifted Cinderella's glass slipper on the steps to his castle. In a way, they were similar, for no other hand fit into his like Cali's did. It was as close to a declaration of love as he had ever received from her. Inscribed on the interior of the sculpture's wrist was a simple message.

My hand and my heart are yours whenever you need them. –Love, Cali

Love, Cali. He traced the words with his finger. Deliberate in all her dealings, Cali would not have used that word unless she meant it. This gift was a declaration of love. Where he hid away in cowardice, she showed her bravery.

As if on cue, his cell phone rang an unfamiliar 917 number. Perhaps if he hadn't been so shocked and elated at the gift, he would have let it go to voicemail. Who picked up a phone call from an unknown number anymore?

"Hello?"

"Hi! Is this Simon Goldberg?" A female voice sounded relieved on the other end.

"Speaking."

"I'm so glad I got you. My name is Gina Russell. We haven't met, but I enjoyed meeting your lovely girlfriend, Cali, at the Robin Hood gala. She told me about your comic, and when I mentioned it to my son, he got so excited. He's a huge fan! Now, I can tell you it can be hard to get through to a teenage boy when you are an over-fifty-year-old woman, but I'm not someone to look a gift horse in the mouth."

"That's...very flattering. Thank you."

But Gina had barely paused to take a breath as she continued steamrolling. "Thank you for giving me something to connect with my son about! I digress. It's my son's birthday in early January, and I was hoping I could commission a custom illustration of him with the Magnificent Zap. I want to give it to him as a framed piece of artwork. You know kids these days—all they want are money and gift cards, but I think gifts should be thoughtful, don't you?"

Simon caressed the cool stone of the model Cali had gifted him with his thumb. "I agree." He paused. "How did you get my number?"

"Oh, it turns out your agent, Joanne, has a son in my son's class! And he introduced my son to Zap! Such a small world. Joanne's son, Jason, has Tourette's, and apparently, he introduced Joanne to the comic as well. Isn't it funny how everything falls into place? Anyway, Joanne gave me your number. I hope that's okay."

Simon's eyes widened as he absorbed the stream of consciousness Gina Russell let forth, including the knowledge that Joanne's son had Tourette's. Why hadn't she shared that information with him?

"Would you be willing to create a piece of artwork for my son? Of course, I'll pay for your efforts. You can quote me your private commission rate."

"Yeah, sure. I should give you my email address."

"Joanne already gave it to me, the sweetie. She wanted me to call you first to make sure you would be okay with taking on more work. I told her I can be very persuasive when it comes to getting something I want!"

"Send over a photo of your son and anything else you want to share–sports teams he likes, movies, TV shows, etcetera. I'll put together a draft for your approval this week."

"Oh, thank you! I'm going to win so many cool points for this gift, and with a thirteen-year-old son, you can imagine I haven't been considered cool since he was in the second grade."

Gina Russell dropped off, and Simon returned his attention to the model Cali had sent him. The fingers weren't warm or malleable. He couldn't press his thumb into her palm as he liked to do or kiss the inside of her wrist as he did whenever he tried to take gentle affection and turn it into mutual passion. But he was soothed by the shape, the knowledge that some of her cells had surely attached to the mold from the plaster model. What he wouldn't give to have her here in his arms. What he wouldn't give to tell her he loved her.

Simon fell back on the bed, clasping his fingers around the model as he considered the barrage of knowledge he had absorbed–Joanne's son having Tourette's, passing along Simon's work to his mom. It reminded him of Cali's advice several weeks ago.

"You need to reframe the narrative. There is a whole other audience out there rooting for you. Wouldn't you have liked seeing someone like you on the news as a kid? Someone who could have made your journey a little more bearable?"

Simon hadn't wanted to be inspiration porn. He'd only wanted to write a comic others would enjoy, but at least one thirteen-year-old kid out there got more out of his efforts. And Joanne... Was there an ulterior motive for her efforts on his behalf? Even if those motives were ultimately benign?

He'd been pushing himself as a way to win a race against the demons that plagued him in his youth, but that gave him no pleasure, no satisfaction, no peace. That's why he freaked out and rebelled against the forces pushing him forward, whether they be Joanne, or Cali, or even his run-in with his childhood bully. But this, knowing what he created, could mean something to more than just himself–that felt worthwhile. Even if he went on television and couldn't control himself, it would be worth trying. If it went to shit, it wouldn't be a failure, only a step forward–something to learn from and grow on.

The urge to be with Cali all at once overwhelmed him. The beautiful gesture of the stone model only served to remind him what he might have lost for his stubbornness.

Setting it down with great care, Simon grabbed his suitcase.

And prayed for a Hannukah miracle.

Cali was going to murder her brother. She was going to slay, assassinate, snuff, waste, massacre, and slaughter her brother. Was she out of her mind to be following relationship advice from a college student? Despite his remarkable emotional maturity, what could he possibly know about adult relationships?

She'd sprung for the overnight shipping. She followed the package through pickup in Phoenix, a brief stopover in Dallas, landing in Miami, and dissemination to Delray Beach, Florida for delivery at 11:02 a.m. EST on December twenty-fourth.

And now it was 7:05 p.m. The holiday lights in her neighborhood gave the streets a friendly glow that further angered her. Their magical twinkle mocked her.

He hadn't gotten it yet. He was doing something with his family. They went to an early movie or a walk on the beach. They were home but didn't hear their doorbell. It would be sitting out there for hours. A porch pirate stole it. A porch pirate had her romantic gesture in a box in the back of his Hyundai Elantra!

Or worse.

He'd received it. He hadn't gotten around to opening it because she disgusted him. He wanted nothing to do with her. He opened it, but thought it was the weirdest thing he'd ever seen. Her hand? What a weird gift! He needed to move away from the stalker that she was.

Oh God, she was going to have to move!

"You okay, Cali?" Michael asked from the floor of their living room while Will Ferrell screamed on the TV screen about his love for Santa Claus. Grace and her dad were off having Christmas Eve cocktails with their neighbors.

"I'm contemplating methods for ending your life."

"What have you landed on?"

"Defenestration or immolation."

"Please go with defenestration. I'd much rather be pushed out a window than sacrificed. What would you even sacrifice me to?"

"I never should have sent that gift." Cali stood up and paced across the carpet of their living room.

"Oh, you definitely should have sent the gift." Michael grabbed a handful of popcorn, shoving it in his mouth, watching her walk back and forth like a cat watching ping-pong. "This is the most fun you've ever been."

"He hasn't called me yet."

"Let it marinate. He's going to call."

"How can you possibly be so sure?"

"It's a guy thing."

"How do you feel about being hanged, drawn, and quartered?"

Michael stretched and grabbed another handful of popcorn. "Seems like a lot of trouble. You should just stab me."

She stopped and looked at her brother, her hands itching to do as he suggested. "Don't. Tempt. Me."

When the doorbell of her parents' home rang, Cali practically jumped in response.

"That's my cue to avoid your assault," Michael said, standing to get the door. "My money is on Dad forgot his keys." Cali watched Michael's retreating form before sitting on their couch. She twisted her fingers into the fabric of her leggings while her heart pumped loudly in her chest. How long before angst turned into misery? Sadness, she could handle, but the unknown? She shook her head and forced herself to take a deep breath.

"Oy, Cali! Come here," Michael called from the front door, startling her. "Package for you."

A package? Cali felt something shift inside. Her fingers felt numb as she brushed one hand against the wall, turning to the hallway leading to their front door.

Clad in shorts and sandals, Simon looked as though he had been directly transported to her family home from the beaches of South Florida. Only his eyes gave away the extent of the effort he had made to travel there–tired but relieved, drinking her in. Michael stood off to the side, murmuring something about three being a crowd before making himself scarce.

"I got your gift, Mad." He grimaced, his voice hoarse, though his eyes never left hers.

Her lips bent inward, her chin wrinkling as emotion threatened to overwhelm. Simon was here. He strode in, wrapping his arms around her, holding her to his chest. She pressed her head against him for a moment while he soothed her gently, and she backed up to look him in the eye, pointing an accusing finger at him.

"You are such a jerk," she said, and the tears spilled over. He wiped one away.

"I know, I know. I'm so sorry." He kissed her head. "I'm such a jerk."

"And a coward."

"And a coward," he agreed.

"So am I." She gave a watery laugh.

"No, you're not. You're my brave pirate princess. You're the one who said how you felt, even when I was a jerk and a coward."

"Yeah, well, I love you."

"I love you too. I love you so much." He claimed her mouth with his, and she encircled his neck with her arms, pulling him close. She remembered Simon telling her that holding her hand and embracing her calmed his tics to some degree. As his warmth enveloped her, she understood. His touch was the balm she'd craved since he'd stormed from her apartment ten days prior. The agita causing her sleepless nights grew quiet in his arms. She pulled away from his kiss and let him hold her in the entryway of her parents' home.

"I'm still angry at you," she whispered. She bent her head into the curve of his neck, warmth suffusing her as she breathed in the familiar smell of him. "But I'm glad you're here."

"Oh, Mad." He sighed into her hair. "Me too."

CHAPTER 29

Retrouvailles: *(noun) the joy felt when reuniting with a loved one after a long separation*

IN HIS FANTASIES, the reunion with Cali would have included making love, but between being in her parents' home and their mutual exhaustion, they fell asleep almost instantaneously that night. When they woke up on Christmas morning, Simon groaned at the discomfort of lingering stiffness from the five-hour flight and the eight hours spent in one position in her full-sized bed.

And he couldn't remember the last time he'd felt so content.

Grace pretended his appearance was no big deal, but Michael offered a surreptitious fist bump. Cali's father grunted in disapproval and commented on the disrespect of unexpected guests. Still, his expression had shifted quickly enough to a smile when Cali gave her father a warm Christmas morning hug and kiss.

"Don't do it again," Mitchell spoke quietly when the rest were out of earshot.

"No, sir," Simon said quickly, nodding nervously.

After Christmas breakfast, Cali gave Simon a walking tour of her neighborhood, taking the opportunity to talk privately for the first time since their fight had put such distance between them. The middle-class homes were festooned with holiday decorations. However, for a person from the northeast, it was incongruous to see Santa amidst the environmentally friendly plants of the Southwest that flourished in the drier conditions.

"Are those holiday lights on a cactus?" Simon put his hand out tentatively to ensure it was a real plant. "How in the world do they do that?"

"The same way porcupines make love—very carefully."

Simon looked back with raised eyebrows and quirked lips. "This is where you moved to after your mom...?" He didn't know how to finish that sentence.

Cali nodded. "Yes, I went to school two blocks from here." She nodded toward the school building, which he could make out in the distance. "My high school was a little further away."

"Did you like growing up here?"

Cali sat on a low wall bordering the local park, her lips pursed. "I don't know that I was capable of it. Liking it, I mean. My goal was limited to not being seen as the class weirdo."

"I understand. You're describing my schooling until I hitched my wagon to Anton, Kat, and Ben."

"You're braver than I am. Standing up for yourself. Making friends. I just tried not to make enemies."

"How can you say that? You're the brave one—putting yourself out there. I'm the chickenshit who ran with his tail between his legs the minute things got challenging."

"And I let you. Even though it killed me not to call you, I let you leave. I would have called and yelled at you if I were braver."

"Then why did you send the gift?"

"Michael talked some sense into me. He made me realize the fear of you discarding me kept me from trying to be with someone who made me... Everything I've done to keep myself from being miserable has done *nothing* to make me happy." Cali closed her eyes as the sun shone on her cheeks, making her more luminous than usual.

Simon lifted his hand to touch her cheek, but he held back.

"And if you didn't want to be with me, at least, I could take some contentment in the realization that there's more out there for me than safety." She tilted her head and opened her eyes, reaching for his hand.

"I can't tell you how happy your gift made me." He took her outstretched palm and shook his head. "No, not happy. Relieved."

"When I didn't hear from you for eight hours after the package arrived, I threatened to kill my brother." She laughed ruefully. "You're the first man I've ever missed." She let the confession sit between them and Simon's breath caught.

"I missed you, too. I knew I would from the minute I left your apartment."

"Then why...?" She swallowed. "Why did you leave?"

"I was scared and resentful."

"Of me?"

"Of..." Simon paused. "I thought I was scared of not being enough for you, and resentful that you wanted more from me. I was wrong though. It wasn't about you. I'm scared of failing again; of not being enough for myself."

"I'm sorry for suggesting...that I needed you to be anything more than who you are. It was my issue with my mom, and I took it out on you. She abandoned me, and I put that fear on you. It wasn't fair. And I'm sorry I didn't tell you about my sorority sisters. But I can't honestly say I would have told you until I knew you were ready to hear it. I didn't see the point of making you feel small when their opinion means nothing to anyone. Would you want to tell me something hurtful someone said about me?"

Simon thought about her question. "No, I'm not sure what I would do. Either way, it was a convenient excuse because I didn't want to tell you how stressed I felt about everything. I should have told you. Instead, I looked for something to be upset about, and your sorority sister's wedding was the justification I needed to bail."

"I don't like that you left without warning."

"And yet the hand model is a pretty romantic gesture."

"No one has ever accused me of having excessive emotional intelligence." She harrumphed lightly. "I didn't want to give up on us, and if you did, at least I would have an answer."

"What do you want to do?"

"Part of me wants to ask you if I can trust you won't freak out on me again because I'm trying to protect myself."

"If I promised, would you believe me? I mean, would a promise be enough to quiet your doubts?"

"No, but I don't think that's your fault. I need to talk to someone—a therapist, probably—about what Michael says is my 'avoidant attachment style.'" Simon gave her a quizzical look in response. "I had to google it. It's 'a pattern in which individuals avoid emotional closeness and intimacy in relationships.'" She looked up as she recollected the definition and turned her attention back to him. "But our first fight as a couple had you jumping on a plane. That's not okay."

Taking a deep breath, Simon noticed his tics were oddly subdued, given the tension of the conversation. It should make him anxious, making his premonitory urges go haywire, but yet...

"Why are you smiling when we're having this serious discussion?"

"Because I'm with you. Because I know you want us to be together. I'm willing to work with you on everything else. Because being with you is superior to being apart, so please tell me what we'll need to do to rebuild trust. If it's time, I'll give you the time you need. If it's therapy, I'll go with you and hold your hand. And if we do all that and you still want to kick me to the curb, I'll be grateful for our time together because you make me a better person."

"I'm better for you in my life too." She looked up at the sky. "What do you need from me? You were upset with me as well."

"Don't hide truths from me, even if you're scared I won't like them. I don't need a protector. I need a partner."

"I should probably tell you, my dad is pretty pissed off at you for breaking the heart of his baby girl."

"Yeah, I could tell." Simon sat next to her on the wall, still holding her hand. Cali rested her head on his shoulder. "You think he'd warm up if I sent him a cactus wrapped in holiday lights?"

Cali giggled. "You're too smooth, Zap. I still want to be mad at you, but you're making it difficult."

"I know. I feel bad for you. I'm going to make you laugh every time we argue." Simon pressed his forehead to hers, stuck his lower lip out, and made puppy dog eyes. "Is this doing it for you at all?"

"Don't you dare." Cali laughed. "This laughter is not replacing my justifiable anger at you."

He scooted closer, his comic expression dropping into sincere imploring. "But we'll start again, Mad?"

Wrapping her arms around his neck, Cali pulled him forward for a tender kiss.

"Yes, Simon. Let's start again."

Over the next several days, Cali and Simon enjoyed their reunion. With her parents' blessing, she borrowed their SUV and took him on a three-day jaunt around the Southwest, visiting the Grand Canyon and Sedona, neither of which Simon had seen. Cali enjoyed showing him the art galleries of Sedona and hearing his professional artist's opinion of the different works. At a local glass-blowing studio, Simon bought Cali a belated Christmas gift of a tree ornament shaped like a pirate ship.

On the long drives between destinations, they alternated between talking, listening to podcasts, and enjoying how the Phoenix metropolitan area gave way to increasingly beautiful desert vistas.

The Grand Canyon provided more adventure when the budget hotel they'd booked featured shower stalls separate from the bedrooms. Walking down the hallway, Simon spotted a small black cat with its head poked out from the shower room. Kneeling in an attempt at affection,

Simon and Cali were equally horrified when the black cat emerged with a large white stripe along its back and the tell-tale smell of a...

"*Skunk*!" Cali yelled. Simon fell back onto his palms and crab-walked backward before returning to his feet and racing after Cali for the exit. The skunk plodded off peacefully in the opposite direction, as if unaware of the drama it had caused. After making it to safety, Cali and Simon laughed long and hard until Simon's chest hurt from the exertion. He looked over at her, mesmerized by her flushed skin and happy expression. Grabbing her close, he kissed her passionately before they carefully found their hotel room.

"These beds are horrible," Cali complained as Simon jumped on after her, his arms bracketing on either side of her head. The squeak of the springs suggested the mattresses had last been replaced in the Clinton administration.

"Try not to think about it." He kissed her neck while she giggled. "My ego isn't so secure that it'll withstand you laughing at me, Mad." Chuckling, he lifted his head to look down at her. Her eyes glowed gently, and she ran a hand through his thick brown hair. Their laughter died in the poignancy of that stare.

"I love you, Simon."

"I love you too."

He met her lips with tenderness rather than passion. He opened her mouth with his in small degrees, tasting her, letting her taste him. She wrapped her arms around his back while he kissed a path down her neck to her chest. He wanted her skin against his and removed his shirt while she did the same to her own. Sometimes his tics set his nerves on fire with their premonitory urges, but this was another sort of electricity. Where the former paralyzed, this one set him on fire. He couldn't stop touching her, kissing her.

He traveled down the length of her body with his mouth, refamiliarizing himself with the smooth skin of her stomach and thighs. The soft sighs she made spurred him on, and when she reached to grab his hair, he made his home between her thighs, all other desires second to making her come. He transmitted his love for her, and with every kiss, every caress, every cry, he felt further emboldened. Resting his tongue upon her clit, he maneuvered it back and forth, gently at first and with incrementally greater pressure and speed until she cried, begging to come.

And then she did.

"Simon!" Her legs tensed around his head as her orgasm claimed her. Disengaging from her core, he climbed up her body and kissed her. She pulled him close, pressing them together from head to toe, and guided him into her. They had made love before, but even those instances were nothing compared to the closeness he felt now. He breathed harshly as he thrust into her. Soaking wet, she welcomed him. He wasn't going to last more than a moment.

"Simon," she whispered as if in disbelief. "I'm going to come again."

"Thank God." He claimed her lips as he fell into her, his nerves firing with release. He muffled his cries against her mouth. As his body quieted, he loathed to let her go, to break from the closest he had ever felt to another person.

"That was..." she whispered at length. "That was... I've never felt anything like that before."

"Me neither," he whispered in response, the room quiet but for their breaths and heartbeats.

Over the next few days, Cali continued showing Simon the different parts of where she came from. After hiking the Grand Canyon, they returned to her parents' home to tour other landmarks of her childhood, from her favorite outlook on Camelback Mountain to a tour of Arizona State University. She took him to her favorite bar, called the Bookstore—famous because parents were sure their children were buying things from the school bookstore whenever credit card charges came through for the local pub.

"But they have the best buffalo wings in the area," Cali confided as they reviewed the students taking advantage of their parents' lack of insight.

Simon extended his stay through January first so he and Cali could ring in the New Year holiday together. They stayed up late with her brother and some of his friends in her parents' finished basement. A few beers, midnight pizza, and a horror movie marathon later, Cali and Simon passed out at 2 a.m., Cali still wearing her ASU T-shirt but peeling off her leggings and bra. Simon passed out in his boxers.

A high-pitched but undoubtedly happy squeal woke him on New Year's Day.

"Oh my God!" he heard in a whispered hush. "Simon, oh my God!"

Simon blinked at the bright morning light, lifting his forearm to cover his eyes. "What happened?" He looked at her with bleary eyes.

"I got a Happy New Year's text from my boss from last night—I think based on the time stamp, he might have been a little drunk." She showed the phone to Simon.

"Happy New Year, Cali! Look forward to celebrating your P-Club win in two weeks!"

Simon tried to remember why this would excite her. "What's P-Club?"

"P-Club—President's Club!" At his blank stare, Cali explained, "It's this event they hold every April for the top company performers. It's at a luxury resort in Hawaii, and the company's senior executive team and top reps attend it. If he's saying I'm going to P-Club, it means I won Rookie of the Year. That's the only way someone of my tenure would get to go. I get all expenses paid! Flights, accommodations, meals, all of it—for me *and* a guest!"

"You say if? Sounds like you won."

Cali shook her head. "They don't announce it until the January kickoff meeting, but some managers know the winners beforehand." She looked at Simon with a feigned casual mien. "It was probably a mistake. I'm not going to count on anything."

"Are you kidding? Certainly, it was a drunk text, but there's no reason to think he's wrong. We should be celebrating your win!"

"Nope, not assuming anything." She stared at the phone, rereading the message and shaking her head. "I won't believe it till they announce it on the big stage at kickoff."

"Suit yourself, Cali. In the meantime, I'm imagining you in a bikini." He closed his eyes but cracked one open to spy on her, still scanning the phone for answers not immediately forthcoming. "You said you get to bring a guest?"

"Yes." She climbed across him to lie on his bare chest. "That's right. Can you imagine the two of us in Maui? Walking along the beach? Staying at The Four Seasons?"

"With your senior executive team?" His hands caressed her upper arms. "I'd rather it be the two of us..."

"Ah, but it wouldn't be all expenses paid."

"Point taken." He paused, his eyes alternating between widening and narrowing several times. "Are you sure I'm the one you'd want on that beach with you?" He brushed her hair out of her eyes. She looked disheveled from their earlier revelries. He loved her like this, messy and unaffected.

Cali poked him in the chest. "Don't put this on me. I wouldn't have invited you if I didn't want you there. If you want to come, come. If you don't think you're ready, I'll accept that too."

"But you'll be disappointed."

"Well, I'm sure you don't want me to be happy if you don't go?" She gave him an arched eyebrow, but at his solemn expression, she took a deep breath. "Of course, I'll be disappointed, but I won't be angry. I'll accept this is something you're not ready for." She paused, her mouth open, as if weighing how to proceed.

"There's a but... Tell me what you're feeling. We promised to be open with each other."

"You're right, we did. Here's the thing, Simon. The training program is designed for the company to ship me around to some degree. I'm in NJ for a regional rotation now, but there's no guarantee I'll be there long-term. In fact, it's highly unlikely. Eventually, I'll work at one of the corporate locations–maybe Chicago, San Jose, or Raleigh. I signed up for that when I applied to the program."

"I didn't know..." Simon sat up, lifting her from him. The comforter dropped to his lap. His right hand patted his thigh, and Cali responded to his anxiety amping up at the realization by taking his hand.

"I get it, Simon."

He didn't turn when she called his name, and she put a hand on his cheek to force his face to look at hers.

"Simon, I want to be with *you*, but even more, I want to be *with* you. You can be an artist anywhere, but my dream means I'll be moving about a bit, at least initially. You don't have to join me in Hawaii, but I want you to take some time to think about whether you'd be willing to come with me and start a new life together at some point."

"Or what? We break up?" He gave her an incredulous look, alarmed and hurt.

"No!" she quickly reassured him, but paused, her head tilted. "I love you so much. I want you to know my future so you can decide if you want to be part of it." She kissed his cheek. "And I hope you do."

"I love you," he said, grabbing her hand from his cheek and kissing the inside of her wrist.

"I love you too." She straightened as if remembering her anxiety. "Anyway, this is all hypothetical until the kickoff meeting."

"Whatever gets you through the day," he commented, biting the inside of his cheek while he stared fondly at her and processed this new information.

CHAPTER 30

Volition: *(noun) the power of using one's will; conscious choice*

"DAMMIT!"

Simon bit his lip as his tics went haywire. With the new year came a return to media training with Alex. Joanne had yet to arrive, so the two of them were working until her arrival.

At the glare of the lights, the premonitory urges filled the space behind his eyes with the kind of lightning he imagined Zap would feel prior to attacking a villain–only Simon's electricity focused inward, damaging only himself. He patted both thighs while he grimaced and rolled his eyes in quick succession. He would suppress for a minute or two while answering Alex's questions, only to give in to the urges when Alex asked the next question.

Simon stood up, throwing his hands in the air. "Ugh! It's no good. I sit here, and my body is primed to go off the rails." He looked at Alex. "I should give up. I'm going to make a fool of myself and fuck up the book launch."

He rubbed one hand over his eyes, pinching the skin at the bridge of his nose. Simon inhaled roughly and looked toward Alex. "I'm sorry. You're trying to help me, and I'm acting like a child."

"Please don't apologize," Alex began, then paused. "I know you're stressed over this, so I did a bit of research over the holidays. I read an article on actors with Tourette's..."

"I already know about Dan Akroyd, Seth Rogan, and Billie Eilish." Simon shook his head. For some reason, people without Tourette syndrome often demonstrated their knowledge by mentioning celebrity names associated with the condition. It was annoying.

"Billie Eilish? Interesting. No, I was going to say many actors with Tourette's find they can gain some slight control over the urge to tic while acting, thanks to the state of focus they enter. Perhaps treating these interview answers like scripts you need to memorize might help you gain some power over the situation."

The memory of his haftorah portion lingered in his brain, and Simon nodded. Yes, memorization could help. Having a strategy at a time when he sorely needed one felt like a victory.

"Can we obtain a copy of the interview questions in advance?"

Alex gave a slight shake to his head. "They won't do that, but we can get an overall outline from the segment producers."

Simon considered how he could memorize the necessary answers to potential topics. "That's a decent strategy."

"Great, let's start again and take notes. We're not practicing interviews anymore. We're drafting your script."

Over the next ninety minutes, they compiled a list of likely questions while Simon drafted the answers that felt natural to him. Somewhere around the half-hour mark, his tics resumed their typical patterns, showing Alex had him in a more productive headspace, if nothing else.

"What would you say if the interviewer asks about how you overcame your Tourette's to be such an inspiration?"

"I'm assuming projectile vomiting would be inappropriate?"

"Not if you want to be invited back when volume two comes out next year." Joanne's voice echoed in the dark portion of the room, outside the glow of the lights of the false studio. “Happy New Year! I come bearing good news!”

Joanne’s larger-than-life personality made up for her lack of stature, but it was never more noticeable than when she unsuccessfully tried to suppress herself. At five feet even, there was nothing small about her presence.

“I spoke with a segment producer at *USA This Morning*! They want you on their nine o’clock hour. They want to interview you in the square at Rockefeller Center.” She tried to keep her voice calm, but Simon saw the excitement she reigned in for his sake.

Simon’s jaw dropped. *USA This Morning* meant colossal exposure. Over the holiday break, he’d been subjected to the banal back-and-forth of the hosts over breakfast with both his and Cali’s families. He understood the reason they were such a highly rated television program. Anything featured on *USA This Morning* became mainstream.

This means several weeks of bestseller status, a decent royalty check, and a down payment on a house or condo in the future.

“That means a live television appearance, doesn’t it?” Simon took a deep breath in and let it out in a slow exhale. He had been warned of the possibility, but *USA This Morning* wanting to interview him seemed about as likely as the film version of his book starring a young Brad Pitt.

Joanne was saved from responding by Alex giving him a hearty pat on the back.

“Great news, my man! It couldn’t happen to a nicer and more deserving guy. We’ll get you so ready for this that you'll be buttoned up tighter than the red carpet at the Met Gala.”

“When do they want to do this?”

“January fifteenth. It’s a perfect day—a Friday. We’ll catch the crowd working from home before the holiday weekend. It’ll be a larger audience than usual. We’ll bookend it with some in-person book signings around the area.”

“Joanne, I know you’re hoping to steamroll past my freakout phase, but you’ll have to let me process this before you plan the next three months of my life.” He gave her an alarmed expression and sat down on a nearby bench, looking out at the makeshift studio Alex had created. His hand tapped at his thigh lightly but quickly.

"Fair feedback, Joanne," Alex called out from behind one of the larger lights. "You know what, I need about twenty minutes to fix this setup. Why don't you head next door to Starbucks and get us all some lattes?"

Joanne grumbled as she and Simon walked to the neighboring building and waited in line with the commuters getting their coffee orders filled.

"I got a call from Gina Russell over the holiday," Simon said before Joanne could start in on him again.

"Yes, she badgered me for your phone number during church services. That woman has the instincts of a hawk." Joanne nodded her head in consideration. "She'd have made a great agent."

Simon nodded, considering her point. "Why didn't you tell me about your son?"

Joanne stood there, turning her head to look up at him. "Gina told you, huh?" Simon kept his peace while she continued. "I didn't tell you because one, it was none of your business, and two, you would've thought he was the only reason I became interested in your work. I'm not altruistic. I saw demand for the product, and I wanted my name attached to its success. If you want to write another graphic novel with a superhero who doesn't struggle with a neurological disorder, be my guest. As long as it meets the same quality standards as your current work, I'll get it published for you."

"How is your son doing?"

"Better than you most days. On the golf team. Takes piano lessons twice a week. At twelve, his angst level is approximately twenty-five percent of what yours is on a good day, and *he's* going through puberty. But he's been reading *The Magnificent Zap* since he was eight years old, and I read it with him. Your early stuff lacked finesse, but you hit your stride about two years back. I couldn't believe it when I found myself reading ahead of my son because I wanted to see what happened next. That's when I reached out to Webcomicz for your contact information."

"Your son sounds like he's got his shit together a lot more than I do."

"Frankly, Simon, he does. It took him about two years after his diagnosis to realize what he has is not all he is."

"Just like Zap..." Simon whispered, thinking of how that had been his goal with the hero all along.

"Just like Zap," Joanne agreed. "He's my son, so I taught him to stand tall. Growing up shorter than ninety-five percent of the population, like I did, means you either get trampled or step over people. Fortunately, Jason gets his father's stature. Imagine having Tourette's and being the shortest kid in your class."

"Your son would make it work for him."

"Damn right, he would," she said right before ordering an Americano with two shots of espresso. "He responded about as well as you might imagine after his diagnosis—that's to say, not great. But after he read your comic, he said to me, 'The thing Tourette's is stealing from me is being unnoticed, so I might as well try to be noticed for things I'm happy doing instead.'"

Cali's words from their reconciliation in Arizona came to mind, unbidden.

"Everything I've done to keep myself from being miserable has done nothing to make me happy."

Would he let his condition steal happiness from him? Safety didn't equate happiness. Cali made him happy. His friends and family made him happy. His work made him happy. The rest was noise.

"Joanne." Simon looked at her after she had placed her order. "We'll have to make sure my calendar is clear for April. I have a planned vacation with Cali. We're going to Hawaii."

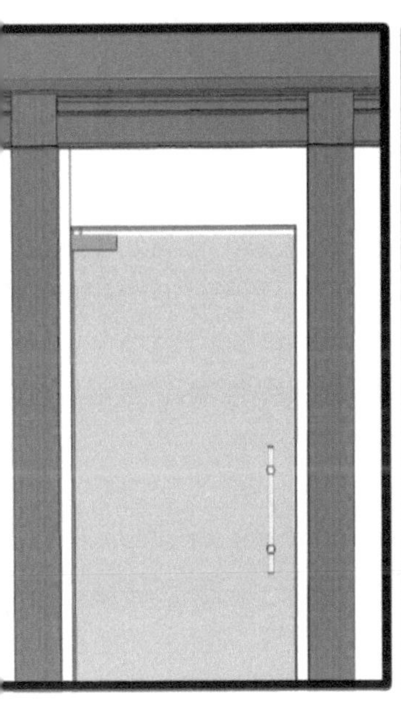

MY FATHER NEEDS ME BACK...
BUT WHY? YOU'VE DONE AMAZING THINGS HERE – WE SAVED THE CITY!

AYE, BUT I MADE HIM A ROMISE THAT D COME HOME O HIM AFTER VE STOPPED...
A PIRATE CAN'T BREAK HER PROMISE.
THEN LET ME COME WITH YOU.

IT'S MORE THAN FIGHTING TOGETHER THOUGH I'VE NEVER BEEN BETTER THAN I AM WITH YOU. I LOVE YOU. I'LL FOLLOW YOU ANYWHERE.
I'LL LEARN HOW TO BE A PIRATE IF IT MEANS YOU'LL TAKE ME WITH YOU.
JUST TELL ME WE CAN BE TOGETHER AND I'LL BE WHEREVER YOU NEED ME TO BE.
I....

CHAPTER 31

Billet-doux: *(noun) a love letter*

NINE DAYS LATER, Cali stared at the beauty of the wildflower-covered California coast as her Uber took her from the airport to the downtown hotel that would host her company for several days.

Of course, for all the beauty of the city, the only part of San Diego that the sales and marketing teams would be enjoying was the windowless conference rooms of the Downtown Hilton. This was not a sightseeing trip, and often Cali wondered why meetings like this weren't hosted somewhere equally accessible but less tempting to explore. If you were going to be locked down for eight hours a day, why not pick something in the middle of nowhere?

Most of the attendees at the Marcus & Meyers annual kickoff event had a love-hate relationship with the standard format. Days spent learning annual strategy were only tolerable as evening events at restaurants and bars in the Gaslamp Quarter capped them. Salespeople were social animals, and sitting in one place for extended periods drained them as much as camaraderie energized them.

For Cali, the opposite was true. She enjoyed the strategy and role-play sessions with colleagues, in which they took turns being customers and reps, trying out new talk tracks to influence potential sales. She enjoyed this part. At the end of the day, she longed to return to her hotel room and either text Simon or hit up the hotel gym, but the dinners were mandatory, especially since she had a team to corral from place to place.

Comprised of Jesse and five other reps, Cali's team endured the strategy sessions gracefully. Role-plays were tedious exercises in the best of times. Still, Cali tried to get them all involved by making feedback a team endeavor. Everyone could learn from anyone, and anyone could learn from everyone. At night, Cali suffered in loud venues with too many people squashed into private dining spaces. She sipped her seltzer and tried to make the best of an emotionally draining activity.

By the end of the dinner on the third night, the teams dispersed to connect with colleagues from around the country, and Cali found herself sitting with Lauren and Matt at the hotel bar where they were staying.

"So, can you tell me what happened with Ryan?" Matt asked as he sipped his beer. "The dude reached out to me on LinkedIn and said something about bullshit feminism. I blocked him, and that felt fucking good."

"Let's just say that some of his less savory behaviors came to light in a spectacular fashion. He called Cali the B-word and the W-word and insulted her boyfriend. George was not happy."

"I'm sorry he treated you like that." Matt nodded at Cali with kind sympathy.

"Lauren here came to my rescue." Cali gave Lauren a fist bump. "Thanks to her, I kept my reputation intact, though not Ryan's shirt, which is probably still sporting the resulting glass of wine I 'accidentally' spilled on him." Cali used air quotes for the word *accidentally* and Lauren did a spit-take of her wine.

"This is the problem with living in Buffalo. I'm too far away from where all the fun stories happen," Matt whined. "Maybe I'll get a management role somewhere closer to the action. San Diego wouldn't suck. Wish we could've explored the city some."

"At least tomorrow night's final event is on Coronado Island. That's a pretty spot in the city," Cali offered. "Can't wait to go home. I fly out first thing the next day. Simon is going to be on *USA This Morning* that day!" Simon had passed on the news several days before. He had sounded...resolved, but not in a way suggesting he dreaded it. He sounded more determined than she had ever heard him before.

"How is Simon doing, Cali? You must have been flattered by that last episode of Magnificent Zap."

"What are you talking about?" Cali looked at her. "His season is on break."

"You didn't see it? He released a surprise episode last night. I assumed you must have seen it since...well...it's super personal." Lauren looked over at Matt. "Her boyfriend is a graphic novelist." She flipped to the app, pulling up *The Magnificent Zap* for Matt to peruse.

"I hadn't heard about any new episodes." Cali grabbed her phone and loaded the Webcomicz app in the next minute while Lauren distracted Matt by showing him her phone. Cali looked over her shoulder, as if afraid the moment would be interrupted before excusing herself to the privacy of the ladies' room. Locking herself in a stall, she opened *The Magnificent Zap*. In the previous episode, Zap and Mad had worked together to defeat Mirror Zap. It had been the ideal end to the season, culminating in Mad and Zap kissing.

This episode began anticlimactically. Zap visited Mad in his civilian gear as she packed up boxes and belongings from her apartment. She explained she had to leave. Mad's father needed her to return home. Zap's palpable heartbreak led to the profession of his love for Mad. Zap offered to follow her and come with her wherever she went. Zap was telling her—*Simon was telling Cali*—he loved her and would follow her anywhere she wanted.

He committed himself to her and their future life together, begging her to trust him.

The final image of the comic featured a close-up of Mad. Her lips were parted in surprise, and her green eyes were bright, reflecting Zap's outstretched hand, silent in the face of Zap's offer.

It was one hell of a cliffhanger. Even Cali wanted to know how it ended.

The swift realization came upon her–Simon was telling her in the best way he knew how that he would be there for her, with her. He would follow her wherever her job took her.

Lauren had known the comic was meant for Cali. Probably anyone who knew them–their story–would know the meaning of the episode. Simon was making himself vulnerable, not only in his comic strips, but also when he would appear on live television in two days.

Both she and Simon had spent the last few months trying to break the bonds of their respective pasts, and they had done so together. Yes, they'd had steps forward and backward, but they'd tried, and in trying, they'd grown. She couldn't have done it without him, and she knew he couldn't have done it without her.

And in forty-eight hours, he would be trying again–on live television!

She wanted to be there for him. She *needed* to be there for him.

One phone call later, her flight, scheduled for two days out, was changed to a red-eye the night before. She would go straight from the gala to San Diego International Airport. If her flight landed on time, she would get there just as Simon began his interview.

Her next call was to Anton.

"Hey, Cali–to what do I owe the honor of this call?" Anton sounded pleased.

"Anton, I need a favor."

CHAPTER 32

Denouement: *(noun) the final part of a play, movie, or narrative in which the strands of the plot are drawn together and resolved*

A BALDING MAN NAMED Rob pinned a microphone to the lapel of the dark blue wool winter coat Joanne recommended he wear for the interview, and that connected to a unit attached to the back of his pants. The weather was unnaturally kind for mid-January New York City—a practically balmy fifty degrees.

"That comfortable for ya?" Rob asked, then turned away before Simon could answer.

"First time on television?" his segment producer—a tall woman named Sonia with tan skin and a taut ponytail—asked.

"Trial by fire," Simon agreed, looking at the tourists outside the studio where they would film his segment.

"Did my assistant walk you through the process?"

Simon nodded. "I get the newbie?"

"Yes, our new entertainment reporter, Lisa Woods. She came to us from *Entertainment Tonight*."

"Any advice?"

"Be yourself. Your agent sent the talking points. Lisa will ask about your book, your inspiration, what's coming next, etcetera."

Simon nodded to himself, his hand patting absently at his thigh. He pursed his lips together, wishing he could control his body in a way that he had not done since sometime around the ninth grade. Something about that wish niggled at his brain like a song stuck there he couldn't quite identify. He tried to identify the feeling of almost déjà vu when Sonia guided him to his mark on the square outside in Rockefeller Center. A smallish crowd stood about, wearing a random hodgepodge of I LOVE NY T-shirts and holding signs advertising their schools and towns from around the country. Lisa worked the crowd, introducing herself to those hoping to get their posters on the air so their friends and family back home could see them. The reporter wore bright blue pants, a silky top printed with silver flowers, and a leather jacket.

Joanne watched from behind the camera setup. He got the sense he shouldn't regularly expect her accompaniment but that she wanted to provide additional support, which both made him appreciative and vaguely infantilized. She had done everything short of offering him snacks and a juice box. If more interviews were forthcoming, he would be doing them on his own.

Simon closed his eyes, trying to ground himself. He remembered the night of the gala and how he had imagined painting Cali's face, and how it had helped him to calm down. He wished Cali were there with him. She hadn't said anything to his comic confessional yet, but it *was* a very personal confession, and she was away at her work event. She would be back tonight, and they would talk.

And tear each other's clothes off. That would happen too.

"You ready, Simon?" Lisa asked, indicating he should stand on his mark.

"Yes, thank you." He reached out his hand to shake hers, and she smiled politely.

"As for me, I'm a bit nervous. I'm new here myself, so I got caught up in the research for this interview. I read your book and some of the more recent episodes online. Love the dynamic between Mad and Zap!

They're so cute together! I'm going to try and weasel some spoilers out of you."

"I'll see what I can do." Simon shook his head, a bit overwhelmed by the sensory overload that was Lisa Woods, who had clearly consumed way too much coffee. Simon's tics temporarily worsened, his mouth grimacing, and Lisa's eyes darted to his hand, patting his thigh in repetition.

"Fantastic! Did you know Billie Eilish and Dan Akroyd have Tourette's too? So many famous people do!" Her tone suggested that Tourette syndrome was a trend everyone was getting in on.

Something dropped in Simon's stomach. Lisa was perfectly nice but emotionally clueless. In some ways, this could be even worse than outward cruelty. Clueless people said hurtful things, but you weren't 'allowed' to be angry at them because their intentions weren't malicious. Simon considered that Lisa's extensive research had not included sensitivity training.

"I did know that," he finally answered, but Sonia distracted Lisa by calling for her attention.

"All right, we're on in ten!" Sonia called out, and Simon looked about, all his prep work flying out of his head. Simon watched the countdown with wide eyes and a dry mouth.

"Thank you, Charlotte! Today, we are joined by Simon Goldberg, whose graphic novel, *The Adventures of the Magnificent Zap*, is hitting shelves in two weeks!" She looked over at Simon. "Thank you for joining us!"

Simon managed to close his hanging jaw in time not to look stupid. "Good to be here, Lisa."

"Simon, I don't read comics, but I could *not* put your book down. I read it cover to cover!" The way she said *cover to cover* indicated how surprised she'd been by her enjoyment of the work.

"I'm glad you liked it?" Simon couldn't help the questioning lilt to his voice.

"Loved it! Zap is such a fun superhero! Like a neurotic Spider-Man."

"That's not a bad description." Simon nodded, appreciating that for all her faults, Lisa attempted to make him comfortable.

"Tell me where you got your inspiration for Zap. I understand you've been working on it since art school." Lisa put on an interested face while she waited for Simon to answer.

"I think every kid thinks about what it would be like to be a superhero, so I tried to create a character that every awkward kid could see themselves in."

"But Zap is more than awkward; he has Tourette syndrome."

Simon paused, feeling as though he were getting ready to parachute out of a plane. The conversation he dreaded was upon him. "That's right."

"I understand you have Tourette's. I can see that you're ticcing with your hands right now."

Simon let out a kind of breathless, surprised laugh at her audacity. Behind the camera, Joanne's fists were clenched. "Yes, well, I was diagnosed with Tourette's at age nine, so I thought it would be fun to combine that with Zap's superpowers, but I think the story is more about how the character balances his secret identity with–"

"Yes, and he does have a hard time with it. Do you think your story serves as an inspiration to others? So they understand how difficult those with Tourette's have it?"

And here came the inspiration porn! She wanted him to tell a sob story. Simon tamped down the urge to curl his lip in disgust. He thought about what Cali would say, recalling her words from the day they ran into his high school bully at the grocery store.

"I think..." He pressed his lips together and began again. "I think the message is broader. There's a word I learned recently, sonder. It's the realization that everyone, be it a graphic novelist, an entertainment reporter, or a tourist from" –Simon looked back at one of the signs–"Delevan, Wisconsin, has struggles, battles, and an entire inner life at any moment in time. The only difference between me and them is that one of my struggles is out there for everyone to see–but Tourette's is not the entirety of who I am, it's just a part of what makes me...me."

"Simon, that's beautiful and so true."

"What we have, what we experience, is not the same as who we are."

"You make an excellent point, and we can see from our crowd out in the square that you have quite the fan base." Lisa waved at the cameraperson to follow as they pulled in close to the railing. Sonia shooed them on to follow the path of the voices, as if sensing a viral moment in the making. Simon saw Anton first, then Ben, Sheila, Kat, Aoki, and–oh my God–his parents, and finally Cali. They were all in homemade costumes, portraying various characters from his graphic novel. His father wore a Zap T-shirt and a mask. Anton, Ben, and Sheila wore hastily made shirts with logos of the villains on them.

And there stood Cali, dressed in full pirate regalia with a corset and tricorn hat. Her blond hair flowed down her back in messy waves as if she had been flying all night, which she almost definitely had. Her green eyes were bright, terrified, and exhilarated. Their eyes met, and Simon had to bite his lip to keep from laughing outright on live television.

"We even have Zap's love interest here. Speaking of which, are we going to see more of Mad McSwiggans? You ended the latest episode on a bit of a cliffhanger."

"Tell me we can be together, and I'll be wherever you need me to be."

"I think..." Simon cleared his throat. His eyes met with Cali's, and her beaming grin reflected his own. "Things are looking good for Mad and Zap."

EPILOGUE

***Epilogue:** (noun) a section or speech at the end of a book or play that serves as a comment on or a conclusion to what has happened*

THE HEAVY SMELL OF FLOWERS and sunscreen perfumed the humid air. The Uber pulled into the driveway of the Four Seasons Hotel. Simon studied Cali, and she smiled as she took in the sight of the pristine staff awaiting the arrival of guests from across the Pacific.

Simon admired the large sign. After flying all night, the bright sun of Hawaii had startled him, given it was still 3 a.m. in his head, but the air wafted so pleasantly that it mellowed the accompanying stress.

Welcome, Members of the Marcus & Meyers Presidents Club!

"They go all out for this event, don't they? It's like something out of *The White Lotus.*"

Cali gave a raised eyebrow at his remark.

"Minus the dead body, of course," he quickly added.

"I should think so. Top performers get the top treatment!"

Cali and Simon would spend the next seven days being wined and dined with the other award winners at the Four Seasons in Maui. In addition to hotel, food, and airfare, the week promised to be filled with other fun activities, such as snorkeling, whale watching, and hiking. Cali confided in Simon her intention to sneak away for at least one spa treatment each day.

"I plan to be pampered beyond all measure. I need something to spend the latest spelling bee money on, right?" Cali had won all but one of the last four spelling bees. Two months prior, she lost to a seventy-year-old retired mail carrier who had been cheered on by his grandchildren. Cali happily surrendered her title with a hug and a series of photos with the temporary new champion. She'd regained the title at the next competition.

Cali looked over at Simon, who stared, intrigued by the display of corporate excess.

"You look okay. Are you feeling okay? Maybe I want you to be okay?" Cali looked over at him nervously.

"What would your therapist say to this?" he teased her.

Cali scowled. "She would say, leave the girl alone from too much emotional introspection on her vacation." Cali pulled him forward by his shirt and gave him a quick kiss on the lips. "Now answer the question, Zap."

"I'm okay." He nodded as if realizing it himself. "*My therapist*"—he gave her a supercilious look that made her smile—"and I have been talking at length about managing any stress I might experience. And honestly, I'm looking forward to seeing your friend, Jesse." It pleased Simon that her colleague had also won an award for the prestigious event, if only because they would both have a friendly face awaiting them poolside.

"Yes, and Gina Russell, of course. You know she's going to try to strong-arm you into some selfies for her son."

"I never thought I'd say this, but it'll be less stressful for me when her son outgrows comic books."

"Don't even joke like that! You don't want to jinx your sales numbers!" Now that the first volume had been released, Simon's focus shifted to formatting more recent issues, including those with Mad McSwiggans. Ever the businessperson, Cali kept a close eye on trends in his marketplace. She and Joanne were a fearsome pair, but since it kept

Simon focused on his art, he didn't mind offloading that responsibility to the two of them. When Cali went overboard, Simon reined her in with a reminder that his success shouldn't be the cause of a stomachache.

"I can honestly say I'm not worried. If the meetings with the TV executives at Comic-Con in June go as well as Joanne seems to think they will, I'm reasonably confident sales will continue to increase. Now, no more shop talk, Mad. I mean it. We both earned this vacation. Let's try to have fun this week."

The valet attendants opened the door to the red Mercedes sedan that drove them from the airport—another company perk.

"Well, a little shop talk, maybe. I got tickets to Pirate Ship Adventures. It's a whole pirate experience with sword fights, canons, the works."

"I hope you packed Dramamine."

"In my medicine bag." She patted her carry-on bag as they entered their room.

Simon's eyes locked upon the view of the Pacific Ocean from their balcony while Cali, bless her neurotic heart, busied herself with hanging up all clothing items that would require ironing or steaming later, grumbling good-naturedly about how everything had gotten wrinkled during the flight.

"Oh look, they sent champagne," he called out, and she poked her head out of the bathroom where she was unpacking her toiletries.

"Yes, please."

Simon poured them each a glass, and Cali joined him on the balcony. He took her hand in his and breathed deeply. For several minutes, they enjoyed the view.

"What are you thinking about?" she asked as the sun dipped low onto the horizon.

"If you must know, I'm annoyed."

"Annoyed? At what?" Cali let out an incredulous laugh.

"I'm annoyed because this is far and away the most perfect place I've ever seen to propose to my girlfriend, but it is simply way too soon to do so."

"I see," Cali responded with mock seriousness. "That sounds difficult for you. I suppose I can try to win the President's Club again, though the location next year is in the Bahamas."

"No, I'll have to come up with someplace rivaling Hawaii for when I pop the question."

"Paris is nice. I've always wanted to go."

"Even with your lactose intolerance?"

"I'll eat the bread, skip the cheese. I'll live on chocolate croissants and crepes."

"I suppose I'll have to check out flights when we get back. Maybe for Christmas."

"I suppose you will," she agreed, maintaining a bland tone, but her nose crinkled.

Looking over at her, the orange rays bathing her in a glowing light made his hand itch. In the past few months, he'd undertaken painting as an additional pastime. It reminded him of his enjoyment of art apart from his work as a graphic novelist.

Of course, the graphic novels paid the bills for the time being, though he had been brainstorming a new idea. Nothing formal yet. First, he'd have to have Zap propose to Mad, leading to a happy and satisfying ending for the readers who had been there from the beginning. Then, well...he had a story in his brain about a group of supervillains who come to regret their actions and, through a support group, try to change their lives for the better. He had an idea for the first person he could call for character research. Cali would undoubtedly approve.

"I love you," he said, feeling joy so potent it felt like a physical being within his chest.

"I love you too," she said, her eyes flickering to his briefly before returning to the view.

Then, they toasted their champagne, enjoying the sunset before them.

ACKNOWLEDGEMENTS

THE AWKWARD AGENDA was a labor of love, and I have so many people to thank. First and foremost, I want to thank the Tourette Syndrome community on Reddit. When I first had the idea of a romantic hero with Tourette's, I knew that research would be paramount to ensure his story was accurate and nuanced. The Tourette Syndrome subreddit was generous with both information and experience, and I will be forever grateful for the stories they shared. I'm particularly thankful to my sensitivity readers: Halli and Naomi.

Thank you to my excellent development editor, Maria Connor, and line/copy editor, Emily Laughridge, who made my story better on every level. Thank you also to my proofreader, Raazia. Thank you to my beta readers, Alyson and Angela, who took the time to provide me with valuable feedback.

Thank you to my illustrator, Stacy Williams, who transformed my preliminary designs for Zap and Mad into beautiful comic illustrations. Thank you to my cover art designer, Michael Ardan.

As much as I would love to turn writing into a full-time career, it is only one of my many responsibilities in addition to my job and children. My next thank you is to my husband, Joel, who not only supports my dreams but takes the time to provide much-needed advice. He's the one I go to when I want to spitball ideas and determine if they are emotionally valid. Thank you also to my kids, Ellen and James, who occasionally lose their mommy to a computer screen during my creative binges. I love you with all of my heart!

ABOUT THE AUTHOR

RAISED ON LONG ISLAND, New York, Beth received her BA in Dramatic Literature and MBA in Marketing and Sales at New York University. She currently lives in New Jersey with her husband, two kids, a cat, and two fish. In her spare time, she enjoys writing and reading romance novels, binging the Great British Bake Off, and rooting for the Seattle Seahawks. You can read her debut novel, Phantoms, Ghosts & Other Heartbreaks, a modern retelling of The Phantom of the Opera, on Amazon now.

www.ingramcontent.com/pod-product-compliance
Lightning Source LLC
LaVergne TN
LVHW091249110826
845146LV00002BA/675

* 9 7 9 8 9 9 1 9 3 6 5 5 2 *